THE
RUNAWAY

BOOK YOUR PLACE ON OUR WEBSITE AND MAKE THE READING CONNECTION!

We've created a customized website just for our very special readers, where you can get the inside scoop on everything that's going on with Zebra, Pinnacle and Kensington books.

When you come online, you'll have the exciting opportunity to:

- View covers of upcoming books
- Read sample chapters
- Learn about our future publishing schedule (listed by publication month and author)
- Find out when your favorite authors will be visiting a city near you
- Search for and order backlist books from our online catalog
- Check out author bios and background information
- Send e-mail to your favorite authors
- Meet the Kensington staff online
- Join us in weekly chats with authors, readers and other guests
- Get writing guidelines
- AND MUCH MORE!

**Visit our website at
http://www.kensingtonbooks.com**

THE
RUNAWAY

LISA CHILDS

ZEBRA BOOKS
KENSINGTON PUBLISHING CORP.
www.kensingtonbooks.com

ZEBRA BOOKS are published by

Kensington Publishing Corp.
119 West 40th Street
New York, NY 10018

All Kensington titles, imprints, and distributed lines are available at special quantity discounts for bulk purchases for sales promotion, premiums, fund-raising, educational, or institutional use.

Special book excerpts or customized printings can also be created to fit specific needs. For details, write or phone the office of the Kensington Sales Manager: Attn.: Sales Department. Kensington Publishing Corp., 119 West 40th Street, New York, NY 10018. Phone: 1-800-221-2647.

Zebra and the Z logo Reg. U.S. Pat. & TM Off.

First Printing: November 2020
ISBN-13: 978-1-4201-5021-6
ISBN-10: 1-4201-5021-9

ISBN-13: 978-1-4201-5023-0 (eBook)
ISBN-10: 1-4201-5023-5 (eBook)

10 9 8 7 6 5 4 3 2 1

Printed in the United States of America

Prologue

She had to get away. She knew that if she didn't escape, she would wind up like the others.

Dead.

Or worse.

But, in order to escape, she had to fight the elements, too.

A bitter wind swirled around the rocky bluffs, blowing spray from the sea onto the rocks, leaving them slick and icy. The wind hurled shards of ice from the dark sky. The sleet stung as it struck her face and arms. She flinched, but she forced herself to keep moving up from the bluffs and the water, up the steep slope. She grabbed at the trunks of pine trees, bark biting into the palms of her hands while the dusting of snow already on the ground seared the bottom of her feet. That burning sensation spread up her legs, which were bare but for the damp hospital gown clinging to her thighs.

The higher she climbed the louder the howling grew— not of the wind but of the coyotes. They yelped and then released high-pitched howls that sounded like screams of pain or terror.

She held in the scream of terror and pain that clawed at the back of her throat. She didn't want to reveal her location.

The tracks in the snow would do that, though—would lead them right to her. She had to keep moving—had to run. But her legs were so heavy and the ground was so uneven and slick. And the sleet kept lashing down at her, blinding her even more than the darkness, stinging like needles.

The needles . . .

She'd fought those. If she hadn't . . .

If they'd drugged her . . .

She wouldn't have made it out of that dungeon of horrors. But she wasn't safe yet—from them or from the coyotes. The animals called out to one another, their howls echoing in the woods around her, echoing off the bluffs and the rocks. They were getting closer and closer.

The wind wasn't the only thing rustling the trees and brush. Something or someone was following her and drawing nearer with each slip of her sole against the snow. She cleared the top of the bluff only to find the slope on the other side steeper and more treacherous. As she started down it, her frozen feet slipped from beneath her. She fell hard to the ground and a cry escaped her lips.

She wanted to lie there in the snow, wanted to close her eyes. But they were too close. So close that they could probably hear her panting for breath and the mad pounding of her heart.

Fear propelled her to move again, and she pushed herself up from the ground. Her legs, numb now, buckled beneath her, and she fell again. But she couldn't stay down.

If they found her, she would never be seen again.

Chapter One

The long bridge shuddered in the wind, creaking and groaning as the car traveled along it. The car shook as well, and Rosemary grasped the steering wheel in tight fists, fighting to keep the tires straight, fighting to keep the vehicle from blowing right off the bridge into the icy water below. The wrought iron railings were low and too spindly to provide any real protection for a car or a person.

If someone had tried to walk across this bridge . . .

She glanced across the passenger's seat and over that railing to the icy water far below that swirled and frothed around huge outcroppings of jagged rocks. She didn't want to think about what would happen to something or someone that fell from the bridge.

But because of the rocky shore, the bridge was one of the only ways on and off Bane Island, which was located three miles off the coast of Maine. Helicopters could land on the island, too, but it was too rocky and uneven for planes. And ferries only braved the distance from the mainland in the summer when the waves weren't quite as high and the water as icy. At least that was what Rosemary had discovered when she'd tried to make travel arrangements to Bane Island—to her sister.

If only she'd gotten the message sooner . . .

Her cell was tucked into the console of the rental car, charging. The weak reception drained the battery here just like it had when she'd been in New Zealand the past week. That was why she hadn't played the message sooner—because she hadn't even heard the call. Since the phone had been dead, it had gone directly to voicemail.

Even if she had dared to take one hand from the wheel, she didn't need to play the message now to remember what it said. It played over and over again in her mind, haunting her:

Rosemary . . .

Help me . . .

Mom and Dad sent me away to this horrible place, and I'm scared. So scared . . .

She hadn't had to say it. Rosemary could hear the fear painfully in her voice, making it shaky and high-pitched. Nearly hysterical . . .

And even though she was a teenager, Genevieve was never hysterical. She wasn't overly dramatic or emotional. Growing up in the same house as Rosemary had, it wouldn't have been allowed.

Because Rosemary had once been sent away, too, and it hadn't been within the same state like the place where Genevieve was. Bane was just a few hours north of Portland where Rosemary's family still lived. Rosemary did not.

She shuddered just as the bridge did when the car traveled along the last few yards of the three miles of flimsy metal and finally struck solid ground. Rock-solid ground. The tires skidded over the slick asphalt, and she clenched the steering wheel even tighter. But she didn't jerk it; she just gripped it and rode out the skid as the car careened dangerously close to the WELCOME TO BANE ISLAND sign. When the car straightened, she expelled a ragged breath.

She wasn't going to be able to help her sister if she crashed before she even found her. She knew where she was, though.

They sent me to this treatment center called Halcyon Hall. More like House of Horrors . . .

Then her voice had cracked with sobs as she'd pleaded with Rosemary.

Please come get me!

The minute Rosemary had played the message she'd tried calling her back, but then Genevieve's phone had gone directly to voicemail. Seeing the remoteness of this place, Rosemary could understand why. It was a miracle that Genevieve had been able to make the call at all.

"I'm here," she whispered into the cold interior of the car. "I'm here . . ."

Genevieve wouldn't be able to hear her, but would she sense it? Although Rosemary was so much older than her sister that they hadn't grown up together, they were close. Despite not living together, they shared a special bond.

So why hadn't Rosemary known Genevieve was in trouble? What had the girl gotten into that Mother had thought it necessary to send her for treatment? Or had she just done that to get her out of the way for the holidays? Rosemary had chosen to go away on a trip, too, because she hadn't wanted to come home to Portland for Thanksgiving—for the awkwardness that ensued whenever she was around her mom and stepfather.

They had taken a trip for the holiday, too, leaving on a European cruise once they had shipped off Genevieve to what she'd called the House of Horrors. From what Rosemary had found when she'd googled the place, she didn't think her sister was being overly dramatic now either.

The history of Halcyon Hall, formerly known as Bainesworth Manor, sounded like the plot of a horror movie complete with a curse and the ghosts of the cursed. The place had once been a psychiatric hospital for young women whose families had committed them for treatment. Treatments that, even if she wasn't a psychologist, Rosemary would have considered atrocious and inhumane. According to the articles she'd read, many of the patients had not survived those treatments, and legend claimed that for decades their ghosts had roamed the ruins of Bainesworth Manor. Even though the buildings and grounds had recently been renovated and advertised as a new age treatment center, its history and maybe its ghosts continued to haunt the property.

She shuddered again in revulsion and because of the chill that permeated her sweater and the tights she wore beneath a long skirt. The rental car's heater wasn't overly generous, or maybe it just couldn't keep out all the cold of this remote place with its miles of rocky shore, bluffs, mountains, and pine trees. But as she continued driving down the road from the bridge, she came upon a collection of buildings and houses and more streets intersecting the main one.

Halcyon Hall wasn't the only thing on the island. There was a town. She even passed a hotel as she continued down the street. Not that she was going to stay there or anywhere else on Bane Island. She intended to collect her sister and leave as soon as possible.

First, she had to find the damn place, though. Since it was on an island, it shouldn't have been that hard. According to the directions she'd downloaded before her phone died, the hall was on the main street that started at the bridge and ended at a pier that extended from the rocky shore to the water.

She reached the pier without finding it, though, and when the tires skidded on the icy pavement, she nearly wound up driving onto the pier. Instead of riding out the skid, she twisted the wheel and swerved as she braked. The car slid toward the rocky bluff and the waves crashing against it. With a sudden jerk, it finally stopped, and Rosemary's breath whooshed out with relief. Her hand trembling, she pulled her cell from the console. Even though the phone showed fully charged, nothing came up on the screen. There were no bars. No reception.

She drew in a breath now and turned the wheel again, steering away from the pier to head back toward town. Someone there would be able to tell her how to find the hall. To reach town, though, she had to travel back along that long stretch of empty road with only pine trees lining it. The road didn't remain empty for long, though. Before she reached town, lights flashed onto her rearview window and a siren pealed out, breaking the eerie silence.

She hadn't noticed the police SUV behind her or anywhere else along the road. It had appeared out of nowhere. And why was it now pulling her over? She'd done nothing wrong. This time . . .

But she dutifully pulled to the shoulder of the road, which was just a thin strip of gravel between the asphalt and the trunks of the pine trees. The police SUV didn't pull over as far, nearly blocking the lane behind her. Then the door opened, and an officer stepped from the vehicle. He was tall, clad in a dark uniform and, despite the overcast sky, dark sunglasses as well. As he approached her side of the car, she fumbled with the unfamiliar controls to lower the window.

"I'm sorry, Officer," she said. "This is a rental, so I don't know where everything is." In the car or on Bane Island. Maybe he could help her.

However, he stared at her with no expression on his face, his lips pressed in a tight line and his square jaw rigid. Finally he spoke. "Sheriff. I'm the sheriff."

Then why was he wasting his time making traffic stops? Not that there was any traffic on the road. Just her car.

"I'm sorry, Sheriff," she corrected herself. "I don't understand what I've done wrong."

"You were driving carelessly," he said. "You nearly went over the edge back by the pier."

"I slid," she said.

"You were driving too fast for conditions."

"I didn't realize how icy the roads are," she admitted. She shouldn't have been surprised, though, since it was late November. Michigan, where she lived now, got snow and ice storms before winter officially started, too.

"The roads are always icy this time of year."

Was he always icy? There was nothing welcoming about his demeanor, and he had to have guessed that she was not from Bane Island. He probably knew everybody on the island, and maybe that was the real reason he'd pulled her over—to find out who she was.

Because his next comment was, "License and registration, please."

She reached inside her purse and pulled out her wallet. After taking out her driver's license, she reached across the console for the glove box. "I don't know if the registration is in here or not."

"This is fine, Ms. Tulle," he said. And with her license

in his big, gloved hand, he turned and walked back toward his SUV.

The cold was blasting through her open window, but she hesitated to raise it. She didn't want to piss him off any more than he appeared to be. She drew in a breath of air so cold that it burned her lungs. Even though it had proven ineffectual, she reached over and cranked up the heater. The fan rattled as the air blasted from the vents. But the air wasn't hot. It was barely warm.

A cough startled her. She jerked against her seat belt before turning back toward her open window. "I didn't hear you come back," she murmured. And she hadn't expected him so quickly. She held out her hand for her license and whatever citation he was going to give her.

But he passed back her license alone. "What is your business here, Ms. Tulle?"

"Halcyon Hall."

Behind those dark glasses, he studied her face for a moment before nodding. "Of course."

"I'm here for my sister," she said. "To pick her up from the treatment center." She doubted Genevieve needed treatment for anything but Mother's overprotectiveness.

He shrugged, as if he didn't care or didn't believe her.

"Can you tell me where it is?"

"Here," he said.

"I know it's on the island but . . ."

He jerked his thumb behind him. "It's here," he said. "Behind those trees and the stone wall."

She peered around him. And now, stopped, she was able to study the trees and catch glimpses of rocks behind the trunks and pine boughs. "Oh, how do I get inside?"

"Are you sure you really want to?" he asked.

"I'm here for my sister," she reminded him.

He jerked his thumb farther down the road. "You'll find the gate if you drive slowly enough."

"I—I will," she assured him, and she waited for that ticket, which he must have realized.

"I'm letting you off with a warning this time," he said. "You need to proceed with more caution, Ms. Tulle. Much more caution."

Did his warning actually pertain to her driving or to something else? He didn't clarify, though, just turned and headed back toward his SUV.

Before she could raise the window, another noise startled her. This wasn't a cough but a cry—a high-pitched, forlorn cry.

Was it human?

"What was that?" she called back to the sheriff.

He stopped next to his vehicle and listened. Then his mouth moved, curving into a slight smile. "Coyote."

Shivering, she raised the window to shut out the cold and the cry. The sheriff got into his SUV but then just sat in it, as if waiting for her to pull away. So she did, slowly, just inching along the road until she found the wrought iron gate in the middle of the rock wall. Pine boughs stretched almost across the drive, obscuring the gate.

Didn't they want anyone to be able to find the place?

The gate was closed, but an intercom system was mounted onto the stone wall next to the gate. She could have lowered the window again, but she wouldn't have been able to reach the controls. So she opened her door instead and stepped out of the car.

And that cry echoed around her, that forlorn cry. Her finger trembled as she punched the button on the intercom panel.

"Halcyon Hall, how may we help you?" a melodic voice

greeted her. The woman sounded upbeat and welcoming, completely opposite of everything that had greeted Rosemary since her arrival on Bane Island.

She breathed a sigh of relief. "I'm here to pick up my sister, Genevieve Walcott."

"Your name?"

"Rosemary Tulle," she replied.

A long silence followed, so long that she pressed the button again. "Hello? Are you still there?" she asked. The wind kicked up, blasting icy bits of snow at her face as her long skirt swirled around her legs and her long hair whipped around her shoulders. She pulled a black strand from where it had tangled in her eyelashes and peered through the gate—at where a narrow driveway wound between more trees and rocks. "Hello?"

The speaker cracked, and the voice sounded nearly as cold as the wind when it replied, "Ms. Tulle, you are not on the list."

"List?"

"You are not on the visitor list."

"Genevieve called me," she said. "She asked me to come get her." Pleaded was more like it, desperately pleaded.

"You are not on the list." A click emanated from the speaker now as the intercom was shut off.

Rosemary repeatedly jabbed the button and called out, "Hello? Hello? Open the damn gates! Open them now!"

But the gates didn't open, and nobody replied to her. Nobody answered her but the coyote that cried out again—so forlornly. Rosemary stepped closer to the gates and peered through the wrought iron. A shadow fell across the driveway on the other side. It could have been from one of the trees or the boulders. But the shape of it looked more human than that—like someone stood there, watching her. . . .

The frozen ground crunched beneath the soles of his shoes as he walked across the grounds of the manor. Except that it wasn't the manor anymore. It was a hall now. A treatment center to help instead of harm.

But no matter how much renovation and remodeling had been done to the stone mansion and the other buildings on the property, the place would never fully escape the past. And no person would ever fully escape from Bainesworth Manor.

He hadn't.

Where was the cop—the *sheriff*—now when she needed him? As she traveled back to town, Rosemary didn't catch so much as a glimpse of another vehicle. But then she hadn't seen the sheriff either until his light had flashed in her rearview mirror.

Instead of looking for him, she should have just dialed 9-1-1 while standing at that gate. But the shadow falling across the driveway on the other side had unnerved her, and she'd rushed back to the rental vehicle. That must have been how Genevieve had felt when she'd left that voicemail—desperate to escape.

It wasn't just the treatment center property that was creepy, though. The entire island with its rocky landscape was cold and forbidding with gray clouds hanging low, casting shadows over everything and everyone. Maybe that was all Rosemary had seen—just the shadow of a cloud.

She doubted it, though. She'd *felt* someone's presence . . .

until she'd jumped back into the rental and locked the doors. Ever since then she'd felt alone, as if she was the only one left on the island. No cars passed her; no people walked along the road.

Then she drew closer to town, and a few cars drove along the streets intersecting the main one. She was not alone. She wasn't sure if that was reassuring or not, though—not here—on this godforsaken island.

Despite the brightly painted clapboard exteriors of the old buildings lining the streets, the town didn't appear any more welcoming than the rocky coast had as Rosemary had driven across that rickety bridge. Many of the awnings had been rolled back with closed-for-the-season signs posted on the front windows. She wasn't looking for a place to buy souvenirs or fudge, though. She was looking for the police department.

If the firehouse, a two-story brick building with a turret and fancy garage doors, hadn't drawn her attention, Rosemary might have missed it. The flat-roofed one-story building was squeezed in between the firehouse and a two-story Victorian house with a diner sign dangling from the gingerbread trim of the front porch. Light shining from the windows of the diner cast a glow on the front door of the short building and on the sign, in the shape of a badge, that adorned the tall steel door: BANE SHERIFF'S OFFICE.

A breath of relief slipped out of her lips and hung, like one of those gloomy clouds casting shadows over the island, inside the car. Maybe the heater had stopped working entirely. She didn't reach for the controls, though. Instead she gripped the steering wheel and turned the car into the lot on the other side of the diner. Ignoring the DINER-ONLY PARKING signs, she pulled into a space.

Her heart beating fast with fear for her sister, she pushed open the door and rushed toward the police department. As she passed the diner, the smell of roasting chicken wafted across the porch; her stomach rumbled, reminding her it was empty.

She hadn't eaten that day. She'd barely eaten since she'd played that message. Maybe once she got Genevieve out of Halcyon Hall, they would stop here before they left Bane Island. Or maybe Genevieve would just want to go home.

Home . . .

Rosemary's stomach churned, but it wasn't with hunger now. It was with dread. She didn't want to bring Genevieve home any more than she wanted to leave her here. Determination surging through her, she pushed open the door to the sheriff's office and stepped inside the building. Not that she felt like she was inside when faced with another wall—with another door and window in it. She gripped the knob of that door, but it didn't turn no matter how hard she twisted. So she stepped over to the window. A desk sat behind it—an empty desk.

She tapped on the glass and called out, "Hello!" Urgency rushing through her, she pounded harder. "Hello! Hello!"

A door behind the desk opened, and a man in the same blue uniform the sheriff had worn stepped through it. He wasn't the sheriff, though. He wasn't as tall or as broad, or maybe the sheriff had only seemed that way because she'd been sitting in the car. The officer pressed a button on the desk, and his voice echoed throughout the small reception area. "How may I help you?" he asked.

"You can help me get into Halcyon Hall."

He gestured at the window with his index finger, making

a pointing motion. She glanced around and noticed a speaker and button next to the glass—which must have been sound-proof and probably bulletproof. The security was nearly the same as at the hall. Pressing the button, she repeated her request.

The man's mouth curved into a slight grin. "You and everyone else . . ." he murmured. "The hall is a private facility. We have no jurisdiction there no matter how much . . ." He trailed off again, leaving her to wonder what he left unsaid.

"My sister is at the treatment center," Rosemary explained. "But they won't let me in to see her."

"You're not on the list."

She tensed. "How do you know that?"

"You don't get inside unless you're on the list," he replied matter-of-factly.

She narrowed her eyes and studied the officer on the other side of that glass. He was younger than she was, probably still in his twenties, or maybe he looked that young from the fullness of his face. He wasn't broad like the sheriff, but he was stocky, his belly straining the buttons of his uniform. "You know a lot about the hall despite having no jurisdiction there."

He shrugged and remarked, "Bane isn't that big an island."

Not big enough to justify bulletproof glass in the police department . . . unless it was a more dangerous place than it appeared, which increased Rosemary's sense of urgency. "My sister called me to pick her up," she said.

He shrugged again. "Then she should have put your name on the list."

"I—I'm sure she did," she insisted.

He shook his head. "Then you would have been on it."

"They must be lying," she said.

"They?"

"The hall—whoever picked up when I pressed the intercom button." Like the button she pressed now—to speak to the officer. "They're lying."

"Why?"

"I don't know," she said. "That's why I'm here. They're holding my sister hostage in that creepy place."

"People pay a hell of a lot of money to go there. They don't need to hold anybody against their will."

"They're holding my sister," she said. "I have a voice-mail from her to prove it." But when she reached for her phone, she remembered she'd left it in the rental car—charging. She'd been so anxious to get help. She suspected the officer wasn't interested in helping her, though. Maybe once he heard the voicemail . . .

"I'll go get my phone," she said. "You'll hear it in her voice—the fear. She wants out of that place."

"Why doesn't she just check herself out then?" he asked. "Or better yet, why did she check herself in there?"

"She didn't," Rosemary said. "Our parents put her in there." So they could go on their vacation without worrying that she'd get in trouble . . . like Rosemary had.

His brow furrowed. "Your parents? How old is your sister?"

"Seventeen," she said.

His lips curved again into another slight smile. This one felt patronizing. "Oh . . ."

"She's being held prisoner," she insisted. "She was put in there against her will." Just like the girls she'd read about, the ones who'd been committed to the manor all those years ago. "You need to help me get her out of there."

He shook his head.

"Why won't you help?"

"Because it's not a police matter, Miss," he said. "It's a family matter. You need to talk to your family."

"I tried," she said. "The damn hall won't let me through the gates."

"Your parents," he said. "You need to talk to them. They must have a reason for admitting her for treatment and a reason for not putting you on the visitor list."

That dread churned in her stomach again. "I tried talking to them," she admitted. She'd left voicemails for them like Genevieve had left for her. But they hadn't returned her calls.

He shrugged. "This is a family matter."

The door behind her creaked open, and a woman stepped into the small reception area with her. She also wore a navy-blue uniform. How many officers did this small island have? Just how the hell dangerous was it?

"Can you help me?" she asked the older woman. Her face was softer and kinder than the male officer's and certainly more so than the sheriff's.

Before the woman would answer, that voice emanated from the speaker again. "I've got this, Margaret. She's here about the hall."

The woman's soft expression hardened then. She juggled containers in her hands as she reached for the door Rosemary had tried opening just moments ago. The knob turned easily for the woman, and she pushed open the door to step inside what appeared to be an even narrower foyer than the reception area. Rosemary considered following her, but she doubted it would matter what she said to these officers. She wouldn't be able to convince them to help her.

Not unless . . .

But she wasn't ready to share her secrets with strangers; she hadn't even shared them yet with a friend. Most of the time she wouldn't admit them to herself.

The door closed behind the woman, locking Rosemary out again. She pressed that button again and asked, "Where's the sheriff?" Maybe he would help her. After all, he had told her where to find the gate to the hall.

"Sheriff Howell is not on duty tonight," the male officer told her.

"But—but he pulled me over just a short while ago—near the hall," she said.

The officer's already small eyes narrowed. "He's not supposed to be out there. . . ." Something about his tone implied that it wasn't just because he hadn't been on duty but for another reason, something to do with that damn place.

"Why not?" she asked.

His jaw tightened momentarily before he replied, "It's a private facility, Miss. We have no jurisdiction there." As if that was enough of an explanation, he stepped away from the glass, through the door that must have led back to where the female officer had gone.

Rosemary could have hit the intercom button again, but she suspected that, just like at Halcyon Hall, nobody would answer her call for admittance. Nobody would help her. So she would have to figure out another way to get her sister out of that creepy place.

Chapter Two

A knock rattled the front door, startling Bonita so that she dropped the teacup she held. It struck the saucer with a clatter and spilled milky tea onto the tablecloth.

"I'm sorry," she said, tears glistening in her glazed blue eyes.

Evelyn reached across the table and patted her sister's hand. "It's fine, honey."

Even now, all these years later, sudden noises frightened Bonita. That wasn't all that scared her, though.

Evelyn forced a smile for her sister as the doorbell pealed out now. Their visitor must have found it behind the brown ivy that wound around their house like bindings. Too bad the landscaper had moved out before taking care of the invasive vines. For a reduction in his room and board costs, Theodore Bowers had promised to take care of the grounds. Evelyn should have known better than to trust the young man, though.

She should have known better than to trust anyone anymore. She squeezed her sister's hand before rising from the table in the parlor. She walked through the open pocket doors into the foyer and drew in a breath before pulling open the door.

She forced another smile for the stranger standing on the front porch. Evelyn knew everyone who lived on the island, and this woman, with her long black hair and bright blue eyes, was not a local. "Hello," she greeted her. "How may I help you?"

"Do you have a room available?" the woman asked.

Evelyn hesitated. Theodore's room wasn't the only empty one in the house—the big house that cost a fortune for heat and electricity and property taxes. She couldn't afford to turn away a prospective boarder no matter how much she suspected that she should, especially after the call she'd taken earlier.

"The hotel in town is closed," the young woman said, her voice cracking with frustration. Dark circles of exhaustion rimmed her eyes. Except for those dark smudges beneath her eyes, her skin was so very pale. "I don't know where else to go."

"The hotels on the mainland are open," Evelyn said, "if you're just looking for a place for the night."

"I—I don't know how long I'll be here," the woman replied. "I'm trying to get into Halcyon Hall."

"They don't have any vacancies?" Evelyn asked.

Color flushed the woman's face now. "I—I didn't think about just trying to check in." She thrust her hand into her purse and pulled out a cell phone.

Instinctively Evelyn reached out and covered her hand. "Don't," she said, and her voice trembled now. "Don't stay there. Stay here. We have a room available."

"Which one?" Bonita asked shyly as she joined them in the foyer.

She was older than Evelyn, closer to seventy than sixty now. Even though her hair had turned a beautiful shade of snowy white, no lines marred her skin, which was pale like their visitor's. Despite the white hair, she looked much younger than her age, younger than Evelyn, who only had one thick streak of white in her auburn hair. Evelyn felt no envy for her sister, though, only love.

And pity . . .

"How about the rose room?" she asked.

The young woman tensed, and her blue eyes narrowed slightly with suspicion. "That's my name," she said. "Rosemary. Rosemary Tulle."

"What a coincidence," Evelyn said—of her slip-up which the woman had very nearly caught. "Then it's meant to be that you stay in that room." And not at the manor. Evelyn couldn't call it the hall—because she knew what it was, what it would always be: cursed.

Evelyn extended her hand to the young woman. "Nice to meet you, Rosemary. I'm Evelyn Pierce and this is my sister, Bonita."

Bonita didn't hold out her hand, and she dipped her head down to avoid meeting the stranger's gaze. She hadn't always been like that—hadn't always been so shy and scared. She'd once been effervescent and energetic and a little wild . . . until she'd been sent to Bainesworth Manor.

"Nice to meet you," Rosemary replied as she shook Evelyn's hand. She turned toward Bonita and warmly said, "Nice to meet you, too, Bonita. What a lovely name."

Bonita glanced up then, and a slight smile curved her lips.

"And a lovely smile," Rosemary added.

Somehow she knew exactly how to treat Bonita— gently, with kindness, instead of ignoring her as so many others did. Maybe having the young woman stay with them wouldn't be so bad . . . and her money for board would help pay some of the bills.

"Do you have any bags?" Evelyn asked.

Rosemary nodded. "Yes." Now she drew a key fob from her purse. "I'll get them."

"I'll help," Bonita eagerly offered. Whenever anyone showed her any kindness or attention, she responded with the same.

"While you two are getting the bags, I'll heat up some soup for you," Evelyn said. "We had clam and corn chowder for dinner."

An almost lustful-sounding sigh escaped Rosemary's lips. "That sounds wonderful. Thank you." Her blue eyes glistened like Bonita's had earlier, as if tears were welling in hers as well.

Evelyn's heart warmed with sympathy for the young woman. She had a reason for being on the island; anyone who came this time of year wasn't here as a tourist. That was why the inn was closed in town. The only thing that drew business now was the manor, and their guests stayed there—not at the inn.

Evelyn shivered and not just because of the cold breeze that blew in the door Bonita had opened. The thought of the manor chilled her . . . and terrified her.

The cell phone vibrated in his pocket, and he quickly pulled it out and pressed the accept button. "Yes?"

"She came here," the caller said in such a raspy whisper that Evelyn Pierce's voice was barely recognizable. "She took a room."

He cursed—even though he'd known—Rosemary Tulle wasn't going anywhere—not without her sister.

"I—I had to rent it to her," the older woman said, defensively. "We can't pay the taxes and utilities for the house without boarders."

"I know," he assured her. "It would have been better if she hadn't stayed, though."

"Better for whom?" Evelyn asked.

"For her," he replied.

"She wants to get into the manor," she said, her whisper cracking with fear now.

"I know."

"That would be a mistake," Evelyn said.

He wholeheartedly agreed. "That's why it would have been better for her if she left."

Because she was determined to get into a place where nothing good ever happened . . .

Would the same woman answer the phone who had answered the intercom at the gate?

Rosemary considered ways to disguise her voice, but eventually she would have to give her name and her credit card to book a room. Like she'd booked this lovely room at the boardinghouse. Wallpaper, with tiny rosebuds on it, stretched between the creamy white wainscoting and the tall ceilings. The same tiny rosebuds adorned the bedspread on the shiny brass bed.

She wanted to pull back that comforter and crawl into bed. The delicious chowder had satisfied her hunger, but she was tired. Even as exhausted as she was, though, she wouldn't be able to sleep—not until she spoke with Genevieve.

If she wasn't on the list to see her, she probably wasn't on it for phone calls either. What had happened to the girl's cell, though? Like most teenagers, Genevieve was never without her phone.

Why did all Rosemary's calls go directly to her voicemail? She tried it again, just to confirm, and now the recorded message informed her that the voicemail box she'd dialed was full.

She probably wasn't the only one who'd left messages for the teenager. Undoubtedly Genevieve's friends had as well. Had she played any of them? Did she even still have her phone?

What the hell had happened to the girl?

What had they done to her at the treatment center? They claimed to use only diet, exercise, and counseling to help people deal with a wide range of ailments: eating disorders, drug/alcohol abuse, anxiety, and post-traumatic stress disorder. Which had Mother claimed that Genevieve had?

Her fingers trembling, Rosemary searched for the number for Halcyon Hall and pressed the button to connect. A female voice answered, but the woman didn't sound exactly the same as the one who had answered the intercom earlier.

"Halcyon Hall, how may we help you?"

Rosemary bit her bottom lip to hold in the words—the accusations—she wanted to utter. After clearing them from her throat, she replied, "I'd like to make a reservation."

"When would you like to seek treatment?" the receptionist asked.

"As soon as possible," she replied. Like now . . . She could definitely claim to have anxiety right now; she was so damn worried about Genevieve.

"The earliest opening we have is May," the woman said, and then she read off the beginning and end dates for the week.

"That's six months away," Rosemary said. "You must have something sooner."

"We only have that opening due to a cancellation," the woman replied, and some of the pleasantness left her voice.

"Halcyon Hall is exclusive, so we would need to approve your stay before we could book that reservation for you. We have an online application process for appro—"

Rosemary disconnected the call. She wasn't waiting six months to get into the place. She needed to get inside now. But that was unlikely to happen tonight.

Frustrated and chilled, she pulled back the comforter and crawled beneath it. The bed was as soft as it looked and smelled subtly of roses as if the flowers on the wallpaper and comforter were real. As if she was in a garden . . .

Her eyes drifted closed, and darkness enveloped her. *She couldn't see much—just glimpses—of his face. She could feel his arms around her as he carried her.*

She stared up at him, stared at the cleft in his chin, the way a lock of blond hair fell across his forehead, and in his green eyes, her image reflected back at her. She looked so disheveled, her hair tousled, her eyes wide.

"What—what happened?" she asked.

She remembered having a drink.

Or two . . .

That was stupid. Drinking was stupid. She realized that now. But she'd thought it would loosen her up, that it would get her to relax because he always made her so nervous.

She was nervous now.

But he smiled down at her, and a dimple pierced one of his lean cheeks. "Nothing . . ." he murmured. "Nothing happened . . ."

She closed her eyes again, shutting out his handsome face. The darkness was deeper when she opened her eyes again. She couldn't see him. She couldn't see anything.

She could only feel—the hands holding her down—the

pain shooting through her body. She thrashed and tried to get away.

Pain . . .

So much pain . . .

Tears burned her eyes. And a scream burned her throat.

She awoke—sitting upright in that room with the roses on the walls and the bed. This wasn't where the dream took place. That had been at home.

When it had felt like home.

Before that night . . .

After that night—that night she remembered always with pain and fear—nothing had ever been the same.

Chapter Three

Whittaker Lawrence stared across his desk at the campaign manager. With his bald head, thick neck and muscular body, Martin Snowden looked more like a boxing manager than the renowned political strategist that he was. But from what Whit had learned in his years as a district attorney and now a judge, boxing and politics weren't all that different.

That was why the thought of running for governor had adrenaline coursing through Whit's veins. He was ready for a fight.

"Is there anything you need to tell me about? Anything that the press is going to dig up about you?" the campaign manager asked.

"Nothing that they haven't already dug up," he said. Not that it had ever been a secret that he was the bastard son of a maid and her millionaire employer. That millionaire had never claimed him but had paid for his prep school. Once Whit had learned the truth of that *affair*, though, he had refused anything else from the man. Whit had put himself through college and law school.

"The reporter who asked to interview you—she's not known for fluff pieces," Martin warned him.

Whit expelled a breath of relief. "Good." He wanted to talk about issues, about law, not about the past . . . *anything* about the past. Not how he'd come into the world and not how his late wife and child had gone out of it.

"No, not good," Martin said, his gravelly voice even gruffer. "Edie Stone only does a story if she thinks there is a story to tell. A salacious story. I think we should cancel the interview."

Whit snorted. "I can handle a reporter, Marty. I've been handling them for years." He'd personally taken on every high-profile case that had come up for prosecution and not just because he was a damn good lawyer—although he had been.

Still was . . .

He'd been wasted as a judge. But pride had made it impossible for him to go backward—to prosecuting. Then he'd realized he'd rather be making laws than just enforcing them.

Martin shook his head almost pityingly.

Whit had had enough of people's pity. "I can handle this reporter," he insisted.

"She likes to dig up dirt and expose everyone's nasty little secrets," Martin warned him.

Whit shrugged off the other man's concerns. "There's nothing for her to expose." Nothing that would hurt him.

"Every man has something or someone in his past that haunts him," Martin persisted.

Whit could not deny that. . . .

Despite the softness of the bed and the comfort of the room, Rosemary awoke unrested—exhaustion hanging heavily around her shoulders with her guilt. So much guilt . . .

She dragged herself up from the mattress, surprised to see that she still wore her clothes. The long skirt, the sweater . . .

No wonder sweat dampened her hair and her tank top beneath her sweater. She needed a shower. She needed to wake up—to shake off the sleep. No. Not the sleep . . .

She needed to shake off the dream. But it wasn't a dream. It was a nightmare. One that always left her feeling the need to shower it off, to try to wash it all away.

But it never completely left her mind. The darkness lingered, just like those gloomy clouds hanging low over the island. After crossing the room to the window, she pushed the curtains aside to stare out . . . at the gloom. Today it was a thick fog that wrapped tightly around the house like a curtain wound around the entire exterior.

Suddenly claustrophobic, she sucked in a deep breath, but it didn't feel as if she got any air in her lungs. They ached . . . like her heart ached . . . for Genevieve. She had to get back to the treatment center. So she grabbed her bag and headed across the hall to the bathroom, and she showered off the last of that nightmare.

But it still felt as if there were hands on her flesh, touching her against her will. So she turned the water colder until it was like ice against her skin. Her teeth chattered, and she shivered but she endured it for a moment longer before she twisted off the faucet. Then she stepped out of the claw-foot bathtub. Her wet foot slipped against the small, marble hexagon tiles, but she caught the edge of the pedestal sink and stopped herself from falling.

She had to be careful. She couldn't get hurt—not when Genevieve was counting on her. Using one of the towels, which was as soft and fluffy as the bed had been, she dried off quickly and reached for her bag.

After clasping her bra and pulling up her panties, she stepped into a pair of jeans, loose jeans, in case she had to scale that damn stone wall today. She would—if she had to, if they wouldn't let her in.

They had to let her in.

Dread churned in her stomach. She knew who could put her name on that damn list. Who should have already put her name on that damn list.

A knock rattled the bathroom door and reminded Rosemary that she was not alone. There were probably other boarders in the house. But a soft voice called out, "Miss Tulle, breakfast is ready if you're hungry."

She shouldn't have been—not after eating so late the evening before. But her stomach rumbled. "I'll be right down," she said. But first she applied some makeup, so her dark circles wouldn't scare the Pierce sisters.

After cleaning up the bathroom and putting away her bag, she headed down the elaborate, winding front stairwell to the foyer. The house reminded her of the one in which she'd grown up—with tall ceilings and windows and elaborate woodwork. But the house where she'd grown up had been meticulously maintained—because her mother believed they had an image to maintain, a façade of perfection.

This house showed its age with scuff marks on the hardwood floors and some water spots on the ceiling. Those imperfections made it more welcoming to Rosemary, though, than that perfect house her mother and stepfather still owned. Because it was truly anything but perfect . . .

Just like their so-called family. Mother wanted so very badly for everyone to believe they were close and happy. But, after Rosemary's father died, that just hadn't been possible—not with how quickly her mother had moved on and how she'd behaved. Desperately . . .

Was she that scared of being alone?

Rosemary found that she preferred it. It was safer than trusting someone only to be disappointed or . . . destroyed. No. She hadn't been destroyed, but their sorry excuse for a family had been. But had that been her mother's fault or hers?

"We'll be ready in a moment," Evelyn called through a crack in what must have been the kitchen door. It was on the other side of the enormous dining room. Instead of having one long table in the room, there were a few. One was a small round table tucked into the curve of a bay window that looked out over what must be the garden when the plants were alive instead of brown and dormant. Bonita stood over that table, carefully placing silverware next to three delicate-looking china plates.

"What a beautiful place setting," Rosemary praised her.

The woman turned and smiled widely at her. The smile barely brightened her blue eyes, though, which still appeared glazed as if she'd been drugged. The psychologist in Rosemary kicked in, wondering what condition the older woman had. Despite her age, she seemed so childlike. Perhaps she had a developmental disability.

Given her age there might have been a complication during her birth that the doctor or the hospital, especially if she'd been born on the island, hadn't been equipped to handle. Maybe the cord had been wrapped around her neck, denying oxygen to her brain. Maybe she'd been premature; she was still quite petite.

"Everything all right?" Evelyn asked, her voice a little sharp with concern and protectiveness, as she joined them. Her gaze ping-ponged between Rosemary and her sister.

She was taller with a musculature to her build that bespoke the hard work she did around the boardinghouse.

Rosemary smiled at her with reassurance. "Yes, I was just complimenting Bonita on what a good job she'd done setting the table."

Evelyn released a shaky little sigh and forced a smile. "Yes, she is amazing. I don't know what I'd do without her. I certainly wouldn't be able to take care of this place on my own."

Bonita turned toward her sister. "You need *me*?"

"Yes, I do," Evelyn assured her.

A pang struck Rosemary's heart at the genuine love between the sisters.

"I need you *and* my baby," Bonita murmured.

Rosemary looked at Evelyn.

"She's talking about a doll," she explained. "She keeps misplacing it."

Noticing the large tray weighing heavily on Evelyn's arms, Rosemary stepped back so the older woman could settle it onto the table. There was a carafe with the aroma of rich coffee drifting from it, and covered serving dishes from which other smells emanated, like cinnamon and bacon.

"Are there more boarders joining us?" Rosemary asked. "That looks like so much."

"We—we don't have other boarders at the moment," Evelyn said, and her brow furrowed with concern. "Will you be staying?"

Rosemary settled onto the upholstered chair Bonita had pushed back from the table for her. "Yes," she said with a nod. "For now."

Evelyn sat across from her and Bonita took the chair between them, staring out into the dead garden. As she held out the carafe of coffee, Evelyn studied Rosemary's face. "You weren't able to get a room at the . . ."—her throat moved as if she was choking down something before she managed to finish—". . . hall?"

Rosemary shook her head. "No."

"Hall?" Bonita asked. "Why would you want to stay in a hall?"

"It's actually a facility where people go to feel better," Rosemary told her. At least that was how Halcyon Hall advertised itself with no mention of the psychiatric hospital the property had once been.

"Are you sick?" Bonita asked with concern.

Rosemary shook her head again. "No. My sister is there. My parents booked her into the place, and they won't let me inside to see her."

Another shaky breath slipped between Evelyn's lips, and her skin, which must have been flushed from the heat of the stove, grew suddenly pale. "Oh, no, it's happening again."

"What do you mean?" Rosemary asked. "What do you know about Halcyon Hall?"

Evelyn shook her head. "Nothing." She reached for a serving dish, but her fingers trembled when she lifted the cover. "You should eat before the French toast gets cold."

Rosemary's hunger had turned into a cold knot of dread in her stomach. "What do you mean that it's happening again?"

Evelyn had to be referring to the young women committed to the place when it had been called Bainesworth Manor, when all those horrible things had been done to them. Experimental procedures. Lobotomies. Shock treatments. But those treatments were no longer used. None of those things were being done now.

To Genevieve . . .

Her pulse quickened as fear tripped it. It was almost as if her parents had committed Genevieve like those families had committed the young women decades ago.

Evelyn turned toward her sister and stared at her for a long moment. Bonita, making patterns with syrup on her French toast, didn't notice the other woman's interest. Evelyn turned back to Rosemary and shook her head. "I *can't* talk about it."

Was that what had happened to Bonita? Had she been committed to the manor? Had she been hurt there? If so, Rosemary could understand neither of them wanting to discuss it.

But Rosemary had no choice. "I need to talk about the place. I need to find out how to get inside. I *can't* leave my sister at Halcyon Hall."

Bonita paused with the syrup bottle gripped tightly yet in her hand. "Halcyon Hall . . . the manor?" That glazed look in her eyes turned from one of confusion to terror. "No! No!" she cried out as she dropped the bottle. Then she jumped up from the table and nearly tripped over her upended chair as she ran from the room.

"What?" Rosemary asked. "What's wrong?"

"That's why we can't talk about the manor."

"Bainesworth Manor . . ." Rosemary murmured. Genevieve had called it House of Horrors. Several articles had referred to it as that, too, because of what they'd done there. To Bonita?

Rosemary wanted to ask if she'd once been committed there, but before she could, Evelyn jumped up from the table, too, presumably to go after her sister. But she stopped and looked back at Rosemary. "Don't talk about that place. And don't go anywhere near it. It's cursed."

* * *

Abigail Walcott gripped the cell phone tightly in her hand as she stared down at the screen—at all the missed calls from her daughter. From Rosemary . . .

Why wouldn't she give it a rest?

Because it was about Genevieve . . .

Of course Genevieve had called her for help—almost as if she knew. Maybe she did. The girl needed help but not the kind that Rosemary could give her.

Abigail sighed.

"Rosemary again?" Bobby asked. He was so handsome with his golden blond hair and deeply tanned skin. Ridiculously handsome . . .

And young, nearly two decades younger than Abigail was. She knew why he'd married her; she was under no illusions that her bank account had been more of a draw than her fading beauty. But she had once been beautiful . . . like Rosemary.

Rosemary was so beautiful.

And so stubborn . . .

"She's not going to stop calling," Abigail said with dread. Eventually she would have to pick up; she would have to talk to her, explain. But she really shouldn't have to explain herself to Rosemary; that wasn't their deal. A deal made so long ago . . .

The phone trilled almost on cue. But it wasn't another call this time.

"She left a voicemail," Bobby said as if Abigail couldn't see that on the screen that illuminated a small circle of their dark bedroom.

She didn't want to hear her daughter's voice, hadn't wanted to hear it for many years now. But knowing

Rosemary wasn't going to give up, she clicked the play button: "Mother, you don't need to call me back . . ."

Abigail released a shaky breath of relief that she wouldn't actually have to speak with her daughter.

Rosemary continued, "You just need to call Halcyon Hall and tell them that I can take Genevieve out of that godawful place. I don't know what you were thinking to send her *there*."

Abigail shook her head. How couldn't she know? How couldn't she understand—after what Rosemary had done? She should know that they couldn't have trusted her . . . *Genevieve* . . . to stay alone while they'd gone on that cruise. A cruise they'd had to cut short because of her. The girl was getting as wild as Rosemary had once been. Maybe even wilder . . .

"I am going to get her out of there—with or without your help," Rosemary continued. "But if you don't help, I will be forced to take action. I will be forced to tell the hall and the authorities the truth. If you want to keep your damn secret, you need to call them right away."

Abigail sucked in a breath. "She wouldn't . . ."

They'd had a deal—a pact, really.

Bobby's face, usually so tan from the bronzer he liberally applied, suddenly grew pale in that eerie glow from her cell screen. "She can't, right?"

He'd heard what Abigail had—the determination in Rosemary's voice. She was on another one of her damn crusades—a rescue mission. This person mattered even more to her than those sick people whose problems she listened to.

Genevieve really mattered to her despite Abigail's best efforts to keep them apart. Rosemary mattered to Genevieve as well, or she wouldn't have called her for help.

Would they be as close if Genevieve knew the truth?

Was Rosemary really willing to take such a risk?

"She won't," Abigail murmured, but she wasn't totally convinced. Rosemary sounded very concerned about Genevieve and she didn't even know everything, didn't know that she was already too late to help her.

"Of course not," Bobby said, and he nodded so sharply that a lock of hair fell over his smooth brow. "She doesn't really know anything. And what she does know, she can't prove." He released a ragged sigh of relief. "Nobody's going to believe her."

Unlike Abigail, Bobby had managed to convince himself, but she knew her daughter better than Bobby did. She knew how stubborn Rosemary could be—how determined. Just like her father, she was obstinate and cared too damn much. Being like that had sent him to an early grave, which was where Rosemary would wind up as well—if she didn't stop meddling.

Abigail gripped the phone more tightly. Should she call her back? Should she try to deter her?

But what would she say?

Even the truth wouldn't stop Rosemary. She wouldn't believe what Abigail did—that it was already too late to help Genevieve. She would keep trying. And that might put them all in danger . . .

Chapter Four

The wrought iron gates rose high above her into the fog hanging ominously over the island. She'd passed the place and had nearly landed in the ocean again. This time the sheriff hadn't pulled her over to warn her to be more careful. But the Pierce sisters had both cautioned her again before she'd left the boardinghouse.

"It's too dangerous," Evelyn had reiterated.

"Cursed," Bonita had murmured.

Rosemary suspected it wasn't just the place Bonita considered cursed as those glazed-looking blue eyes had momentarily focused . . . on her. Bracing herself against nerves and the cold, she drew in a deep breath as she stepped out of her rental car to push the button for the intercom.

"Welcome to Halcyon Hall, how may we help you?"

Welcome? Hopefully, this time they would.

"I'd like to see my sister, Genevieve Walcott," she replied.

"Name?" the voice crackled out of the speaker.

Was it the same person who'd answered the intercom yesterday or the one who'd answered the phone the night before? Rosemary wasn't certain. And it really didn't matter—as long as she was on the list this time.

"Rosemary Tulle," she replied. Then she sucked in another breath, of frosty fog air, and waited for those enormous gates to open, but the wrought iron didn't budge. Something moved, though, a shadow shifting in the fog. Like the day before, someone stood inside those gates. Watching her?

Finally the speaker crackled again. "I'm sorry. You're not on the list."

Hadn't she given it enough time?

"My mother was going to call and authorize you to let me visit Genevieve," she said. Abigail had to call . . . if she wanted Rosemary to keep her damn secret.

Not that Rosemary intended to keep it anymore—not after her mother had failed to uphold her side of their agreement. She had promised to always make sure that Genevieve was safe and happy. And then she'd put her here . . .

While it claimed to be a new age treatment center, it seemed very like the psychiatric hospital it had once been—where parents had committed their wayward daughters. But Genevieve had not been wayward. She wasn't like Rosemary at all.

"Has she called?" Rosemary asked. "Has Abigail Walcott called?"

"I'm not at liberty to reveal guests' call logs."

"My mother isn't a guest. Has she called you or the director or whoever the hell controls this damn list?"

The speaker crackled now with a sigh. "You're not on the list, Ms. Tulle."

So either her mother hadn't called, or she had called and denied Rosemary access to Genevieve. Her frustration turned to fury, heating her skin despite the cold, damp fog hovering all around her—like that damn shadow hovered on the other side of the gates.

"You have to let me inside," Rosemary persisted. "I have to see my sister. I have to make sure she's all right."

"You are not on the l—"

"Your list be damned!" Rosemary shouted as she pounded her fist on the intercom panel. "You have to let me in!"

"You will not be allowed inside, Ms. Tulle," the voice replied. "And you need to leave the premises, or we will contact the authorities and report you for trespassing."

The sheriff hadn't given her the citation for reckless driving, but he might give her one for trespassing. Maybe that was why the officer hadn't helped her yesterday— because the police department's allegiance was to the hall, which was probably the biggest employer and taxpayer on the island. Who else did they employ? Security guards— to keep guests inside and unwanted visitors out?

Was that who was hovering on the other side of those gates?

She walked away from the intercom to squeeze in between the car's front bumper and the wrought iron. The scroll design was so tight that there was no way she could get through the metal. The gates were so high, like the stone wall on either side, that she wouldn't be able to scale them. She gripped the cold metal in tight fists and shook it.

That shadow moved closer toward the gates, and a man stepped from the fog. He was tall and lanky with a knit cap pulled low over his weather-chafed face. He was young.

"Hello!" she called out to him.

He didn't look like a security guard. He was probably

one of the groundskeepers since a pair of long clippers dangled from one gloved hand.

"Can you open the gates?" she asked, as she rattled the metal again.

He shook his head. "No."

"Please," she implored him. "I need to get inside. I need to see my sister."

He just stared at her.

"Genevieve Walcott," she said. "Do you know her? Have you seen her?"

He shook his head again. "I don't see the guests."

It was so damn cold that it was unlikely any of them had been out walking the grounds.

"I need to talk to her," Rosemary said. "I need to get inside."

"They won't let you in?" he asked.

She shook her head now, and a lock of her hair caught in the wrought iron. She pulled back, and the black strands clung to the metal. "I need your help."

"I can't," he said again.

Did he not know how to open them? Or was he afraid to? She rattled the metal again.

"Don't do that," he warned her as he glanced uneasily around them. "The guards will come."

His warning chilled her and confirmed her suspicion about the hall having security guards. But why did they need them? To keep people out or to keep people in?

Before she could ask him anything else, he slipped back into the bushes and into the fog. Not even his shadow remained.

He was gone. He wouldn't help her. Who would help her?

Dare she act on her threat to her parents?

She had no choice. She had to get Genevieve out of this place—because she was beginning to believe Bonita. It was cursed. Or maybe Rosemary was because she now had to relive her recurring nightmare during the day. In order to secure Genevieve's future, Rosemary had to face the horror of her past.

"You don't look nearly as ferocious as I've been told you are," Whit mused as he leaned back in the chair behind his desk and studied the reporter sitting across from him.

Edie Stone was petite and blond and young—too young for the reputation she'd already earned. Her lips curved into a slight smile. "I was just thinking the same thing about you, Mr. Lawrence."

He chuckled.

"Or should I call you Your Honor?"

"You're not in my court," he pointed out.

"Considering your reputation as the hanging judge, that's a good thing." She glanced around his office. "But I am in your chambers."

"Would you have rather we met somewhere else?" he asked.

She narrowed her eyes and studied him like he'd been studying her. "Should I?" she asked. "Am I in any danger being alone with you?"

He grinned. "From all I've heard about you, I am the one who's in danger."

She chuckled now. "Only if you have something to hide, Mr. Lawrence."

"Whit," he told her. "And I have nothing to hide."

She smiled now and shook her head. "Everyone has something they'd like kept secret."

He nodded in agreement. "That might be so. But I don't think secrets are possible nowadays, not with reporters like you."

She tensed in the chair and lifted her pointy chin. "Are you one of those politicians who resent and vilify the press to detract from your scandals?"

"What scandals, Ms. Stone?" he challenged her, but as he did, a frisson of unease chased through his stomach. Was challenging her a mistake?

She narrowed her eyes again as she considered him. "That's what I'd like to know, Mr. Lawrence," she said.

"I'm sure you already know everything about me," he assured her. "I'm tough on crime. But I'm only as tough as the law allows me to be. That's what I would like to change as governor. I'd like to introduce some new legislation that would—"

"I am well aware of your campaign propaganda," she interrupted him. "Mr. Clean made sure I had the party line."

A laugh sputtered out. "Mr. Clean?" But he could understand why she had given Martin, with his bald head and brawny build, that nickname.

Her face flushed slightly, but she smiled. "Yes, he also told me about the tragedy you overcame—not that I haven't heard about it from every other interview done on you. I'm not here to cover those articles, Mr. Lawrence. I'm here to find the story."

That frisson of unease passed through his stomach once again. Martin had been right—this had been a bad idea. Edie Stone was only going to run a piece on him if she could dig up some dirt.

"Then you're wasting your time and mine, Ms. Stone," he replied, and he stood. "I'll show you to the door." He walked around the corner of his desk, but as he did, the intercom buzzed. Maybe his clerk had been listening and had known it was time to end the interview. He clicked a button. "Yes, Dwight?"

"Sir, I hate to interrupt you, but someone is insisting on seeing you right now," Dwight replied, his voice rising with discomfort.

Whit didn't care; he'd take any excuse to get out of this meeting with the reporter who was looking only for a scandal. "Who is it?" he asked.

"A Miss Rosemary Tulle," Dwight replied.

"Rosemary Tulle?" Whit had to be dreaming. She couldn't be here, this close, just a door away from him.

"Yes," Dwight replied. "I told her that she should have made an appointment, that you're very busy, but she insisted that I buzz you. She insists that you will see her."

"He will!" a voice shouted so loudly that Whit heard her through the door as well as the intercom.

"Dwight, give me a moment," he said, but a moment might not be long enough, though, to get rid of the reporter and to gather his wits about him again. Why was she here? Now? And why did she sound so angry?

"Who is Rosemary Tulle?" Edie asked.

Whit narrowed his eyes and focused on her face; she was studying him just as intently. What the hell was going on?

"Someone who obviously wants to meet with me," he said. "You and I have nothing further to discuss anyway. I can't give you what you want for this interview."

She hesitated a long moment before finally standing. "I'm not so sure about that now."

What the hell did she think she knew? Fortunately, his office had two doors, one to the reception area where his clerk worked, and another that opened directly to the hall. He walked to the hall door and closed his hand around the knob for it. "It was nice meeting you, Ms. Stone," he lied.

She must have known because she laughed. "So much for your honest politician image . . ."

He wasn't going to argue with her. He just wanted her gone, so he pulled open the door and held it for her. She took another moment before she walked across the room and exited. When he closed the door, he made certain to turn the lock. He didn't want her sneaking back inside, didn't want her interrupting this meeting with Rosemary.

His intercom buzzed again, so insistently that he wondered if Rosemary was pushing the button herself. But why was she so determined to see him now?

Whit walked back toward his desk and pushed the intercom button.

His curiosity got the better of his common sense. "Show her in, Dwight," he said as he dropped into the chair behind his desk. Then he turned toward the door and prepared himself to face his past.

He preferred to live in the past—back when the estate had been a manor and the hall a psychiatric hospital. Hell, he would have preferred the ruins it had fallen to after the state had shut them down to this . . .

Dr. James Bainesworth stared out his window at the perfectly manicured grounds covered with a dusting of snow. The snow couldn't whitewash everything, though; neither could the renovations. While it looked different, it hadn't really changed.

While he looked different, he hadn't really changed. He'd just gotten older, and unfortunately there were no renovations for him. Nothing that could help him regain the physical strength he'd once had. But as for his mind . . .

It was as sharp as it had ever been. He knew what was going on; nothing escaped him. Nothing had years ago when he'd run Bainesworth Manor, and nothing escaped him now.

The new management could not say the same. They should have come to him, should have asked for his help.

Not that he would have given it to them. He wanted them to fail. He was looking forward to it. He'd rather have the place fall to ruin again than to become what it was now: a playground for the rich and spoiled.

But soon . . . when the truth came out . . . everything would be spoiled, not just the guests. The curse had struck again. Just nobody knew it yet . . . but him.

Chapter Five

"You can go in now," the young male secretary repeated. Or was he called a clerk? "His Honor said he'll see you."

His Honor . . .

There was nothing honorable about Whittaker Lawrence. How had he become a judge? And a district attorney before that?

She'd moved away from Maine after college, so she hadn't known then about his elections. She certainly wouldn't have voted for him. She might have even . . . done what she should have done all those years ago.

But it was too late now for that . . .

Rosemary couldn't make herself move toward the door. It was as if she had no control over her own muscles, over her own body, like that night so long ago. That night that haunted her so many years later . . .

Like the man haunted her.

"He said for you to show yourself in," the clerk added.

Shouldn't he open his door? Shouldn't he come out here to greet her—where there was a witness—someone to protect her if he tried anything again?

Not that he would try. She wasn't the stupid sixteen-year-old girl so besotted with puppy love that she hadn't been able to see what kind of person he truly was. She was older now and wiser, thanks to him. She was in control now.

She drew in a deep breath and forced her limbs to move, to walk across the reception area to that door. But when she reached out for the knob, her fingers trembled, and a chill raced down her spine despite the warmth of the office. And it was warm—with a fire burning low in the hearth of a fireplace between two couches on the end of the room across from the receptionist's desk. She hadn't sat down on the couches, though; she hadn't warmed herself at that fire despite the chill in her bones.

The chill she'd had since coming to Bane Island and Halcyon Hall. Because of the fog she'd barely been able to see the bridge she'd driven over to get back to the mainland. Then she'd had to drive three and a half more hours to get here, to his office, to him.

But now that she was so close . . .

She couldn't quite bring herself to turn that knob and push open the door. She closed her eyes, and instead of that nightmare, Genevieve's face flashed through her mind. So young, so beautiful . . .

So vulnerable. Like Rosemary had once been. She'd had nobody to protect her.

Genevieve had *her*, and Rosemary would not let her down.

She gripped the knob, twirled it, and shoved open the door. The inner office was nearly as expansive as the reception area, so much so that the man behind the desk didn't look that big. Until he stood . . .

He was even taller than she remembered. Taller than he'd been at eighteen at least. He was broader now, too, his shoulders stretching the seams of his tailored suit. "Rosemary . . ." he murmured. "I didn't expect—"

"Expect or hope that you'd never see me again?" she interjected; the anger coursing through her chased away the chill and the fear she'd momentarily felt. She wasn't afraid of him anymore.

"It has been a long time," he said, and his gaze traveled over her.

Revulsion coursed through her like that chill had moments ago. Not fear. And definitely not attraction. It had to be revulsion. She didn't find him attractive any-more—not like she had when she'd been a kid. But he was probably even more handsome than he'd been as a teenager, his features even more chiseled. His hair was a darker gold than it had been, but it was thick and full with a lock falling over his brow, emphasizing the deep green of his eyes.

"It hasn't been long enough," she said. "I would have never come to you—if I'd had any other choice." Her mother had taken away the last option Rosemary had when Abigail hadn't put her name on that damn list.

"What's wrong?" he asked, and he stepped around his desk as if to approach her.

She instinctively stepped back and glanced at the door. It was closed now. She hadn't done that; his clerk must have.

"Did he lock that?" she asked, her heart pounding fast and frantically in her chest. "Did you have him lock that?"

"What?" Whit asked.

"The door," she said. "Did you have him lock me in here? Is that part of his job description to lock women in with you?"

"That's ridiculous. You're the one who insisted on seeing me now."

She flinched. "I didn't want to see you," she said. "I never, ever wanted to see you again after that night. . . ."

The color fled from his face, leaving it starkly pale—probably like hers.

"But I do," she said. "So often in my nightmares, I see your face as you're carrying me up to my room." She shuddered. "I hate what you did . . . I hate you for that . . . but I can't hate . . ."

"What are you talking about?" he asked, his brow furrowed.

She continued as if he hadn't spoken—because she had to get it out. She had to confess what she'd never admitted to anyone. "But I can't hate our daughter. In fact I love her so much that I would ask anyone to help me rescue her—even my rapist."

His eyes widened with shock.

Feigned shock. It had to be; he couldn't actually be surprised. Maybe he'd thought, because of whatever he'd slipped in her drink, that she wouldn't remember. He'd probably been counting on it, or he wouldn't have gone into politics.

All it would take was a DNA test to prove what he really was. The very thing he was known for prosecuting and now for sentencing—a criminal.

Then she would have to tell Genevieve the truth. Rosemary had promised her mother that she would never reveal that she was actually Genevieve's mother. Not her sister. Abigail had made her a promise in return, after putting her and Bobby's names on Genevieve's birth certificate as her parents, that she would take care of Genevieve, that she would protect her from all harm.

She'd broken that promise when she'd sent her to Halcyon Hall. Rosemary had to get her out of it.

"I need your help," she said, the plea sticking in her throat, making her voice gruff with emotion. "I need you to help me find our daughter."

He shook his head. "You're crazy," he said.

"No, I'm not," she said. "I'm determined to do what's right for our daughter—even if I have to threaten you to do it."

"You're going to threaten me?"

"I'll go to the press," she warned him. "I'll let them know what kind of man you really are."

"What you don't have is proof, Rosemary. You have nothing to back up your wild accusations. Nothing. You'll make a damn fool of yourself."

"A DNA test will prove it," she said, "will prove that you're my daughter's biological father."

He arched a dark blond brow as he chuckled again. "Really? Bring it on, then. What do you need? A cheek swab?"

She tensed. "I shouldn't be surprised that you know so much about paternity tests. Not with the kind of man you are."

He snorted. "A well-informed one? One who's watched television? Just because I know how it works doesn't mean I've ever had one. But I'll take one now if you want. And your daughter . . . ?"

The chill rushed through her again as she realized why he had agreed to the test so quickly. "You know . . ." She gasped. "You know that I can't get to her. You know she's being held in that place. . . ."

"What place?" he asked, his brow furrowing again.

"Halcyon Hall," she murmured. "Bainesworth Manor. Who told you? My mother?" Abigail was the only other person who knew who Genevieve's father was. Or at least that was what Rosemary had thought.

But had her mother told Whit all those years ago? Had he learned he'd gotten her pregnant? Was that why he'd stayed away? Her mother had probably threatened him. What she should have done was have him prosecuted. But she'd talked Rosemary out of calling the police, had said that it would be too hard on her to relive that night.

Hell, Rosemary had relived that night so many times without going to the police that a few more times wouldn't have made much difference to her. But justice . . .

She should have gone after justice then. For herself . . .

For Genevieve. But then Genevieve would have known that she'd been conceived of a rape, and Rosemary hadn't wanted her baby to bear that stigma. Abigail certainly hadn't wanted that either—for herself more than for her grandbaby. She'd convinced Rosemary that everybody would have blamed her—like she'd blamed her—for hosting that party while they were gone, for being so besotted that she would have done anything Whittaker Lawrence had asked her to do.

Heat rushed to her face with embarrassment that she'd once been such a fool. Even though she'd acted rashly, she hadn't deserved what had happened to her. She hadn't deserved what he'd done. And then the hypocrite had become a prosecutor and now a judge when he'd eluded justice himself for so long.

He stared at her; his brow furrowed yet. Then he spoke to her softly and slowly as if she was as crazy as he'd accused her of being, "What is Halcyon Hall or Bainesworth Manor? What are you talking about?"

The heat suffusing her now was rage. "You know what I'm talking about!"

Didn't he?

He shook his head. "No, I don't."

Tears stung her eyes now, but she had resolved long ago to stop crying over him. "You better remember," she warned him. "I kept your dirty secret long enough. You owe me."

"You want money?" he asked. "That's why you're here. You're shaking me down."

"No!" she shouted back in his face. "I don't need or want your money."

"What the hell do you want?" he asked.

She hadn't come here expecting an apology or even an admission. "I just want your help," she said. "I need to rescue Genevieve from that place."

"Have you tried the police?"

She blew out a breath of frustration. First he'd treated her like she was crazy, now like an idiot. "Of course I did. The Bane sheriff's department refused to help me."

"Why?" he asked. "Why wouldn't they help you rescue your daughter?"

"They don't know she's mine," she said. "Nobody does. I let my mother list herself as her birth mother."

"So if you can't help her, how do you think I can?" he asked. His handsome features twisted with a grimace of disgust. "Am I listed as her father?"

She hesitated for a long moment before admitting, "No."

"Then how do you think I could help you?" he asked.

Her frustration and fury receded, deflating her. She could only shake her head and murmur, "I should have known better. I should have known. . . ."

He wouldn't help her.

She turned and headed toward the door through which she'd entered. She closed her hand around the knob and drew in a breath, bracing herself in case it was locked, but it turned easily.

It was his voice that stopped her from walking out. "Rosemary . . ."

She tensed, but she didn't turn back. After that night, she hadn't ever wanted to see him again. Coming here had been a mistake. It hadn't helped Genevieve at all. But maybe it had helped her. She wasn't afraid of him anymore, so maybe the nightmares would stop. At least the nightmares about him . . .

Ignoring his calling her name, she started walking again, and she didn't stop until she stood in front of the elevators. When she reached for the down button, her hand was steady. She knew what she had to do.

Whit reached up to brush his hair off his forehead, and his hand shook. He was shaking . . . with fury. She had accused him of being the very thing he hated most: a rapist. He couldn't believe it. . . .

Rosemary Tulle . . .

He hadn't seen her in so long. She'd been such a pretty girl all those years ago. She was a beautiful woman now—despite the dark circles beneath her eyes, even with her long black hair tangled around her shoulders. Why had she been so disheveled with her once pale skin chafed from the cold?

Was she homeless?

Her jacket and jeans had been clean, though. So had her hair, so clean that it had shimmered in the glow of the lights. She was so very beautiful. And so distraught . . .

Was she going through some kind of psychotic break? Or maybe she'd been mentally unstable for years.

All he knew of Rosemary Tulle was the sweet sixteen-year-old girl she'd once been. She wasn't sweet anymore. She was possibly in collusion with the scandal-seeking reporter or using his campaign to extort money from him.

What other reason would have compelled her to come see him now—after all these years? It had to be money.

She couldn't actually expect him to help her break some girl out of what?

What the hell was Halcyon Hall?

And why did he care?

He couldn't afford a distraction like her—not right now. Not when he was just getting ready to run for governor in the next election. He needed to make sure that Edie Stone wasn't going to publicize this crazy story. Maybe the two of them were working for one of his political rivals to discredit him. That was going to prove dangerous and not just for his campaign.

Rosemary Tulle was a danger to herself and to others. She kept running her big mouth, kept causing trouble about the manor. And about Genevieve.

She had to be stopped before she ruined everything.

Thick leather gloves gripped the steering wheel, turning the truck onto the same street onto which her rental car had turned. The street that led to the bridge back to Bane Island.

Only Rosemary Tulle wouldn't be making it back to the island. Now or ever again . . .

Chapter Six

The fog hadn't lifted from the island. Not that Rosemary could see the island. She could barely see the bridge as she steered the rental vehicle toward it. The fog was thicker now as night began to fall along with some fat, white snowflakes that obscured the visibility even more.

Once she hit the metal of the bridge, the tires skidded across the slick surface, and she cursed.

She'd already been gone too long. She needed to get back to the island, back to Genevieve. Even though she couldn't see her—yet—at least she could be close to her.

But not if she landed into the waves crashing against the rocks below the bridge. She couldn't see those now either, though. She could only see the small holes her headlights bore into the fog and snow in front of her vehicle and the lights in the back, burning through her frosted back window and casting a glare on her rearview mirror. She squinted and looked away, blinded by the light and the snow.

And the fear . . .

That blinded her, too, blinded her to the dangers of driving under the current conditions. Warnings emanated from the radio. Weather advisories. Authorities warning against traveling unless it was an emergency.

This was an emergency—getting back to her daughter, getting her out of that damn place. Cursed . . .

That was what it was. But it wasn't just the building that was cursed. Rosemary was as well.

Why had she been so stupid as to think that her mother or Whittaker Lawrence would help her when they hadn't before?

She'd wasted time. Precious time that she could have spent trying to get to her daughter. Her *daughter* . . .

Not her sister.

She wanted everyone to know that—most especially Genevieve.

What would the teenager say? How would she react? Would she hate Rosemary for giving her up—for giving her to *them*?

She hated herself for doing that. But she hadn't thought she'd had any other options then. She'd been so young and dependent on her mom and stepdad. Hopefully, Genevieve would understand.

Needing to see her, needing to explain, Rosemary pressed harder on the accelerator. But the tires skidded again, the steering wheel twisting in her tight grasp. The rental careened close to the flimsy metal side rail of the bridge. Gritting her teeth, she held on and willed the vehicle to straighten up as she eased her foot from the gas pedal.

She had to slow down, had to be careful, or she wouldn't make it back to the island. Unfortunately, the vehicle behind her didn't slow down; the lights got even closer. From the height of them, it must have been a truck or an SUV. She couldn't see anything beyond the light.

Why the hell didn't he slow down? Whoever was driving

must have been in even more of a hurry to get back to the island than she was. Why? And why had he or she started across the bridge the same time she had?

She'd already been chilled from the cold that the weak trickle of heat from the vents couldn't dispel. But now her teeth began to chatter, with fear, as that vehicle drew closer yet.

The front bumper touched the rear bumper of the rental, sending her car and her body jolting forward. The seat belt caught her shoulder, holding her back from striking the steering wheel. But there was nothing to hold back the car as it lurched forward—toward that flimsy guard rail.

A scream escaped her lips, but she tamped down her panic. She needed to speed up—to get the hell away from that truck. But once again when she pressed on the accelerator, the tires skidded and the car swerved, zigzagging across the two-lane bridge.

Rosemary gripped the wheel as tightly as she could, her knuckles aching from her effort to keep the car from crashing into that rail. From the other times she'd crossed the bridge, she knew the metal was old and rusted—maybe rusted enough to break.

Then the truck struck again, sending her into a spin. She screamed as the vehicle bounced off one railing and then into the other lane of traffic. Lights shone brightly in her windshield. Had she spun around to face the truck?

A horn blared. And she swerved back into her lane so far that the passenger's side scraped along that rail. As the vehicle passed, she noticed it was a car.

The truck was gone. Where?

Had it fallen over the bridge?

She drew in a shaky breath and continued the rest of the distance to the island, the metal swaying and creaking beneath the weight of the car and the ice. Where had the other vehicle gone?

She went directly to the police department. This time instead of passing it to park in the diner's lot, she pulled right up to that front door with the badge on it. When she shut off and stepped out of her vehicle, her legs nearly folded beneath her. She had come so close to crashing over that railing.

Had the truck?

Maybe she should have stopped and called for help. But in the moment all she'd wanted was to get the hell off that bridge. To get out of danger herself.

But even at the police department, she didn't feel safe. It wasn't like the bustling police station in Grand Rapids, Michigan, where she lived now. Civilians and police officers were constantly walking in and out of that three-story building that occupied the corner of a vibrant city block.

This building was just the one floor and just that one exterior door that she pushed open before stepping inside the narrow reception area. Like the police station at home, she had to buzz for the inner door to open. But it didn't open to let her in—instead someone stepped into the room where that single desk sat.

It was the older female officer she'd seen arriving with take-out containers the evening before. The woman raised a gray brow and wearily asked, "Can I help you?"

"Is the sheriff here?"

The woman shook her head. "No, ma'am, but if this is still about getting into Bainesworth Manor, he can't help you."

Bainesworth Manor. It didn't matter what it had been renamed; the locals apparently preferred to use the name of the old psychiatric hospital it had once been. The one that had fallen into ruins from the pictures Rosemary had pulled up online, of most of the stone walls crumbling with vines and moss growing all around them.

"I'm not here about that," she said. Not just about that anyway . . .

"Then why are you here?" a deep voice asked.

Rosemary whirled around to find the sheriff standing in the doorway behind her. Cold and snow blew in as well. How had she not noticed the door opening? How quietly had he moved?

"Somebody just tried to run me off the bridge," she said.

"Were you on your way out of town?" he asked.

She shook her head. "I was just coming back from the mainland."

"Maybe you should have stayed off the island," he said.

She sucked in a breath. "Are you threatening me?" Once again she'd come to the wrong place. After the last time the police had refused to help her, she should have known better.

"I cautioned you," he said, "about your reckless driving. Maybe I should have given you that citation, then you might have slowed down."

"I wasn't driving too fast," she said. "Somebody rammed into the back bumper of my rental car. You must have seen the damage when you came in."

From where?

Where had he been?

On the bridge?

She'd thought the vehicle had been a truck, but it could have been a big SUV . . . like the one the sheriff drove. She pushed past him to rush out to the street. His SUV wasn't parked there. Her rental, with its crumpled back bumper and scraped metal, was the only vehicle in the street on which snow was beginning to accumulate.

"I saw it," the sheriff said as he joined her outside. "Looks like you hit the railing and then spun around and probably hit the other side of the bridge with the rear bumper."

She sucked in another breath along with air so frigid it burned her lungs. "That's not what happened," she said. "Another vehicle struck me."

"What kind?" he asked.

"I—I don't know," she admitted. "I only saw the lights, but it stood taller than the rental car—the headlights were higher." And the beams had definitely been brighter. Had the driver had the high beams on the entire time? Was that why she'd been so blinded?

Tears stung her eyes now, tears of frustration and tears of cold. "I'm telling the truth," she persisted, "about everything. I don't know why nobody will believe me."

Maybe Whit had only been acting like she was crazy, though. Maybe he hadn't doubted her at all—because he'd already known. Had he sent that vehicle after her? Or had he been the one behind the wheel?

He was a powerful man with a lot to lose if she went public with what he'd done to her all those years ago. She shivered.

"You should get out of the cold," the sheriff told her.

No place on the island—or anywhere else for that matter—felt warm to her. "Don't you want to take a report?"

"When did it happen?" he asked.

"Just a little while ago," she said. "I drove straight here from the bridge."

"Then I have enough for the report."

"But—but . . ." She'd been in traffic accidents before

where the officer had taken a half hour to fill in the form on his laptop.

"Do you remember anything else?" he asked. "Anything that might help?"

"Help . . ." That was all she'd wanted, but nobody would offer her any. She had no idea what to do now, no idea if she should trust him with the truth. She had no way of proving that she was Genevieve's mother, so she doubted the claim would get the sheriff to act on her behalf. It hadn't compelled Whit to help her. But maybe that was because he didn't want Genevieve free. Maybe she was a skeleton he wanted locked in a closet like those parents had had their daughters locked up at Bainesworth Manor all those years ago. But just as Evelyn had said, it was happening again. . . .

"Are you going back to the boardinghouse?" he asked.

She nodded but then tensed as it struck her that he'd already known where she was staying. How?

"You can't go to the hall again," he advised her. "They're going to press charges for trespassing the next time you show up, and they'll know if you do. They have security cameras at that front gate. Maybe you should have just stayed on the mainland. There's nothing for you here."

"There's Genevieve." She wanted to claim her as her daughter now, wanted to shout it from the rooftops that she'd been freed from that horrible pact with her mother. But she couldn't trust anyone here. Every time she'd reached out for help she'd been turned down. And tonight . . .

Tonight she could have been killed. That attempt made her more concerned about her daughter.

She reached for the driver's door, tugged it open, and slid beneath the steering wheel. Before she could pull the door closed, the sheriff caught the top of it in a gloved hand.

He leaned down, and she finally realized that he wasn't wearing his dark glasses. His eyes were dark—fathomless, unreadable. He didn't need to wear the glasses to conceal his expression. She couldn't read it, so she had no idea what he meant when he cautioned her again, "Be careful."

Was he talking about driving on the slick roads? Or dealing with the hall and whoever the hell had tried running her off the bridge?

Sheriff Deacon Howell stared after the rental car as it drove away. One of the rear lights was broken, but he didn't wave her down. He let her go. And he wished like hell she would keep going.

She was trouble. He'd known it when he'd watched her drive through town the day before and when he'd stopped her and learned she was looking for the hall. . . .

He shouldn't have just given her a citation; he should have locked her up. Hell, it was probably the only way to keep her safe since she was so damned determined to get onto the property of Halcyon Hall.

It didn't matter what it looked like now. Nothing had changed about the damn place. It was still cursed. Nobody knew that better than he did. Except maybe Genevieve Walcott. Was that why the teenager had called her sister begging for help to escape?

He'd noticed something else about the damage to Rosemary Tulle's rental car besides the broken light: paint transfer on the crumpled rear bumper. It wasn't quite black; it wasn't quite gray. It was the weird charcoal color of every vehicle Halcyon Hall owned.

"Are you coming inside?" Margaret asked from the open doorway to the police department.

He shook his head. "No. I need to check out something."

Her eyes widened. "You're not going out there, are you?"

He sighed, and his breath formed an icy cloud in front of his face. "I have to."

"It's a family matter," Margaret insisted. "Her parents didn't put her name on the list of visitors for her sister. They probably had a good reason. Maybe she's a poor influence." His deputy bristled with maternal protectiveness—of him. She obviously thought the teenager wasn't the only one Rosemary Tulle might poorly influence.

"What was their reason for putting their daughter in that place?" he asked.

"I'm sure they had a good reason for that, too," Margaret said. "A reason that's none of our business."

"We're the police," he reminded her. "It's all our business." The majority of the crime calls on Bane Island were domestic disputes. This one just didn't happen to affect the locals.

For that he should have been relieved—would have been relieved—if it hadn't involved the damn manor.

"But you're not supposed to go out there," she reminded him. "Like Warren says, we have no jurisdiction there."

Deputy Warren Cooke had more jurisdiction than Deacon did; he was related to the sons of bitches who ran the place. At least the young deputy wasn't on duty tonight, or he would have called ahead to warn them that Deacon was coming. That was probably the only reason he worked for Deacon—to spy on him and to eventually take his job.

Waving Margaret back inside the building, he headed around the back of it to his SUV. Snow melted and slid off the warmed-up windshield and hood. He hopped back inside and turned on the engine.

The manor wasn't far away, but the roads were slippery

enough that four-wheel drive wasn't even that effective at avoiding skids. Maybe Rosemary had just spun around and struck the bridge like he'd suggested. But the bridge wasn't that charcoal gray color; it wasn't any color now but rust.

The streetlamp under which she'd parked hadn't been that bright, though, not bright enough for him to be certain that he'd identified the color. But the couple of chips he'd scraped from the bumper and dropped into an evidence bag would either confirm or disprove his suspicion—once he got it back from the state police lab. He needed another sample to match it to, though.

As he neared the stretch of stone wall where the gates should have been, he noticed one light burning in the rear of a vehicle parked on the road. Damn. She was trouble.

He braked at the gates and jumped out of his SUV. Storming over to her vehicle, he rapped his knuckles against her frosted side window. It wound down with a lurch. "What did I just tell you?"

"I'm not on the property," she said. "I'm on the street."

He snorted.

"What the hell are you going to do here besides get hit again?"

"Whoever comes or goes, I'll stop them—get them to tell me about Genevieve."

"The employee entrance is farther down the road and doesn't have a security camera," he said, surprising himself that he'd made the admission. "But trying to sneak in there will get you more than a trespassing ticket; it'll get you arrested."

"What are you doing here?" she asked, her eyes wide with hope. "Are you checking on . . . Genevieve?"

His eyes narrowed at that slight pause he'd caught earlier outside the office. Maybe there was a reason she wasn't on that list. Maybe she wasn't really related to the girl at all. The place was marketed to appeal to the rich and famous. That was the reason, or so they claimed, that they were so vigilant with their security.

"I'm here on police business," he told her, "not that it's any of your business." But it was; it was about her.

"Did they already call you about me?" she asked. "I just got here."

"Go back to the boardinghouse." He would have told her to go to the mainland instead, but she'd been lucky to make it across that bridge once already tonight. And she hadn't managed that unscathed. "The sisters are worried about you."

"Did Evelyn call you?" she asked.

He nodded. Last night and earlier that afternoon. "You left your stuff, so they figured you intended to return and were concerned that you hadn't yet and that the weather was bad." That was why he'd been out when she'd arrived at the police department; he'd been looking for her.

A crease appeared between her black brows. "I didn't mean to worry them."

"Then get back to the boardinghouse before anything else happens to you," he suggested.

She sucked in a breath, probably thinking again that he was threatening her. His warnings were actually just good advice, though—advice she seemed intent on ignoring. But after a long, silent moment, she nodded. "Okay, I'll go back to the boardinghouse. Please, check on Genevieve for me, though. Make sure they haven't done anything to her."

"It's some touchy-feely rehab center," he said. At least that was what it was claiming to be now. He knew better, though. Hell, everybody on the island knew better. Instead of being a place where people went to get help with their problems, it just exacerbated them.

Remembering what the place had already cost him, he flinched at the sudden jab of pain. "Just leave," he told her, "and don't come back." He didn't know why he wasted his breath, though. She wasn't listening.

She rolled up the window and drove away, her tires skidding on the road as she did a U-turn and headed back toward town. With the weather worsening, maybe she'd stay away for the night. But she would return in the morning, and so would he, to either arrest or cite her for trespassing.

Wet snow settled on the shoulders of his jacket, adding to the weight of guilt he already carried, as he jumped back into his vehicle. He pressed the button to lower his window and reached out for the intercom. Before the person could even greet him, he said, "Sheriff Howell, let me in."

Whoever it was had the sense not to ask for a warrant this time—just opened the damn gates. He drove through them. Snow had accumulated on the driveway, as if nobody had been down this way for a while. And maybe they hadn't. As Rosemary Tulle could attest, they weren't exactly welcoming to visitors—sometimes even the ones who were on the damn list.

Deacon wasn't here to visit, though. He was here to investigate whoever had run into Rosemary Tulle and taken off. The people who would have been driving one of the Halcyon Hall vehicles used the employee driveway that wound around the back of the main building, so they wouldn't have left tire marks in the snow accumulating on the front drive.

The SUV tires skidded on the slick snow as he drove it around the tight curves on the long drive that wound past iced-over ponds and stands of pine trees. The darkness of those trees gave way as the last turn brought him in front of the manor, which glowed in the floodlights pointed at the enormous stone mansion. It didn't look like a house, though. More like a mansion or a fortress or a prison . . .

Part of Bainesworth Manor—the locked ward—had been a prison for the criminally insane. It hadn't been just that ward that had been locked, though, if the old rumors were true. . . .

And it hadn't been just the criminals that had been mistreated. But that had all been before his time. He wasn't here to investigate old rumors.

Deacon opened the SUV door and stepped back into the cold. As he rounded the front of his vehicle, the ten-foot-high, steel double doors to the foyer opened like a drawbridge coming down over a moat. He wasn't walking across a bed of alligators, though; he was walking into one.

Those doors opening reminded him that there were security cameras all over the property. Except near the cliffs. He would need a search warrant to secure any of the footage, though. Cooke wasn't likely to hand over anything without one.

When he stepped over the threshold into the expansive foyer of the hall, the doors closed automatically behind him. All the security and automation were parts of the renovation that had taken years to complete. Maybe it wouldn't have taken as long if the contractor hadn't been so damn distracted stealing other men's wives.

He flinched again when another pang struck his heart. But the place had literally been in ruins when the renovation had begun; they should have left it that way. He walked through the foyer into the reception area. For a minute he thought it was empty, but then a man stepped from the shadows. Or maybe through some secret sliding door in the dark paneled wall. The place was rumored to be full of secret passageways and chambers.

"Deacon," Dr. Elijah Cooke greeted him, his voice nearly as frosty as the wind howling outside.

The wind wasn't the only thing howling though. Despite the thickness of the stone walls, the wail of coyotes echoed eerily within the hall.

His voice wasn't the only frosty thing about Elijah Cooke. His eyes—a weird pale silver—were like the iced-over ponds on the property. They contracted sharply with his darker skin and black hair. A few strands of silver had slipped into that hair, though, even though Elijah was just thirty-eight, like Deacon.

Hell, Deacon had a few gray hairs himself, though. And not just because of this place.

"What brings you out to the hall at this hour?" Elijah asked him.

"Rosemary Tulle," Deacon replied.

Elijah sighed. "She's not on the list, and I will not violate a patient's privacy. You understand that."

"I do," Deacon acknowledged. "What I'm investigating is her claim that someone tried running her off the bridge on her way back to the island a short while ago."

Elijah sighed again and shook his head. "You can't seriously think anyone at the hall had something to do with that. How would anyone here know that she'd even left the island?"

Heat climbed into Deacon's face. Elijah Cooke had always had this effect on him, had always made him feel like an idiot, since they were kids. The guy was too damn smart for his own good and for anyone else's.

"Did she accuse someone here of trying to run her off

the road? And if so, does she have any witnesses to back up her outrageous claim?" Elijah didn't wait for Deacon's answer before he shook his head in response to his questions. "Of course she doesn't."

Leather creaked as Deacon's hands tightened into fists at his side. He wanted to slam his gloved fist into Cooke's face like he had once or twice when they were kids. That had been before Elijah's cousin David, Deputy Warren's older, bigger brother, had rushed to his defense and before Elijah had hit his growth spurt. Not that Deacon had been afraid of them; he'd just realized it was smarter to control his temper than get suspended for fighting.

"The paint that transferred onto the bumper of her car looks an awful lot like the color of all your company vehicles," Deacon said, and he studied Elijah's face for any reaction.

The guy was too cool—and too damn smart—to betray his thoughts, though. He just shrugged. "It's gray. A lot of vehicles are gray."

"All of the ones on the island that are that particular shade of gray belong to you," Deacon said.

"*She* was coming back," Elijah said. "But that doesn't mean the person who struck her was a local. It could have been another visitor to our beautiful island."

The urge to hit him got stronger. It was good that they hadn't gotten closer to each other, or Deacon might have given in to the temptation.

"What's the deal with her sister?" Deacon asked. "Why'd the parents put her here? Drugs? Eating disorder?"

Cooke shook his head. "I cannot violate our privacy policy."

"Let me talk to the girl then," Deacon urged. "Make

sure that she's really all right and not being held here against her will as Rosemary Tulle thinks."

Cooke shook his head again. "Rosemary Tulle is mistaken and perhaps delusional."

"She seems pretty sane to me," Deacon said. He wasn't a shrink, like Dr. Cooke, but he knew crazy. "Just worried about her sister, worried enough that she's getting me a little worried." Because he was still studying Cooke closely, and despite the distance between them, he noticed the muscle twitch along the guy's cheek, noticed how tightly his jaw was clenched. He was working hard to hide any reaction.

Was something going on? He'd figured Rosemary's sister just wanted out of rehab so she could get back to her bad habits. But maybe there was more to it—if someone from the hall had tried running Rosemary off the bridge.

"Unless your name is on the list or you have a warrant, you can't visit with Ms. Walcott either," Cooke said. "So if you're done . . . I really should get home."

It wasn't as if he had far to go. If Cooke didn't live in the hall itself, he lived in one of several other buildings on the property.

"You should get home as well, Sheriff," he said, "before the roads get any worse and you have a mishap like Ms. Tulle."

"Are you threatening me?" Deacon asked.

Those creepy pale eyes widened with shock—probably feigned. "Of course not."

"Better not," Deacon said. "Threatening an officer . . ."

"For however much longer you're an officer," Elijah remarked.

"My term's not up for a while," Deacon reminded him.

"Before your cousin tries to take my job, I have plenty of time in office to take care of unfinished business."

"You might be the law," Elijah said, "for now, but even you are not above it."

"Nor are you," Deacon reminded him. Even though the son-of-a-bitch was the richest damn person on the island. While he owned most of it, he couldn't do whatever the hell he wanted on it—not like his family had done before the state had finally shut them down.

The sheriff turned and headed toward those doors. But when he touched the handle and pulled on one, it refused to budge. He turned back toward where Elijah had been standing but he must have evaporated into the damn wall again. What the hell was he?

A ghost?

A soft buzz rang out and the doors opened of their own volition. Deacon stepped back to avoid getting hit. But before they could close again and lock him inside the freaky mausoleum, he rushed out.

Why the hell would anyone choose to come here? Especially Holly . . .

He pushed the thought from his mind for now. She was on it entirely too often. He climbed into his SUV and glanced back at the building. He felt like it stared back at him—or at least somebody did.

Cooke?

Or Genevieve Walcott?

Was she being held here against her will?

She wouldn't be the only one who'd had that experience at the hall. But it had been called Bainesworth Manor when that kind of stuff had happened here, when parents had committed their wayward daughters for *treatment*. Just because the name had changed didn't mean the practices had, especially when the same damn family running it now had run the psychiatric hospital.

Back then Elijah's grandfather, James Bainesworth, had been the resident shrink and director. Had Elijah taken over more than the operation of the hall? Was he continuing the manor's gruesome legacy?

Light flashed against the front windows, shining through the drapes. Evelyn rushed to the front door. Pulling it open, she sucked in a breath as the cold air and snow struck her like a hard slap. The motion light in the driveway turned on, illuminating the blowing snow and the car parking beneath it. The back bumper was crumpled, the passenger's side scraped.

"Oh, no . . ."

She'd been right to worry about Rosemary, but she'd been concerned something would happen to her at the manor, not on the roads. She glanced toward the street now, and a strange movement caught her attention. A vehicle passed, but its lights weren't on. She noticed it only in the light spilling from the driveway into the road. It was dark and big, and its front bumper looked as if it had been pushed back, as if it had struck something.

Maybe the accident had just happened. Maybe she needed to call the sheriff to write up a report. But instead of pulling into the driveway behind Rosemary's car, the vehicle continued past, its brake lights flashing as it slowed to turn at the next intersection.

Then it was gone.

"I'm so sorry," Rosemary said as she joined her on the porch. "I should have called. I didn't mean to worry you."

Evelyn's heart warmed, and she released a ragged sigh of relief. "You're okay?"

Rosemary nodded.

"Let's get inside," Evelyn said. "You must be freezing."

The young woman's face was chafed from the cold, and snow had collected on her black hair and in her lashes. Evelyn stepped into the house and tugged her over the threshold. Before she closed the door on the cold, she glanced again at the street.

Had the vehicle come back? Would it return?

"What happened?" Evelyn asked her. "I see that your car is damaged. Why didn't the other vehicle stop?"

Rosemary tensed. "How do you know that it didn't?"

"It just drove past after you pulled into the driveway," Evelyn said. "I thought it was going to stop, but it kept going."

"You saw it?" Rosemary asked.

"Barely," Evelyn replied. "Its lights weren't on, but maybe that was because of the damage to the front of it. Where did the accident happen? I didn't hear it." With as close as she'd been sitting to the front of the house, waiting for Rosemary, she should have heard the collision.

"I was hit on the bridge," Rosemary replied. "But you saw the other vehicle just now?"

Evelyn nodded. "I think so . . ."

Anger flushed Rosemary's face. "I told the sheriff it wasn't an accident."

"You already reported it to him?" Evelyn asked.

Rosemary nodded. "Yes, and he went out to the hall. I

think he knows someone from there must have done it, must have tried to force me off the bridge."

"I told you not to go to the manor," Evelyn reminded her. "It's too dangerous."

"Is it too dangerous for me to stay here?" Rosemary asked. "Do you want me to leave?"

Evelyn shook her head. "No." And it wasn't just because they had bills to pay and no other boarders at the moment. It was because Rosemary reminded her of herself all those years ago when her sister had been put in a place from which she couldn't help her escape.

While physically she'd gotten her back, Bonita had never really come home. She wasn't the person who'd been sent to the manor fifty years ago. She wasn't the sister Evelyn had once known and idolized. Those treatments had destroyed the bright and lively young woman Bonita had once been. She'd returned to them more like a child. That hadn't been what their parents had wanted. Or had it?

Evelyn reached out and grasped Rosemary's cold hands. "Come inside. I saved you some dinner, and I'll make you some hot tea."

"Where's Bonita?" Rosemary asked with a concern that touched Evelyn's heart.

"She already went to bed." She'd been very upset earlier, going into a panic about her missing baby, but more than likely she'd been upset about the earlier talk of the manor rather than a misplaced doll. Evelyn didn't share any of that with Rosemary. She didn't want to make her feel guilty for bringing up the manor—because she knew the young woman would have to bring it up again.

While she didn't agree with Rosemary putting herself

in danger, she understood that she had to—that she couldn't let her sister remain there.

She just hoped that Rosemary got her sister back fully—not like Evelyn had gotten hers back. Bainesworth Manor had broken Bonita—mentally, spiritually, emotionally.

What were they doing to Rosemary's sister?

Chapter Seven

Whit's head pounded and the words blurred on the screen of his laptop. He blinked and focused again, but it didn't matter how many times he read what he'd found. He still didn't like it. And neither would . . .

The door creaked open, alerting him to someone's arrival. Since he'd called the meeting, he was expecting this person. "You were right," he told his campaign manager. "I should have canceled the interview."

Martin dropped heavily into the chair in front of his desk. He rubbed a big hand over his bald head and groaned. "What happened?"

"It was a setup," Whit said. It had to have been. It couldn't have been that sick a coincidence. But then stranger things happened. He filled in the campaign manager on what had transpired the afternoon before with Rosemary.

Martin uttered a louder groan. "I asked you if you had any skeletons . . ."

"I don't," Whit said.

"So nothing she accused you of is true?" Martin asked. Whit nodded.

"Then she's a kook," he said. "And we can easily prove that."

Whit tapped his computer screen. "That's the problem. She's not a kook. She's a shrink. A very highly respected one who specializes in counseling rape victims."

Martin flinched.

"I think there's a strong probability that if Edie Stone goes live with Rosemary's story, people will believe *her*."

"Not just people—voters," Martin grumbled.

Whit wasn't concerned about just the voters. He studied the older man's face for a long moment. "What about you? Do you believe her?"

"You said you had no skeletons," Martin reminded him. "You lied to me."

"I didn't lie," Whit insisted.

"If you'd just told me up front, I could have figured out a way to handle the reporter and Rosemary Tulle."

Whit tensed. "I didn't tell you her name."

"Of course you did."

"No." He was always very aware of every word he spoke, and he'd been careful not to share her name. "How do you know it?" And how long had the campaign manager been aware of Rosemary?

Martin's face flushed. Was he embarrassed at getting caught? Or angry? He shrugged. "I do my due diligence before I take on any client."

Whit furrowed his brow. "What does due diligence have to do with this? I knew Rosemary a lifetime ago. How the hell . . ."

"Some old prep school friends mentioned her name to me," he said.

Whit flinched now. "I had no friends in prep school." When they hadn't tried bullying him, they'd patronized and pitied him for being the bastard son of a maid. He hadn't known the truth yet then, or he would have set them straight.

"They want to be your friends now," Martin assured him. "I didn't think she was going to be a problem."

"She's not," Whit said, "because what she's saying isn't true."

"But you said yourself that people will believe her," Martin reminded him. "She must be stopped." His beefy hands clenched into fists, and he looked even more like a fighter. "I'll take care of her."

Whit shook his head. "No." He didn't trust the man now and wanted him nowhere near her. "I'll deal with Rosemary." Once he figured out how the hell to do that . . .

The other entrance to Halcyon Hall had been even harder to find than the visitor one. The gap between the tall pine trees lining the road was even narrower, and so was the gate in the stone wall that encompassed the grounds of the estate. There was no room for Rosemary to park on the driveway or the road on that side, so she parked across from it.

And she waited for employees to arrive.

She'd come early, way before dawn had even begun to lighten the sky, so she wouldn't miss the first shift. But the hours at the hall must not have been the same as other places of employment. Or perhaps everybody lived or stayed somewhere on the grounds.

Maybe, like Genevieve, they weren't allowed to come and go of their own free will. Lights glinted off Rosemary's windshield, alerting her to an approaching vehicle. Her luck it would be the sheriff.

Or perhaps that vehicle from the night before, the one that had struck her on the bridge and then followed her back to the boardinghouse. Had Evelyn really seen it though?

She hadn't been able to describe much of it—except that it was dark, and the front bumper had looked crumpled.

Squinting against the glare of those headlights, Rosemary focused on the approaching vehicle, and her heart began to pound fast and furiously. This one was dark and big and heading straight toward her. She'd shut off her engine and her lights. She didn't have time to restart and move the vehicle, didn't have time to get out of the way.

Just as it was about to strike her, the SUV turned sharply into that narrow employee drive and braked. A man stepped out of the driver's door and stared out at the street, at her vehicle.

Shock gripped Rosemary that she'd come so close to getting hit again and . . . that she recognized the man. At least she thought she did . . .

He'd been a friend and mentor of her late father's and the reason she'd attended the university where he'd taught. She'd always admired the professor. What the hell was he doing here?

Hand shaking, she fumbled with the handle before pushing open the door and stepping onto the street. "Dr. Chase?" she called out to him.

He walked closer to the street and peered at her. "Rosemary? Is that you?"

"Oh, thank God," she murmured. She rushed across the street, slipping on the icy surface, to join him.

Despite it being more than a decade since she'd seen him last, he looked the same. His hair had been white for years, maybe prematurely then, but now he had wrinkles in his face. He'd always been older than her father, but her father was the one who'd died of the aptly named widow maker's heart attack at forty—right before Rosemary's thirteenth birthday. After his friend's death, Dr. Chase had continued to come around to check on her and her mother.

She'd once hoped that her mother would turn to Gordon Chase for more than comfort. But, maybe feeling her own mortality after losing her spouse, Abigail had sought out younger men . . . like Bobby, who was closer to Rosemary's age than her mother's.

"What are you doing here?" she asked him. "I thought you were retired." Some years ago . . . since he had to be seventy.

He shook his head. "Retirement bored me. So I let the hall lure me back into private practice." His voice held a trace of affection, as if he loved the place as much as he loved his career. "It feels great helping people work on their problems. Some people come here just to relax. Some come to work on their problems," he admitted. "Like stress and substance abuse. We have quite a few with substance abuse issues. That's how I help."

"Does the hall really help though? Or does it hurt?" she asked. "Like the manor used to?"

His brow creased, and more lines appeared in his face, betraying his age. "You shouldn't listen to the gossip of the islanders," he admonished her. "This place has done a lot of good—for our guests and for the island."

"I'm talking from my own experience," Rosemary said.

"You've been a guest?"

"No. My . . . sister is." How could he not know that? But perhaps he'd forgotten her mother's current surname. "Genevieve Walcott."

The creases remained in his brow, as if he didn't recognize the name or her.

"Is she still here?" Rosemary asked.

"I can't talk about clients," he said. "I taught you that, remember?"

"She's my . . ." She bit her lip to hold back her secret. Maybe he already knew it, though. Maybe her mother had told him.

She doubted it, or he wouldn't have kept urging her to explore the nightmares he'd learned about while she had been one of his students. He wouldn't have wanted her to relive the horror of that night if he'd known.

"You're not her legal guardian," he said. "So I can't discuss her situation with you."

"Situation?"

He sighed. "You were always persistent . . . with others," he said. "When it came to your own life . . ."

"I didn't become a psychologist to treat myself," she said. "I did it to help people. I want to help Genevieve. She left me a voicemail begging me to get her out of this place."

"You should talk to your mother," Dr. Chase advised her.

"She won't return my calls," she admitted. "Nobody will help me help Genevieve. Will you, please?"

He sighed and pushed his hand through his thick white hair. "If you wanted a recommendation for a job here, I'd be happy to give it to you," he said. "But I can't intervene in this other matter."

Tears stung her eyes, and she turned away from him, like she used to when he'd broached the subject of her dreams. She wished she'd never told him about them, but it had been part of a class assignment—one she wished she'd never done. But since she'd failed to be the perfect daughter her mother had wanted, she'd worked hard to be the perfect student.

"I hear great things about you," he said. "You're very well respected, Rosemary. You could be really effective here."

She turned back toward him and snorted. "They won't let me through the gates to visit my sister. You really think they'll hire me?"

"Dr. Elijah Cooke runs the place," Chase said. "He's an exceptionally intelligent man. He'll see how much you could help some of the guests, more than even I could."

Her lips curved into a smile. "We both know the student hasn't surpassed the teacher."

He chuckled. "I think that's exactly what has happened, Rosemary." He reached into the pocket of his long over-coat and held out a business card to her. "E-mail me your résumé, and I'll present it to Elijah myself."

Tears stung Rosemary's eyes again, but these were tears of relief. Despite his claim that he couldn't help her, he was. He was helping her find another way inside the gates—as an applicant for employment.

"Thank you," she said as she took the card from him. "Thank you."

"Don't get your hopes up," he cautioned her. "Things may not turn out as you want."

Dr. Elijah Cooke stood at the head of the conference table in what had once been one of the formal dining rooms—before his grandfather had converted the family home into a psychiatric hospital. Then it had become a ward filled with mentally ill patients before it had eventually fallen to ruin.

During the renovation, Elijah had had the contractor—

who was also his cousin—turn it into a conference room with the dark paneled walls and coffered ceiling restored to their former glory. Elijah wanted everything restored to its former glory. The manor and the family's reputation.

He gripped the edge of the long table as he stood to disperse the personnel he'd gathered for the morning meeting. The table, too, had been restored after David had found it in storage in one of the many outbuildings on the property. The chef, Jean-Claude Marchand, rose first from the table, intent on returning to his kitchen. Warren Cooke, his security director, filed out after him, probably heading to his other job as the sheriff's deputy. Then Elijah's business partner, Bode James, and his head fitness trainer, Heather Smallegan, filed out at his silent dismissal. The publicist, Amanda Plasky, hesitated for a long moment until Elijah shook his head. He didn't have time for all her concerns right now. He didn't have time for anything. But the psychiatrist, Dr. Chase, remained after everyone else had finally left.

Gordon stayed seated in his chair, which was close to Elijah's, maybe so close that he'd noticed the dark circles beneath Elijah's eyes. He hadn't slept well after his visit from the sheriff.

When the door to the corridor fully closed, he turned toward Chase and asked, "What?"

"She's not going away."

"Who?" he asked.

"Rosemary Tulle," Dr. Chase replied.

Elijah flinched. "How did you hear about her?"

Nobody had mentioned her name at the morning meeting—on his orders. Not that all that many people knew about her trying to get inside to visit her sister. He suspected everybody knew about her sister, though.

"She was waiting outside the employee gate this morning," Dr. Chase informed him.

He clenched his jaw so tightly he had to grind out the words, "She was warned about trespassing."

"She didn't come inside," Chase said.

"But she tried." He narrowed his eyes as he studied the older man's face. "She got to you."

"I know Rosemary very well," Chase said. "I knew her as a child and as a student."

He nodded. "That's right. You know her family. That's why Genevieve was here."

Chase flinched now. "I had no idea how it would all turn out."

"Of course not," Elijah said.

"I do know that Rosemary won't go away quietly," Chase said. "She's not going to give up until she finds out what happened to her sister."

Elijah expelled a shaky breath. "But that won't be the end of it, and you know it."

"I know," Chase acknowledged.

"She won't be happy with what she finds out," Elijah said. He wasn't happy about it.

If the truth got out, it could destroy everything he had worked so hard to restore.

It would bring back all the old stories, all those horror stories . . . and then no one would come to the hall. All the money and time he'd spent would be for naught.

And he would be left with nothing . . .

Chapter Eight

Rosemary stared down at the card she'd set on the table next to her laptop. Would this work? Or had Gordon Chase only been placating her so that she'd leave him—and Halcyon Hall—alone? No. He knew her better than to think she would go away without seeing Genevieve for herself, without making sure that she was all right.

She had to be all right.

"You're here?" Evelyn remarked with surprise as she walked into the dining room.

"I hope you don't mind my using this for a work space," Rosemary replied.

Evelyn shook her head. "Of course not. I'm glad you're here. When you were gone this morning . . ." Her voice cracked with concern as it trailed off.

"I left a note," Rosemary said. She'd taped one to her bedroom door, so that they wouldn't be concerned. But because they'd probably suspected where she'd gone, they undoubtedly had worried.

Evelyn's face flushed. "I don't mean to act like your mother. . . ."

Evelyn actually seemed to care more about Rosemary than her mother ever had. Whenever her mother had seemed to care, it had been more about her own reputation than Rosemary's physical or emotional well-being. Why in the hell had she ever trusted her with her baby?

At sixteen, she'd felt she had no other options, though.

"That's probably why we don't keep boarders," Evelyn said. "Or it's how we feel about the hall. . . ."

"Have you had people live here who've worked at the hall?" she asked. "Or do they all live on the property?" If she was actually hired, she would hate to leave the sisters, too, but she was willing to do whatever she had to in order to see Genevieve again.

"The owners live on the property of the manor, just like they always have," she said.

Rosemary needed clarification. "But aren't the owners of the hall different than the ones who ran the manor?" After all these years and the ruins the property had fallen into, new owners must have purchased the property.

Evelyn shook her head. "No. It's the same family. Just different surnames but the same blood. The same money. The same power."

The same penchant for locking up young girls? Rosemary was right to be so worried about Genevieve.

Evelyn continued, "We did have many of the construction workers stay with us while it was being renovated and some of the employees have lived here until finding more permanent housing. Most recently one of the grounds-keeping staff lived with us." Her brow creased slightly. "Teddy Bowers."

Rosemary wondered if it was the young man she'd seen by the gates the day before.

"A fitness instructor stayed with us for a while, too," Evelyn remarked, "before moving onto the estate. She was a very sweet girl. We warned her about working at the manor, but she didn't listen. We haven't seen her since she moved out."

"And the groundskeeper?"

"He was never around much when he lived here," Evelyn said. "So of course, we don't see him anymore even though he was supposed to work on our gardens for us."

Rosemary glanced out the window at the ice-encrusted brown branches of the shrubs and flowers. "Maybe he'll come back in the spring. . . ."

"Maybe," Evelyn agreed. But she sounded doubtful.

"Where is Bonita?" Rosemary asked.

Evelyn's head tipped back as she looked up at the coffered ceiling. "She's resting now. She got very upset this morning. . . ."

A pang of regret struck Rosemary. "About me?"

Evelyn shook her head. "About her baby . . . she thought it was lost again even after I found the doll for her."

Rosemary furrowed her brow. "You don't think she could be talking about something else . . . ?"

Evelyn sighed. "I don't know what she's talking about half the time. And neither does she." She stepped closer to the table and sucked in a breath as her gaze focused on the laptop screen that displayed Rosemary's cover letter for the psychologist position at Halcyon Hall. The older woman trembled slightly and stumbled back from the table. "I—I didn't mean to look at your computer."

"That's all right," Rosemary assured her. She doubted anything would come of her application, but it was worth a try. Anything was worth a try to get into Halcyon Hall.

Evelyn shook her head. "No, no it's not. You can't apply there. You can't become part of that . . ." She trailed off, her voice choked with emotion.

"Hall," Rosemary finished for her. "It's not what it once was." Or so they claimed.

Evelyn shook her head again. "They didn't change the place. They just restored it to what it once was."

"It's more of a rehab facility now," Rosemary said. "And I'm a psychologist. I counsel people to help them work through their problems. That's what Halcyon Hall does now."

Evelyn shuddered. "Is counseling really their only treatment? Not the kind of procedures they used to do, the things they did . . ."

Rosemary wanted to deny that they still did those things, but she didn't know for certain. Instead she asked, "How do you know so much about the place?"

Tears glistened in Evelyn's eyes. "Just like you, my parents put my sister in that place and wouldn't let me see her."

Rosemary had already suspected as much. "Bonita was there."

Evelyn nodded now. "I think part of her still is. It must be—because the smart, sassy girl she'd once been didn't come home—not after what they did to her."

Tears of sympathy stung Rosemary's eyes now, too. She suspected a lobotomy might have been performed on Bonita, damaging the bright young woman she had been. But nobody practicing in psychiatry today used that archaic procedure. Halcyon couldn't. Dr. Chase wouldn't work there if they did.

"They treat patients now with counseling and exercise and diet," Rosemary repeated the website's claim, trying to convince herself of that as well as Evelyn. "They focus on the body and the mind—on total wellness."

Evelyn shook her head. "I don't care what they claim.

It's still the House of Horrors it always was. And you shouldn't go there."

House of Horrors . . .

"You know why I have to," Rosemary said. More than anyone, Evelyn had to understand.

The older woman drew in a deep breath and nodded. "I wish I would have tried harder to help my sister."

"You must have been just a child then. . . ."

Bainesworth Manor had been shut down long ago.

"I knew she was in danger," Evelyn said, her voice cracking, "just like you know your sister—"

"Genevieve is not my sister," Rosemary said. "I was just sixteen when I had her, so I let my mother and stepfather claim her as theirs. She's my daughter." Admitting it again gave her a sense of relief and pride and fear. Her child was in that horrible place.

"Oh . . ." Evelyn murmured, her eyes warm with concern and understanding.

"I will do anything to get *my daughter* out of there," Rosemary continued.

"That's what I'm afraid of," Evelyn said with a shaky sigh. "That you'll do anything . . ."

"Sheriff, Miss Pierce is on line two for you," Margaret called through the wall that separated the front desk from the rest of the office. "She sounds upset."

She must have been, or this deputy—unlike Warren—wouldn't have interrupted his lunch—such that it was. The fries had already gotten cold. He dropped the soggy spud back into the carry-out box, wiped his hand on the already damp napkin, and reached for his phone. "What's up, Evelyn?"

Or maybe he should have asked what Ms. Tulle was up to, but he already had a pretty damn good idea. Rosemary wasn't the only reason Evelyn called, though. Sometimes Bonita wandered off in search of her missing *baby*, and Evelyn needed help finding her. The older woman never made it very far from the boardinghouse, though, so he was able to help Evelyn.

If only he could help Rosemary Tulle . . .

But her sister wasn't missing. She knew exactly where she was, and that was the damn problem.

"I'm worried about our new boarder," Evelyn said.

"What has she done now?" he asked. And why hadn't the hall called to complain about her yet?

"She's applying for a job at that place," Evelyn said.

He chuckled at her tenacity. "I don't think you need to worry about them hiring her," he said.

"I am worried," Evelyn said. "She could have been killed yesterday."

He glanced down at the pictures he'd taken of her car before he'd stepped inside the station. The damage was severe. He hoped she'd taken out the insurance when she'd rented it.

"She reported it," he said.

"So you're investigating?" Evelyn asked. "It followed her here last night, you know . . ."

His blood chilled. "What did?"

"The vehicle," Evelyn said. "It drove past the house, no lights on, as she pulled into the driveway. It followed her here."

"What kind of vehicle?" he asked.

"Big—like the kind you drive," she said.

"An SUV?"

"Or a truck," she said. "I couldn't see much of it with all the snow and it not having its lights on."

There was only one reason why someone would drive with the lights off at night—because he didn't want to be seen. Who the hell was after Rosemary Tulle?

He already suspected that it was someone from the hall. Elijah? No. He wouldn't do his own dirty work. Warren driving one of the security vehicles? Or maybe David; he was the one who'd always done Elijah's dirty work.

But why go after Rosemary? What the hell had happened to her sister that they didn't want her to know?

Or maybe Elijah was right, and Deacon just wanted it to be someone from the hall.

What if it was someone else? Someone from her past?

Maybe it was about damn time he learned more about Rosemary Tulle.

Chapter Nine

Rosemary pulled the battered rental car up to the tall wrought iron gates at the visitor entrance. Would they call to report her for trespassing? Maybe this was all just a trick to get her arrested or ticketed. Maybe Dr. Elijah Cooke didn't really want to meet with her.

But for Genevieve, Rosemary had to take the risk of arrest or even worse—admittance to the House of Horrors. She opened the door and stepped out of the tepid warmth of the battered rental car, so she could reach the intercom. Cold air blasted her. While there was snow on the ground, it wasn't snowing today. It might have been warmer if it had been. Instead there was just the frigid cold and the gloom that seemed to perpetually hang over the island. Trembling with the cold, she pressed the button and before the person could greet her, she announced herself, "Rosemary Tulle to see Dr. Cooke."

"He's expecting you," the female voice replied pleasantly, and the gates rattled and whined as they slowly opened. That was when she noticed the camera in the stone wall, the lens pointed at the intercom panel. They had been watching her.

Rosemary jumped back into her car, and before the

gates could close and shut her out, she pressed on the accelerator and sped through them. The tires skidded on the slick driveway, and the rear of the car fishtailed, bringing the already crumpled bumper dangerously close to the pine trees lining the driveway. Thankfully, nobody stepped out of them today like the groundskeeper had the other day.

The only shadows on the drive appeared to be from the trees and clouds, and the wrought iron gates as they drew closed behind her, locking her in. Would it be as difficult to leave as it had been to enter? Would she be stuck here forever like Genevieve . . . ?

Her pulse quickened now—not with fear—but with anticipation. Surely, once she was inside the hall, she would be able to see her daughter and make sure she was safe and well. She had to be—or Dr. Elijah Cooke wouldn't have had his secretary call Rosemary to schedule this interview.

If anything had happened to Genevieve, he wouldn't want to risk her discovering it. Unless . . .

Unless he wanted to stop her from trying to find out . . . like someone had tried to stop her from returning to the island the other night. If the railing on the bridge had broken, she would have died.

Could she have been lured here—not for a job—but for her death?

Damn it.

Gordon was right. Rosemary Tulle was perfect.

Elijah had already suspected as much from her cover letter and résumé. Anyone could pad those to look impressive, though, so he'd done some research on his own and had confirmed she was well-respected as a counselor and had already helped so many people.

She could help more.

Here. At the hall . . .

Maybe if she'd been here sooner, she could have saved . . .

He pushed that thought from his mind, having learned long ago he couldn't do anything about the past. He could only focus on the present and the future. The hall had to have a future. He'd invested too much into it—financially and emotionally. It could not fail. *He* could not fail.

"Do you have any other questions for me?" Rosemary asked from where she sat in the chair across from his desk. Light filtered through the blinds at the tall window behind him, casting a glow to her porcelain skin. She was beautiful with her glossy black hair and bright blue eyes.

Since the receptionist had shown her to his office, he'd treated her like any other job applicant, and she'd acted like any other job applicant. But they both knew why she was really here. Unfortunately . . .

"Why are you wasting your time applying for this job when you already have one?" he asked.

The slight smile she'd obviously been forcing slipped away. "Why are you wasting your time interviewing me if you have no intention of giving me a job?"

"I would consider you for the position," he replied, "if I thought you really wanted it."

She drew a shaky-sounding breath. "I would consider accepting the position," she said, "if I knew that this facility has really changed from what it used to be."

"Halcyon Hall has been a treatment center," he said.

"Now," she agreed. "But I know what it was when it was Bainesworth Manor."

He closed his eyes. Would he ever escape it? Would they?

"It hasn't been a psychiatric hospital for decades," he told her. "People need to let go of the past."

"Agreed," she said. "Of the past, not of people . . ."

"That's why you're here," he said. With a ragged sigh, he leaned back in his chair. "You're really here about your sister."

"She's not my sister," she said.

A curse slipped through his lips. "No wonder you're not on the damn list. You're not a relative at all." What was she?

A reporter?

But she couldn't be—not with Gordon Chase vouching for her as a psychologist and her credentials had all checked out, impressively so.

"She's my daughter," Rosemary said.

Skeptical of her latest attempt to see the teenager, he arched a brow. "Really? You can prove that?"

Her porcelain skin flushed with color, but she didn't sound embarrassed when she replied, "No. I can't." She sounded frustrated. "I was a teenager when I had Genevieve, so my mother—worried about a scandal—insisted on putting her name as mother on the birth certificate. She and my stepfather are listed as Genevieve's parents. But they're not. I am her mother."

"Your mother was worried about a scandal. . . ." he murmured. He understood that very well.

"My mother worries about everything," Rosemary said. "That's probably why they put Genevieve in this place— to protect her from making the same mistakes I did."

He closed his eyes again, trying to hide his reaction— trying to hide the truth. But maybe it had been hidden long enough. Maybe it was time . . .

He pushed back his chair and abruptly stood up.

She jumped up as well. "Dr. Cooke—"

"Stay here," he told her. Needlessly. He doubted she was going to go anywhere until she saw her daughter. Maybe it was her résumé and the recommendations he'd received regarding her. Or maybe it had been the emotion when she'd spoken of her, but he believed Genevieve was her child. As her mother, she deserved to know the truth—no matter how painful it might be to her.

Her vehicle with its crumpled rear bumper and scraped sides was parked in the visitor lot right in front of the damn hall with its many windows. Anybody could see what he was about to do . . . if they looked out.

So he had to move fast.

He couldn't be seen.

She couldn't see what he was doing. Squeezing beneath her car and the snow-covered asphalt, he snipped the line leading to her brakes. If she saw what he'd done or noticed the fluid that dripped onto the snow-covered asphalt, she wouldn't get back into the vehicle. She would call the sheriff's department instead.

He had to stop her from going to the police. Not just about the car but about Genevieve. *Nobody* was going to take anything else away from him. He had already been denied too much that should have been his. That, by birthright, was his.

Like Bainesworth Manor . . .

But he would never get the chance to claim it, if they discovered what he'd done. If they locked him up, like those girls had been locked up all those years ago . . .

He was not going to get locked up. So he had to stop Rosemary Tulle from interfering anymore. He had to stop her like he'd tried on the bridge. But unlike that night, this time he could not fail.

Rosemary Tulle had to die—before she ruined everything.

Chapter Ten

Once the door closed behind Dr. Elijah Cooke, Rosemary dropped back into the chair from which she'd sprung up. Her knees trembled. She was as shaken as she'd been when the truck had tried to run her off the bridge. Or worse yet, as shaken as when she had confronted Whit Lawrence. She'd survived those confrontations, though; she would survive this one, too. Not that it had felt much like a confrontation.

It had felt like the job interview his secretary had claimed it was—until those last few minutes. Until he'd asked why she'd applied . . .

She couldn't lie. Not anymore . . . She'd kept secrets for far too long.

Did he believe her, though? That she was Genevieve's mother?

If he did, maybe he had left to get her daughter—to bring her to Rosemary.

And if he didn't . . .

Had he gone to call the sheriff's department? Or his own security team? What would they do to her, escort her off the premises? Or somewhere else?

She hadn't seen much of the estate—just the winding drive up to the huge building in front of which she'd parked. And of the building, she'd seen only the foyer and the director's office, which had been right off the foyer. The only other person she'd met besides him was his secretary, and the young woman had seemed more like a mannequin than a human. Beautiful but devoid of emotion . . .

Dr. Elijah Cooke was the same. She had not expected him to be so young or so incredibly good-looking. He was the epitome of tall, dark, and handsome except for his eyes. Those were strangely pale—not blue like hers—but an odd silvery color like the ice on the roads or the fog that hung over the island. And totally unreadable. Or perhaps just devoid, like the secretary had seemed, completely devoid of emotion.

The two of them were almost more like robots than humans. Maybe only robots could survive this place. Maybe that was why Genevieve wanted out so badly.

The longer Rosemary waited in that office the more she wanted to leave. Her pulse began to quicken, and a heavy pressure settled on her chest, making it difficult to draw a deep breath into her lungs. Where had he gone?

Why hadn't he returned?

She stood up on legs that trembled slightly beneath her weight. She was not going to be locked up in this place, not like Genevieve had been. She headed toward the door the receptionist had opened for her earlier, but when she closed her hand around the knob, it didn't turn. He had locked her in . . . just as she'd feared.

She clasped the knob more tightly, but it didn't budge. Where the hell was the lock? It must have been on the outside. Just as she loosened her grasp, it began to turn. Something clicked and the door opened, pushing her back against the wall behind her.

Dr. Cooke's strange silver eyes widened with surprise. She considered pushing past him and running from the room, from him. But would she be able to get out of the hall? Past the security the groundskeeper had warned her about? And did she want to—without Genevieve?

No.

"I wondered where you'd gone," she said.

"I'm sorry," he said. "I needed to do something."

In the middle of an interview? Not that it had been only an interview as they'd both acknowledged.

The phone on his desk buzzed, and he walked around her, letting the door swing shut behind him. Rosemary stared at it, at her chance of escape, but she let it snap closed in the jamb. Heard the lock click . . .

Expelling a shaky sigh of resignation, she turned and followed him back to his desk.

He stood beside it and reached down for a button on the phone. The receptionist's too perfect voice filled the office. "The call you had me place has been returned, Dr. Cooke," she said. "They are on line three."

They?

Was he checking her references now?

Was he going to offer her a job?

He pressed another button and spoke. "Thank you for returning my call, Mrs. Walcott."

Rosemary gasped. He'd called her mother.

"Do you have any news?" she asked.

"I have Rosemary in my office," he said.

"Rosemary?"

"She's told me that she's Genevieve's mother."

A pause so long ensued that Rosemary wondered if

her mother had hung up. But finally she replied, "She can't prove it."

Rosemary spoke up then. "DNA will prove it. Stop lying, Mother. Stop preventing me from seeing my daughter. Is that why you put her here? To keep her away from me?"

"You are a bad influence on her," Abigail said. "She already acts too much like you."

"Because she's my daughter," Rosemary maintained.

"That's why she's there," Abigail said. "Because she got into partying, too. She got suspended from school for it—"

"So you shipped her off to avoid a scandal," Rosemary said. "Or just to get her out of your—"

"I haven't called to mediate a family matter," Dr. Cooke interrupted their tense exchange. "I've called for you to grant me permission to tell Rosemary the truth."

"You don't want to do that, Dr. Cooke," her mother warned him.

"You don't want to force me to contact the press," Rosemary said. "I'll tell anyone who will listen that Genevieve is my daughter, and that you stole her from me."

Her mother gasped now. "You liar!"

"I won't stop," Rosemary warned her. "Not until somebody believes and helps me."

"I believe her," Dr. Cooke said.

Rosemary stared at him in shock.

"I believe her, and I suspect the sheriff does, too," Dr. Cooke continued. "It's only a matter of time before he gets a warrant and forces the issue."

Her mother's sigh crackled out of the phone speaker. "Very well then. You can tell her. But I warn you, Dr. Cooke, this will not be the end of it."

The line clicked and a dial tone buzzed. Dr. Cooke pressed a button on the phone, and silence reigned.

From the speaker.

Not from Rosemary. Her heart beat so loudly that surely he must have been able to hear it, too. "She gave you permission," Rosemary said. "I can see Genevieve now."

He shook his head. "No, you can't."

"But she said—"

"She said I can tell you the truth," he said. "And the truth is that you can't see your daughter."

"Why not?" Rosemary's head began to pound as intensely as her heart. "What do you mean?"

"She's gone."

Her heart felt as though it stopped beating altogether, and her breath froze in her lungs. Finally the shock receded, and she asked, "Are you saying that she's dead?"

"No, no," he quickly replied.

Maybe a little too quickly. A little too defensively.

"She's left the hall."

Rosemary released a shaky breath. "She got someone else to pick her up." Of course. Genevieve had many friends. One of them must have driven out to the island before Rosemary had arrived.

But why wasn't Genevieve answering her phone? Why hadn't she called to let Rosemary know she was okay?

"I am sure that is the case," Dr. Cooke replied.

"Who?" Rosemary asked. "Who else was on the list to visit her?" Since Rosemary hadn't been.

He shook his head. "No one."

"Then how . . ."

"I don't know how she did it," he admitted. "I just know that your sis—your daughter ran away."

Rosemary shook her head. "But why isn't she answering calls? Did she leave her phone here?"

"Nothing," he said with a slight shake of his head. "She left nothing behind."

But if she had her phone and charger, she would have been able to make calls. She would have contacted Rosemary, especially after Rosemary had left her all those voicemails. She wouldn't have let her worry about her.

"I want to see her room," she said.

"Of course," he complied. Too easily . . .

Was that where he'd gone? Had he cleaned it out and hidden her things, her phone, so that Rosemary would believe him? Moments later she stood in the doorway to an opulent suite. With thick luxurious carpeting and soft furnishings, it looked comfortable and empty.

"This is where Miss Walcott had been staying," he said.

She shook her head. "Genevieve is a teenager. It wouldn't have been left this neat."

"Of course, it's been cleaned."

"How long has she been gone?"

He shook his head. "Almost a week."

"What day?" she asked.

"Last Tuesday."

The day after she'd called Rosemary. Why hadn't she waited for her? Why hadn't she trusted that Rosemary would come—would help her?

She shook her head again. "No. She didn't run away."

"She was furious with her parents for bringing her here for treatment," he said. "She was furious with you for allowing it to happen."

She flinched as if he'd slapped her. Genevieve hadn't sounded angry with her on the voicemail, though. She'd just sounded desperate and scared.

"That's why she ran away," he said.

Rosemary doubted that, but she had another question. "Why haven't you reported her missing then?"

"I asked your parents if they wanted to report her missing, but they said that she already threatened to declare herself an emancipated minor. And at nearly eighteen, she would be able to do that and check herself out of here."

"But she didn't check herself out," Rosemary said. "How did she get out of here? How did she do it?"

How?

Elijah had been asking himself and his staff that question since Genevieve Walcott had disappeared a week ago. He'd been especially hard on his security advisor, his cousin Deputy Warren Cooke, but the man hadn't been able to answer the question. How the hell had she escaped from the hall and the grounds?

Not that the place was necessarily designed to keep people in—not like it used to be. Now it was designed to keep people out. Unwanted guests. Reporters.

The security measures were to protect the guests. They hadn't always proven successful, though. Not for Genevieve Walcott and not for . . .

He shook off the wayward thought to focus on Rosemary. Through his window, he watched as she walked the grounds around the hall—as if she would find her daughter hiding among the trees. If Genevieve had been out there for the past week, she would have died already of hypothermia. The temperatures on the island often dipped below zero at night even though it was still November.

Also whatever tracks she might have left behind as she'd walked away from the hall would have been obliterated long ago by the wind and snow. The only tracks Rosemary was likely to find were of coyotes, and those would give her no comfort.

Knuckles rapped against wood, and he turned toward the door he'd left open—in case she returned with more questions for him.

She wasn't the one with questions, though.

"Did you offer her the job?" Dr. Chase asked.

"Why would I do that?" he asked.

"Because she's highly qualified, and she would have a better rapport with the female guests than either you or I have been able to form."

"I know," he agreed. He'd surmised that just from reading her résumé. But when he'd met her . . .

"Then hire her," the older man urged.

"She doesn't want a job," Elijah said. "She wants her daughter."

"You mean sister," Chase said.

"No, her daughter."

Gordon snorted. "She told you that so you'd let her see Genevieve."

"It's the truth," he said. "I called Mrs. Walcott."

"And she confirmed it?" Gordon asked.

"Not so much by what she said but by how she said it," he explained. "And she let me tell Rosemary the truth."

"She knows Genevieve ran away?"

He pointed out the window, and Gordon joined him. "What's she doing out there? She's going to freeze."

He shrugged. "She doesn't believe she ran away."

"What does she think happened to her?"

"I don't know," he said. But now he wished he hadn't told her the truth—because she'd refused to accept it. Would she follow through on the threats she'd made to her mother? Would she talk to reporters? Would she press the issue?

The hall couldn't handle any bad publicity—not right now. And an investigation into Genevieve running away might open up another investigation . . . into other things that had happened at the hall in the long ago and not so long ago past.

"Offer her the job," Gordon said. "She'll take it. She's not going to go far until she finds her child."

And maybe if she worked here, Elijah could make her understand that the hall could do so much good now that it could make up for all the bad . . . if it was given the chance.

If he was given a chance . . .

Chapter Eleven

Where the hell was she?

The treatment center she'd mentioned was on a damn island, so it wasn't as if there were that many places she could be. Since she'd said they wouldn't let her into Halcyon Hall, he hadn't even gone there yet. But he didn't know where else to search.

The local hotel was closed for the season. Was she sleeping in her car?

Whit peered through the windshield as the headlamps of his Cadillac illuminated twin spots of light in the all-encompassing gloom of Bane Island. Brick and clapboard buildings lined the street he traveled. He'd found the town. Maybe he would find Rosemary here. He passed the police station, or so the emblem on the door declared the small building. She wasn't there; she'd already said they wouldn't help her. So he pulled into the lot of a diner next to it.

Weren't diners usually gathering spots for the locals? Someone here would know where she was. The lot was nearly full, but he found a spot next to a Jeep. Since he hadn't seen much else open, he wasn't surprised that the restaurant was packed. The din of voices reached him across the porch as he headed toward the front door of the old Victorian house. Once he pulled open the heavy mahogany door, though, all conversation ceased and everyone turned toward him.

Had they stopped talking because he was a stranger? Or because they recognized him? After a quick glance at him, everyone resumed talking and eating except for one person who stared intently at him from a booth on the other side of the room.

Anger coursed through him. He was such a damn fool; he'd started to believe that maybe Rosemary did need his help, that she had been telling the truth about that at least. But not now . . .

Not with *her* here. They must have been in on it together to discredit him. He stalked over to the booth and slid onto the side across from Edie Stone. "Where is she?" he asked.

The blonde tilted her head. "To whom are you referring?"

"You damn well know whom," he shot back at her.

Why would Rosemary do this to him? For money? Revenge? He hadn't been responsible for what had happened to her, though. He'd had nothing to do with spiking her drink that night. And once he'd found out . . .

Edie Stone's mouth curved into a slight smile. "Rosemary Tulle."

"So you do know her," he said. "That's why you're here."

"I'm just chasing down the lead to a hot story," she said.

"Chasing or creating?" he challenged her.

She sucked in a breath. "I don't create. I just report."

He snorted. "There's nothing to report here."

"You're here," she said. "For Rosemary Tulle." She

hadn't asked a question. She already knew. So if she wasn't conspiring with Rosemary, she must have been listening at the door after he'd showed her out. Or maybe someone else had told her . . .

"Who's been talking to you?" he asked. He doubted that Martin had; he was even more desperate—too desperate—to keep Rosemary's allegations secret than Whit was. "Dwight?" His clerk could have been swayed with either her money or her charm.

What else had Dwight told her? He wasn't above listening in on the intercom or at the door. What had he heard that day? Her accusation that he'd raped her? The word was so damn ugly that his guts twisted at just the thought of it, of someone doing that to someone else, to someone he'd once cared so damn much about. She wasn't the only woman he'd cared about who'd been violated like that. His own mother . . .

How had she ever been able to look at him let alone love him? He was a constant reminder of what had happened to her. Once he'd found out how he'd been conceived it had been too late to do anything about it. The statute had run out. That was one of the things he wanted to change when he got elected, if he got elected. . . .

If Edie Stone reported Rosemary's accusation, some people would believe it—even though it couldn't be proven. There was no statute of limitations on scandal.

"Nobody's been talking to me," Edie Stone replied. "Your campaign manager has made certain of that. What's he trying to cover up for you, Your Honor? Or is that why you're here now? You're doing your own dirty work?"

He shook his head. "Not at all. I'm reaching out to someone who might need my help."

She snorted now. "More like reaching out for votes."

He wasn't looking for votes. He was looking for Rosemary Tulle and for the truth.

Running through the open front doors of the hall, Elijah called out, "Stop!" As he rushed toward the parking lot, his shoes slipped on the slick sidewalk, and the cold wind blasted through his suit jacket and dress pants. "Damn it!"

He was too late. Rosemary Tulle's rental car, with its back bumper crushed, headed down the drive toward the road. He wasn't about to chase her down to do . . . what?

Stop her from calling the police? That was probably where she was headed. But Sheriff Howell understood, better than most, that teenagers ran away; when he heard what had happened, he wouldn't be as concerned as she was. And if she talked to reporters . . .

Elijah would just decline to give out any information on a guest. Maybe he shouldn't have told her what had happened. But, damn it, he wanted to hire her, wanted her to work with the guests that he and Dr. Chase weren't able to counsel the way she would be able to. . . .

Was Gordon right about her not leaving the island until she found Genevieve? Would she take the position if he offered it to her? That was why he'd really tried to stop her—to ask.

"Who was that?" a deep voice asked.

Elijah turned toward his business partner. The younger man wore a suit, too, a track suit. Bode James was the head of the physical well-being part of the treatment center, and the fitness expert embodied his role. His black hair was damp beneath the hood of his sweatshirt. He must have been out running.

"The psychologist I interviewed this morning."

"She ran away from your interview?" Bode chuckled. "What the hell did you ask her?"

"It's what I told her," Elijah said. "She's Genevieve Walcott's mother."

Bode shook his head and a droplet of sweat rolled down his face. "No, she's not. I met the mother when Genevieve was dropped off."

Of course he had. Bode always made it a point to meet—and charm—every female who arrived at the hall.

Elijah studied the younger man's handsome face. "Did you meet Rosemary Tulle just now?" he asked.

Maybe she'd had another reason to run off.

Bode expelled a shaky breath. "The sister . . . the one who's been trying to get in to see her . . ."

"She knows the truth now," Elijah said.

"Does she?" Bode mused. "Do we?"

Elijah narrowed his eyes. He suspected Bode might know more than he did. Genevieve was a beautiful girl. Girl . . .

Wouldn't her age have stopped Bode from turning his charm on her, though?

Bode tugged his hood tighter around his face, as if uncomfortable with Elijah's scrutiny of him. "So is she going to stay away now?"

"I hope not," Elijah said. "I'm going to offer her a job."

"Have you lost your damn mind?" Bode asked. "I thought you were kidding about interviewing her."

Elijah arched a brow. "You did?"

Bode snorted. "Yeah, you're right. I should have known better. You don't have a sense of humor at all."

And Bode had too much of one. They were damn unlikely business partners. Even more unlikely brothers . . .

But Elijah had had no choice about either situation. Neither had Bode. Or Jamie, as Elijah called him. The fitness expert had rearranged his first and middle names and dropped his last to sound more marketable, for his brand . . . for the books he'd published and the television programs on which he was a frequent guest. He was smart—smarter than Elijah realized most of the time.

"It's a bad idea," Bode said. "Hiring her . . ."

Probably.

"She's just going to make trouble for us."

They'd both invested so much into restoring the manor and converting it to something new, something special—something that the past wouldn't be able to overshadow anymore. But if the press found out about the recent problems . . .

The curse would come back to haunt them all.

And he and Bode had too damn much to lose . . .

Panic pressed on Rosemary's lungs again—like it had while she'd waited for Dr. Cooke to return to his office, to let her out. Would the gates open as she neared them? Or did she have to stop and request to be released? And would he let her go, or would he keep her inside that damn property like he'd tried to keep Genevieve?

Had she really run away?

Where the hell could she have gone?

And why hadn't she contacted Rosemary to let her know where she was, that she was okay?

Because she wasn't okay . . .

Tears stung Rosemary's eyes, blurring her vision as she neared those tall wrought iron gates. With the wet sole of her boot, she tapped the brakes, and the pedal went down, down to the floor of the car, with no resistance. The tires didn't slow. The brakes didn't engage.

What the hell had happened?

She glanced up, just as the gates opened. Maybe it would have been better had she crashed into them. Maybe they would have stopped her. But she couldn't stop now. She could only wrench the wheel to the right so she wouldn't crash into the trees across the street. The right brought her away from town, but if she'd turned left, she would have had two lanes of potential traffic to navigate.

The car fishtailed, sliding back and forth across the slick pavement, as she fought to get it under control. But she was going too fast, just as the sheriff had cautioned her that first day she'd arrived on the island. She was going too fast for conditions—for having no damn brakes.

What had happened?

And how the hell was she going to be able to stop?

Turning away from town brought her toward that pier she'd nearly struck the first day and all the rocks along the jagged shoreline. She had to stop the car before she launched off the pier and into the frothing icy waves in the ocean.

She jerked the wheel again, this time to the left. She wasn't trying to turn back toward town. She knew she would never make it there. She could only hope that she didn't wind up in the water where nobody would ever find her, let alone save her.

As she turned, at such a high speed, the tires squealed and skidded before two of them left the pavement, and the car toppled onto its side, then its roof, then its side. . . .

Metal crunched, and Rosemary screamed as the car began to collapse around her. She could only hope that it stopped tumbling before it landed in the water. But then something struck her head, sending a wave of pain and blackness crashing over her. And she thought no more. . . .

Chapter Twelve

Deacon leaned against the front counter of the diner, waiting on his lunch order. He could have sent Margaret to pick it up, but it was cold, and he'd needed to stretch his legs.

This time of year was usually quiet on the island. It would have been quiet if not for Rosemary Tulle's arrival. But she wasn't the only unfamiliar face in town. As he waited, Deacon glanced around the booths and tables. Most of the patrons were known. Some smiled and waved at him; others looked away, unwilling to meet his gaze. Some others stared back at him with disapproval and condemnation.

It didn't matter what the state police had ruled; some of the islanders held him responsible for what had happened. They believed the worst. Hell, maybe he was responsible—just not in the way that they thought.

Ignoring the familiar faces and the unfriendly gazes, he focused on the unfamiliar. They were a couple. Both blondes. The woman's hair was nearly as short as the man's and tucked behind her ears, revealing her pointy chin. She looked familiar.

Deacon narrowed his eyes as he focused on the man.

He wasn't completely unfamiliar. Something about him struck a chord in Deacon's memory. He'd seen him before.

Where? When?

And why was he on the island now?

It wasn't exactly tourist season. He could have been heading to the hall or bringing the woman . . .

But why stop in town? Why not head right there?

Cooke had hired some fancy French chef. Deacon had eaten there once—when he'd been the guest of a guest, when he'd been on the list that Rosemary wanted on so damn badly.

Where was she now?

He probably needed to check on her—to make sure she'd not gotten herself into trouble again. He'd just been assuming, though, that she'd found trouble at the hall.

But what if it had followed her here?

What if the danger Rosemary Tulle was in had nothing to do with the island at all and everything to do with the people in her life? Were these people in her life?

Deacon had learned the hard way to not ignore his instincts. These people appearing in town right now—right around the time Rosemary Tulle had—was no coincidence.

He approached the booth the couple occupied. Not that either seemed all that happy with the other's company. Tension radiated from both of them. Was that because of the conservation he'd interrupted or because of his badge?

"You're new to the island," Deacon remarked. "Anything I can help you find?" The man shook his head while the woman asked, "Do you personally greet all visitors to the island, Officer?"

"Sheriff," Deacon corrected her. "And yes, I like to learn the name of every stranger to Bane."

"Edie Stone," she replied. "And this is Judge Whittaker Lawrence."

"Oh . . ." Now he knew why he'd recognized him. The guy had just announced his intention to run for governor next year. Was he already starting his campaign? Why here? Bane didn't have that many registered voters, not like Portland where he was a sitting judge.

"Thank you for the warm welcome, Sheriff," the woman remarked with a dismissive smile.

A grin tugged at Deacon's lips. "Not much warm about the island this time of year," he murmured, "which makes me wonder why you would choose to visit now."

"Is that what's brought you over to our booth, Sheriff?" the woman asked. "Curiosity?"

"Of course."

"Why?" she asked. "You must get visitors year-round with Halcyon Hall on the island."

"Is that where you're heading?" Deacon asked. "You two checking in?"

"You are quite curious, Sheriff," Stone said while the judge remained silent.

He shrugged. "Hazard of my job, I guess."

"Mine too," she said. "I'm a reporter."

A pang of unease struck him. He was not a fan of the press. "A reporter and a politician . . ." Usually politicians weren't fans either, at least not lately.

"Sounds like the beginning of a joke," the judge finally spoke, but it was obvious from the tight expression on his face that he didn't find the situation all that funny.

"What's the punch line?" Deacon asked.

"If she had her way, it would probably be me," Lawrence admitted.

He hadn't imagined that tension. "Sounds like at least one of you might need a stay at the hall," he mused.

"I've heard it's pretty hard to get into," Lawrence remarked.

"You heard right," Deacon said. "I hope you've made a reservation for your stay, or you will probably be turned away at the gates."

Like Rosemary Tulle had been . . .

"I'm not here to check into the hall, Sheriff," Lawrence adamantly replied. Of course he wouldn't want anyone to know that he was checking into what was basically a fancy rehab center.

Before Deacon could challenge the judge with more questions, his cell phone vibrated in his pocket. Margaret was probably wondering what was taking him so damn long to pick up their lunch. The bag sat on the counter. Hopefully, the Styrofoam containers had kept it warm, as warm as it had ever been.

"Margaret," he greeted her. "I'll be right there."

"Sheriff, there's been an accident," she said. "You're needed out past the manor—near the pier."

"Is Warren closer?" he asked.

"Warren's not answering his radio," she replied. "And it's serious. I've already dispatched an ambulance."

Margaret wouldn't have done that for a fender bender. He cursed. "That bad?"

"Rollover," she confirmed. "A rental car . . ."

"Rosemary Tulle?" he asked.

"You know anybody else driving a rental right now?"

Maybe these two, but they were here. They were safe. He turned away from them, dodged a waitress carrying a coffeepot, and headed toward the door. When he pushed it open, somebody caught his arm. He didn't want the damn food now. "I have to go—"

But it wasn't a waitress holding him back. It was Whittaker Lawrence. "What the hell do you want?"

"Rosemary Tulle," Whit said. That was who he wanted. "You said her name."

The sheriff's dark eyes narrowed. "You know her?"

Not anymore . . .

But with how he'd said her name, it was obvious the sheriff did. So she must have tried to get the police to help her, like she'd claimed.

"What's happened to her?" Whit asked, his heart beating fast with concern.

The sheriff jerked his arm free of Whit's grasp. "I'm about to find out. I advise you to stick around Bane, Lawrence, because I'm sure I'm going to have some questions for you." His dark eyes skimmed briefly over his face, the same look in them that had been in Rosemary's—the accusation.

Had she told the sheriff what she believed about him?

Before he could ask, the man headed out the door. He started after him but someone tugged on his arm. "Where are you going?" Edie asked as she shoved her wallet into her bag and pulled out her keys.

He tugged free of her grasp and headed out the door, but she stayed with him as he crossed the lot to his vehicle. The lights flashed on the Jeep as she clicked a fob. "If you're trying to follow the sheriff, my ride will handle these roads better than your fancy car."

His car wasn't particularly fancy, but it wasn't all-wheel drive like her Jeep or the sheriff's SUV that pulled away from the front of the police department with its lights flashing red and blue and its siren blaring. Not wanting to get left behind, he jumped into the passenger's side of the Jeep. Edie Stone drove fast with no fear of the slick roads, the Jeep easily keeping up with the sheriff's black SUV that raced ahead of them.

The sheriff was obviously on his way to an emergency— an emergency that involved Rosemary. What could have happened to her? The sheriff drove so fast that the distance between the vehicles widened.

Edie cursed. "We're losing him."

The road curved, and the SUV with the flashing lights disappeared. Then the Jeep rounded that curve, and Edie slammed on the brakes. The sheriff's SUV had stopped behind an ambulance. A fire truck flanked the road in front of them.

Whit unlocked and pushed open the passenger's door. Where was she? What had happened?

A voice shouted, "Lawrence!"

He ignored it as he walked around the sheriff's SUV, his shoes slipping on the icy surface of the road. To get around the ambulance, he had to step onto the narrow shoulder of the road. His shoes disappeared into the snow. He didn't give a damn about the cold. He barely felt it as he headed toward the fire truck.

The wreck was on the other side of the red engine. The crumpled car lay on its roof, the front windshield shattered but intact. He couldn't see clearly through it, but he knew she was inside it. Her black hair spilled out the broken side window.

Was she dead?

Was she dead?

Rosemary fought her way back from oblivion. Her head pounded, and she winced at the blare of sirens close to her. Help had arrived.

She would be okay.

If she fought . . .

She had to fight just to stay awake. Wincing and moaning against the pain in her head, she opened her eyes. Her vision was blurred—not just from the darkness that loomed over her like those dark clouds over the island—but from the hair that had tangled across her face.

She tried to move her arm, tried to raise her hand toward her face. But the airbag held her arms beneath the steering wheel. Too bad it hadn't protected her from hitting her head. She must have lost consciousness for a while—long enough for the emergency vehicles to get to her.

Where was the help?

Didn't they know she was alive?

She cleared her throat, getting ready to yell. But then fingers brushed across her face, brushing back the hair that had tangled around her head. And she could see . . .

Was she awake? Or was she dreaming? Because the face she stared into was the one she saw in every nightmare she had. Fear rushing through her, she screamed.

Chapter Thirteen

Her scream sent a chill racing over Deacon that had nothing to do with the cold wind blasting across the ocean and the shore and everything to do with the man kneeling next to her car. Deacon jerked the judge to his feet. "I told you to stay out of the way. What the hell are you doing here?"

"What the hell are you doing?" Lawrence shot back at him. "She needs help, and you're all just standing around!"

Maybe that was why she'd screamed. She was crushed between the roof of her car and her seat, upside down with her hair falling over her face. Blood trailed from a wound, dripping out the broken window to stain the snow falling on the road.

He dropped to his knees beside the wreckage. "Are you hurt?"

She peered up at him through her tangled hair. "Sheriff . . ."

"Are you hurt?" he asked again.

She shook her head, and a grimace twisted her beautiful face. A moan slipped through her lips.

"Of course she's hurt!" Lawrence yelled. "What the hell is everybody doing? The fire truck and ambulance are here."

Maybe the judge was used to barking out orders in his courtroom, but this was Deacon's turf now. He stood up and pushed the judge back. "Get the hell out of the way or I'll arrest you!"

Just then a paramedic rushed up with a couple firefighters who carried the Jaws of Life. The paramedic, George Reynolds, said, "You all need to step back, so we can assess her injuries and get her out of there."

The judge finally moved away, but Deacon leaned down toward Rosemary again. "They're going to get you out. You're going to be okay."

She fumbled around the now deflating airbag and reached out the window. "Genevieve . . ."

Of course this was about Genevieve. That was why she'd come to the island, why she kept risking her damn life . . .

"You worry about you right now," he said.

She tried shaking her head again but flinched. "Genevieve . . ."

George tugged at him. "C'mon, Sheriff."

Deacon stepped back, out of the way. The firefighters moved to the other side of Rosemary's crumpled car, but before they did, they put a protective plastic tarp over her.

"No!" Whittaker Lawrence yelled, his face twisting into a grimace of grief. "Oh, my God, no!"

Who the hell was Rosemary to him?

Sparks began to shoot out of the firefighter's machinery as they cut away at the wreckage. "She's not dead," Deacon told the judge and the reporter who stood near him. "They just covered her up to protect her as they work to extract her."

Whittaker Lawrence nodded. Then he turned away, as if he didn't want them to see his reaction. It was too damn late for that. He was clearly out of his mind over her. Why? Because she was hurt? Or because she had survived?

Deacon had no idea how long her car had been here—wrecked—before someone had called in to report it. Nobody traveled this way this time of year unless they were lost like Rosemary had been that first day.

What about today? Why had she come this way today?

She knew where the hall was and which direction town was. Why was she down near the pier? Had she been meeting someone—someone like Whittaker Lawrence?

"How do you know Rosemary?" he asked.

Whittaker was too far away to hear him—more so in his thoughts than physical distance. So Deacon focused on the reporter. "How do you know her?"

"I don't."

He jerked his thumb at the judge. "He sure does. How?"

She narrowed her dark eyes as she studied Lawrence. "That's what I've been trying to find out."

"You don't have to answer the reporter's questions," Deacon informed the judge. "But you need to answer mine. How do you know Rosemary?"

Whittaker cleared his throat and replied, "From school."

"School? College? High? Elementary?" he asked. "Any of them was a damn long time ago. So why are you here?"

The judge glanced at the reporter before turning toward him again. "She came to see me a couple days ago," he admitted. "She wanted help with something."

"Genevieve . . ." Deacon murmured.

He nodded. "Yes. And Halcyon Hall."

Deacon grunted. Everything—everything bad that happened on the island—came back to that damn place.

* * *

Under that thick plastic, Rosemary felt like a corpse. And even though they had her covered up while they were tearing apart the wreckage to extract her, sparks danced before her eyes. Then her head spun dizzily as she went from dangling upside down to lying on her back on a stretcher. Another blanket covered her, this one warm and soft.

"We need to raise your body temperature," a paramedic told her. "You could have hypothermia."

"How long were you there?" the sheriff asked.

"I don't know . . ." She hadn't looked at the time when she'd left the hall, and she hadn't had time before she'd crashed. "But the heater in that thing was never great anyway."

His lips curved into a slight smile. "Hope you paid for the insurance when you rented it."

Rosemary felt a smile tug at her lips, too. She hadn't realized the sheriff had a sense of humor. She'd always been a sucker for a humorous man—like Whit. He'd gone out of his way in school to live up to his name, quick-witted and smart-mouthed. That was why she'd fallen so hard for him. Had she seen him? Or had that just been part of her nightmare?

"What happened?" the sheriff asked.

"I—I thought I saw someone. . . ." She tried to peer around him, but he leaned over the stretcher and was so broad shouldered that it wasn't possible.

"Whittaker Lawrence?"

She shivered despite the blanket covering her. "He was here?"

"Is that who drove you off the road?" he asked, his voice gruff. Anger flashed in his dark eyes.

"No," she said. "I did that."

He groaned. "Were you driving too fast again?"

"I had no choice," she said. "Something happened to my brakes. I think someone cut them . . . while I was at the hall."

The sheriff cursed. "They let you in?"

She nodded, and now dark spots danced across her vision.

"We have to get her a CT scan," the paramedic said. "Now . . ."

She reached for the paramedic and grabbed his arm. "I don't want to leave the island." Because, no matter what Dr. Cooke had told her, she didn't believe that Genevieve had run away.

"We have a hospital on the island," the paramedic said. "It's small but fully equipped."

She released a shaky breath and nodded. Then she reached for the sheriff's arm. "I need to talk to you."

"I need to talk to you," another deep voice chimed in, and Whit's handsome face, tight with concern, appeared over the sheriff's shoulder. "I want to make sure that you're all right."

"I told you to stay back," Sheriff Howell said.

"What—what are you doing here?" she asked.

"I want to talk to you," he said.

"Not now," the sheriff told him. "She's hurt. We need to get her to the hospital." He gestured at the paramedics to lift her into the ambulance.

As the stretcher began to rise, Rosemary reached out again—for Whit. "I'm staying at the boardinghouse in town," she said. "I'm sure I'll be back there soon. I'm not hurt."

Not physically. But she might have been hurt mentally since she was compelled to see him again.

"Why'd you do that?" the sheriff asked as he stepped up into the back of the ambulance with her. "Why'd you tell that guy where you're staying?"

"You don't trust him?" He must have just met him—at the accident scene. How had Whit known she'd been in an accident? Except that she didn't think it was an accident any more than the fender bender on the bridge had been an accident.

She looked out the back doors of the ambulance just as a firefighter pushed them shut. Before they closed she saw Whit's face—saw the concern in his expression.

"As a rule, I don't trust politicians," the sheriff replied.

"Aren't sheriffs elected politicians?" she asked.

His mouth curved into a slight grin. "I was voted into office," he acknowledged. "But I'm a lawman. I didn't lobby for votes like Lawrence does."

"You think that's what he's doing here?" Rosemary asked.

He shook his head. "Not anymore. Not after seeing him with you. You're the reason he's here. What's the deal with the two of you? He said you went to school together."

Her head continued to pound, but at least the hammering was duller now, not as sharp, not as painful. "We did."

The sheriff continued, "He said you asked him for assistance with Genevieve. Bane is outside his jurisdiction. How did you think he could help? Why did you think he would?"

"Because he's Genevieve's father," she said. "She's my daughter. And he's the father." Even though he wouldn't admit it . . .

But he had to be.

The sheriff stared down at her through narrowed eyes. "How hard did you hit your head?"

"I'm fine," she insisted, and she was. "I was just a kid when I had her. Just sixteen."

He flinched and murmured, "Holly's age . . ."

"Holly?"

"My daughter. I can't imagine her having a baby." He cursed. "I don't want to imagine it. Don't want to imagine her ever dating."

"With you as her father, it might not be easy for her to get a date," Rosemary assured him. "Who wants to date the sheriff's daughter?"

"Hopefully no one," he said. "So you believe that Lawrence showed up to help you?"

She shook her head and flinched, just a little bit, at the jab of pain in her skull. "I don't know what to believe. He denied that he could be Genevieve's father. He acted like I was crazy."

Something like a low growl emitted from the sheriff.

"Like you haven't thought the same thing," she accused him.

He sighed but didn't deny it. "I think you're crazy for telling Lawrence where you're staying. When you nearly got run off the bridge, were you on your way back from seeing him?"

She sucked in a breath. "Yes . . ."

"And today . . . what the hell happened today?" he asked.

"I told you—my brakes went out," she said.

"That's why you were down near the pier," he said with a nod. "But were you really at the hall before that happened? They actually let you in?" Now he sounded like Whit, like he thought she was crazy or maybe that she'd hit her head too hard.

"I had an interview with Dr. Cooke," she said.

"Interview?" He snorted. "What—you were going to wash dishes to get inside the place?"

"Counsel," she said. "I'm a psychologist."

"Oh . . ."

"I was heading out of the gates when I tried to use the brakes and the pedal went completely to the floor." Her heart leaped with that remembered rush of fear and panic. "I didn't know what to do."

"Of course not," he said. "Were they wonky earlier? Since the accident on the bridge?"

"That wasn't an accident," she said. "And neither was this. Someone must have tampered with my brakes."

He sucked in a breath. "And both these things happened after you accused the judge of fathering a kid with a sixteen-year-old girl. His career would be over if anyone found out. I don't think he wants to talk to you. I think he wants to shut you up. Permanently."

"I don't care what he wants." She reached out and grabbed the sheriff's arm. "I need your help."

"Yeah, I'll investigate that bastard and—"

"I need your help finding Genevieve."

"They let you in but didn't let you see her?" he asked. "Elijah playing some sick game with you? Not that I'm surprised—"

"He claims she ran away," Rosemary said.

"Claims? You don't believe him?"

"Where would she run?" Rosemary asked. "We're on a damn island."

"With a bridge to the mainland," the sheriff reminded her.

She cringed at the thought of anyone trying to walk across that bridge. Driving was dangerous enough. Genevieve was a slight girl; she could have blown right off it. "No.

She wouldn't have run away—not in this weather." She wouldn't have survived.

"You need to tell the authorities where she lives to look for her. She probably called someone to pick her up and bring her back home with them."

"She called me," she reminded him.

"And when you didn't show, she called someone else," the sheriff said. "She's a teenager. I'm sure she has plenty of friends."

"She does," Rosemary said. "But why isn't she answering her phone?"

"Did she leave it behind?"

She shook her head. "She left nothing behind."

"Then she ran away and doesn't want to be found," the sheriff said. "That's probably why she hasn't called you. She doesn't want you bringing her home."

"I wouldn't," Rosemary said. "I never should have given her to my mother to begin with. Never should have trusted her . . ." Tears stung her eyes, and she blinked furiously to clear her vision and her mind.

"I'll reach out to the authorities back in your hometown," he offered. "See if they can find her hanging out with friends there. Then you'll feel better."

The sheriff was dismissing her concerns about Genevieve again, just like Dr. Cooke had. And Whit . . .

What the hell was he doing here?

Really, after what had happened, after someone had tried—twice now—to kill her, she couldn't trust anyone. Not with her life and not with Genevieve's. She had to find her daughter on her own.

* * *

How the hell had the bitch survived?

Again?

When her car had turned toward the pier, he'd thought it was over—that he would finally be rid of her. With no brakes, she wouldn't have been able to stop on the pier and would have either driven off it or off the rocky shore. The ocean should have sucked her in, sucked the car under, where nobody would ever find her.

Just like nobody would ever find Genevieve . . .

But Rosemary Tulle had survived yet again. At first he hadn't been sure, though, when he'd seen that the car had rolled. She could have died in that crash. But before he'd had a chance to make sure, another car had come along and the driver had rushed to the wreckage before he could. The person had had a camera around her neck, probably going to take pictures of the pier. She'd called for help.

He'd been watching—from the protection of the pine trees—as the fire department, paramedics, and the sheriff had arrived at the crash site. And some other couple—a guy in a suit and a blonde. At first he'd thought Rosemary might have been dead . . . until he'd heard her scream.

Damn it!

If she could scream, she could talk, and she'd keep talking to the sheriff and anybody else who would listen to her. Would anyone listen to him when he was ready to claim what was his? Eventually somebody would, just like eventually somebody was going to believe Rosemary Tulle.

She had to be stopped.

Permanently.

Chapter Fourteen

"Tell me about Rosemary Tulle," Edie Stone said the minute he closed the passenger door on her Jeep. She started the car.

A surge of protectiveness rushed over him. "Rosemary Tulle is none of your business."

"Why is she yours?" she asked.

He sighed. "Good question."

"How well did you know her in school?"

He repeated, "Rosemary is none of your business."

"But I'm interviewing you," she reminded him. "You agreed to that."

"And then I shut down the interview because all you want to report is a scandal."

"Is Rosemary a scandal for you?"

He groaned. "If you're looking for a scandal, look into Halcyon Hall," he suggested. "That is why she came to see me—about the hall."

"What about the hall?" Edie asked.

"They won't let her see . . ." Her daughter. Rosemary had a daughter that she thought was his. What the hell had happened that night after he'd left her house? "Drive me back to the diner," he said, "so I can get my vehicle."

"I'm driving to the boardinghouse," she said as she steered away from the wreckage of Rosemary's vehicle.

She was lucky she'd survived the crash. But how badly was she injured? He should have gone to the hospital instead; he should have gone with her in the ambulance like the sheriff had. But he had no right—no rights at all where Rosemary was concerned. No right to open her life up to a reporter who'd only been given permission to interview him.

"Bring me to the diner," he ordered her.

But she was already pulling her Jeep up to the curb in front of a Victorian house with a sign out front offering rooms for rent. "We're already here. But it's not far to town if you want to walk back to the diner." She shut off the ignition and pushed open her door.

And he cursed. He didn't want her here. But she blithely walked across the porch to the front door and rang the bell before he could stop her.

Everything else passed in a blur as he met the Pierce sisters and was shown into their parlor.

What had Rosemary told everyone about him?

The sheriff had treated him with suspicion. Now the ladies at the boardinghouse eyed him with that same suspicion. He and Edie sat in the front parlor—where visitors were received—according to the one who spoke. The other woman just stared at him—until he looked back at her; then she quickly cast her gaze down at her lap where she clutched a small, crocheted baby's blanket.

He and Edie Stone sat on one faded rose-colored sofa while the sisters sat across a polished mahogany coffee table from them on another faded rose-colored sofa. The legs of the thing were so spindly that he was surprised they held up under his weight. The whole place reminded him of a bedraggled Victorian dollhouse. At least a fire glowed in the hearth near the end of the couch where Edie sat, trying to warm up.

He doubted even a fire could warm him up. He was chilled to the bone—over what had happened to Rosemary. She could have been killed. And even though she'd been talking after they'd extracted her from the wreckage, she could still be seriously injured. Perhaps fatally so . . .

It had been a while, and she hadn't returned like she'd told him she would. "I need to go to the hospital," he said.

Edie leaped up from the sofa. "I'll go—"

"If you're going back to the mainland, you should leave soon," Ms. Pierce advised the reporter. "The bridge is dangerous to travel at night. Miss Tulle will attest to that. This isn't the first accident she's had on the island."

"What?" Whit asked. "She's been in another?"

"Not sure how much of an accident it was," the older woman continued. "Another vehicle struck hers. She's lucky it didn't push her right through the railing and into the ocean."

Tension gripped Whit. She wasn't lucky. She was in danger.

"The person didn't even stop," she continued, and she eyed him with open suspicion now.

"I'm sure the sheriff is investigating," Edie said as she sent Whit a sidelong glance. She was suspicious of him, too. "He will investigate this accident as well."

"He better," Whit said. But the sheriff had already been of no help to Rosemary, and he was one of the islanders, maybe on the hall's payroll. She hadn't reached out to Whit for help for the right reasons, but he wanted to help her anyway. "What do you know about the hall?" Whit asked Ms. Pierce. "About Halcyon Hall?"

"Cursed . . ." The word escaped in a whisper from

the other woman, who clutched that bedraggled blanket. "Cursed . . ." she whispered.

"Cursed?" Edie asked, the reporter's interest obviously piqued. "What is she talking about?"

"The manor," Miss Pierce replied.

"Manor?"

"We all know it as the manor. Bainesworth Manor."

"How is it cursed?" Edie asked.

Before either sister could answer her question, a door creaked open, and heels clicked on the wood floor of the foyer. "Sheriff, you don't need to see me inside," Rosemary said. "I'm fine. The doctor said I'm fine."

His heart pounding, Whit leaped up from the sofa and rushed out to the foyer. Rosemary didn't look fine; in fact when she turned toward him, her eyes widened with shock or fear. Didn't she remember telling him to meet her here? How badly was she hurt? Her skin was pale except for the bruise on her forehead and what looked like bruises beneath her eyes but were probably just dark circles of exhaustion. While she stood, she seemed unsteady, like she might have stumbled if not for the sheriff's big hand cupping her elbow. But instead of being grateful for the sheriff finally supporting her, Whit felt something else— something to which he had no right: jealousy.

The sheriff ignored him and corrected her. "The doctor said that you should stay for observation, just in case . . ."

"In case of what?" she asked. "It's only bumps and bruises—"

"A concussion—"

"A slight one," she said. "I'm fine. And you have work to do."

The sheriff expelled a ragged sigh. "I don't think you have anything to worry about, Rosemary."

"About the accident?" Whit asked.

"It wasn't an accident," the sheriff said. "Her brake line was cut. Know anything about that?"

"Absolutely not," Whit said.

"What about you?" Sheriff Howell asked, and Whit turned to see Edie standing behind him.

"I don't know Miss Tulle," she replied. "The first time I saw her was when we followed you to the accident site."

"I know you," Rosemary remarked as if just now recognizing Edie. If they'd been conspiring together, she would have recognized her right away. "You're a reporter." She looked at Whit again, but now confusion replaced her fear. "You brought a reporter here? Why?"

He shook his head. "I didn't bring her. She was already here." But now he doubted that Rosemary had been meeting with her.

"Why?" the sheriff asked Edie.

"I'm working on a story."

Rosemary gasped. "About Genevieve?"

Edie's brow furrowed. "Genevieve? Is that who the hall won't let you see?"

Whit shook his head. "No. You're not going to interrogate her."

"No, you're not," the sheriff agreed. "I'm going to interrogate the two of you. Where were you two nights ago?"

According to the boardinghouse landlady, two nights ago would have been when Rosemary had been nearly forced off the bridge, probably after leaving his chambers. Edie had been at his office when Rosemary had arrived. Had that just been a coincidence?

"I can provide an alibi," Whit said. "But you don't need it."

The sheriff snorted. "I don't. You do. Everything

that's happened to Rosemary has happened after she contacted you."

"It's happened here," Whit pointed out. "Just as she's looking for her daughter."

Rosemary gripped the sheriff's arm. "Please," she implored him. "Please find Genevieve."

The sheriff sighed. "We'll talk about this tomorrow," he said. "You need some rest." Over her head, he stared down Whit. "You need to let her rest."

Whit detected a trace of jealousy in the other man, or maybe he was just projecting his own feelings onto the sheriff. The familiarity between the lawman and Rosemary had something churning in his gut. When the sheriff stepped out of the house and closed the door behind himself, Whit breathed a slight sigh of relief.

The older women rushed forward now, one on each side of Rosemary. "Are you all right, dear?" the older one asked—at least she looked older.

The younger one smiled. "Evelyn made cookies. I put some on your pillow, so you could have a bedtime snack."

"That was very sweet of you, Bonita," Rosemary told her with a big smile. "Thank you for taking such good care of me."

The woman smiled brightly back at her.

"We're not taking very good care of you," Evelyn said, "since you keep getting in *accidents*."

"Those accidents have nothing to do with the two of you," Rosemary assured them.

The women looked at him now—with suspicion again. Ignoring them, he said, "I would like to talk to you, Rosemary."

She sucked in a shaky-sounding breath, and fear flickered in her blue eyes. Rosemary really believed that he'd raped her. He'd never felt as sick as he did right now, not even when his mother had admitted the truth of his existence. "We can talk here," he offered. Then he remembered the reporter. He did not want her to be part of their conversation. "We can talk in the parlor while Ms. Stone helps the Pierce sisters get you something to eat."

Edie narrowed her dark eyes at him in a glare while the older-looking Pierce sister remarked, "Yes, you must be starved. You left so early this morning. I have some of that crab chowder you like so much." She headed off toward the kitchen.

Before Bonita trailed after her, she touched Rosemary's hand. "You're cold. Go by the fire."

But Rosemary hesitated before walking through the double doors to the parlor.

"You're safe," Whit assured her.

Edie nodded. "You are. The judge is too smart to harm you with witnesses in the house."

Rosemary stared at her for a moment before stepping into the parlor.

"Thanks," Whit sarcastically told the reporter. "But this is a private conversation."

"I know," she acknowledged although it might have been begrudgingly. Then she added, "Be careful with her. It sounds like she's been through a lot."

It did. All those years ago when he'd left her alone in that house that night and now, since coming to Bane Island.

Once Edie headed down the hallway after the sisters, Whit stepped back into the parlor. When he pulled the doors closed behind him, Rosemary tensed and sucked in another shaky breath.

"I won't hurt you," he promised. "Despite what you and

the sheriff think, I have nothing to do with your accidents. And I have nothing to do with Genevieve either."

Would she believe him? Could he make her believe him?

He hoped like hell that he could and not just because of his career. He couldn't bear her thinking that he was like all the animals he'd prosecuted as a DA and sentenced now as a judge. He couldn't bear her thinking he was anything like the man who'd fathered him.

Liar! Rosemary wanted to shout at him. But she didn't have the energy to rage at him right now, not like she wanted. Instead she asked, "If, as you claim, you have nothing to do with anything or anyone, why are you here?"

"I have something to do with you, Rosemary," he said, and he crossed the room to stand beside her at the hearth.

Panic rushed up, stealing her breath away. "Not any-more . . ." She shook her head. "Not since that night . . ."

"Nothing happened that night," he insisted.

"You son of a bitch," she murmured. "How the hell can you say that? I got pregnant that night."

"Not by me," he said. "Genevieve is not my daughter."

"What are you suggesting?" she asked. "Immaculate conception?"

He pushed a hand through his thick blond hair. "I don't know what happened after I left." His voice gruff with what sounded like guilt, he added, "I shouldn't have left."

"You didn't," she said. "You carried me up to my room. I remember that." She cringed as the nightmare played through her mind again. "I remember the dark and the feel-ing of helplessness and the pain . . ."

He flinched as if he was feeling the pain, too. "Damn it. I shouldn't have left you. . . ."

Tears stung her eyes, so she squeezed them shut, blocking his face. She saw him way too often—in her nightmares. "I see you all the time," she murmured. "I know it was you."

"I carried you up the stairs," he admitted. "After you passed out, after those stupid prep school assholes drugged you."

She opened her eyes and narrowed them to glare at him. "You did it."

He shook his head. "They did it. Said it was the only way someone like you—like them with money and class—would sleep with the bastard son of a maid."

She gasped with shock, not that she hadn't heard what others had said about him back then. She'd hated how he'd been treated, but he'd been so strong that he'd never seemed to let it bother him. He'd always held his head high, always had so much class—so much more class than any of those spoiled bastards they'd gone to school with. That class had been another of the many reasons she'd thought she'd loved him.

"I didn't hurt you," he said. "I swear it. I would never hurt someone like that. . . ."

She heard the conviction in his deep voice, but she also heard that guilt. "Then why did I never see you again after that night? Why did you dump me with no explanation?"

He sucked in a breath. "Dump you? I wasn't given a choice. Your mother didn't give me a choice."

"My mother?"

"She and your stepfather showed up that night," he said. "They threw me and everybody else out of your house. She didn't believe that it was the other guys that drugged you, and she threatened to call the police on me if she ever saw me around you again. She swore she would ruin my life."

Rosemary shook her head. "No. She and Bobby came the next morning."

She remembered her mother pulling open the blinds, demanding to know what the hell had happened the night before. And Rosemary crying . . .

Crying so many tears . . .

She'd cried that night. She'd cried out in pain, and nobody had come to her aid. Nobody . . .

"I don't know why she's lying, but she is," Whit insisted. "I can prove I'm not your daughter's father. I'll do that DNA test."

"Genevieve is gone," she said.

His brow furrowed. "She's in that hall you've talked about, the one where you were before the crash today." His green eyes darkened with anger. "That must have been where your brake line was cut."

If it was, it couldn't have been Whit—unless he'd done what she hadn't been able to do, and he'd somehow gotten inside those tall wrought iron gates without being on the damn list.

She drew in a breath of the wood smoke from the fireplace and a faint trace of his cologne, something fresh smelling like rain. "According to the director, she ran away."

"You don't believe that?"

She shook her head. "No."

"That's why you were asking the sheriff to find her."

"He won't look," she said, as she tensed with frustration.

"He believes she ran away and thinks she's already left the island."

"You don't?"

"She's here," Rosemary insisted. She just knew it. "She's here." But was she still alive?

Whit stepped closer to her. "You're scared."

She nodded. "Damn scared."

"Of me?" he asked with such dread.

She studied his handsome face, with the sincerity in his deep green eyes, and admitted, "I don't know anymore. . . ."

"I would never hurt you," he vowed. "Not then. Not now."

"But you left . . . and you never contacted me again."

He flinched and closed his eyes. "I am so sorry. I thought you would be safe with your parents there. I thought everybody else was gone. But when I told your mom that the other guys put something in your drink, she didn't believe they did it." A muscle twitched in his cheek. "She said it had to be me who did it because I was trash. Then she threatened to call the police on me. I thought they would believe her over me, so I left."

She gasped. But she didn't doubt her mother had said those things to him; she'd said it many times to Rosemary.

He's not our kind of people. He's a maid's bastard. He's trash.

"I cared about you," he said. "When I saw that car today and knew you were in it . . ." His breath shuddered out. "I realized I still care about you."

Maybe the sheriff was right. Maybe she'd hit her head harder than she'd thought; harder even than the ER doctor had thought. Because she was starting to believe him . . .

* * *

The sisters were quiet, as if they were listening intently for any hint their boarder needed them. They cared about Rosemary.

So did Whittaker Lawrence . . .

Why the hell else had he risked his career coming here? Too many people had seen him, could talk to the press . . .

To her . . .

Not that these people were all that damn talkative.

"So tell me about this Bainesworth Manor," Edie said.

Evelyn gasped. And the other one—Bonita—dropped the bowl she'd been taking down from the cupboard. It fell onto the counter, rolled off the butcher block, and crashed against the wood floor, breaking into brightly colored ceramic pieces.

"Cursed," Bonita murmured again like she had earlier.

"Be careful," Evelyn said. "Don't cut yourself." As if her sister was a child, she guided her away from the shards of the bowl—to the side of the kitchen.

Bonita *was* quite childlike. Even Rosemary had talked softly and gently to her, as if not wanting to frighten her. Like Edie had frightened her. She had never been good with children even when she'd been one herself.

The woman stared at her with wide eyes—eyes that looked glazed with fear or maybe with drugs. Was she on something?

As a reporter, Edie had seen it all. Or so she'd thought. This island was something else, though, something almost sinister. Maybe the judge was right; maybe her story was here. "Why is it cursed?" she asked them again.

Evelyn gasped again. "We're not talking about it."

"Why not?" Edie asked. She'd googled the place when the judge's clerk had told her that was where he was going today. "It's a matter of public record that this treatment center used to be some old asylum for the criminally insane."

"They weren't criminals!" Evelyn exclaimed. "They weren't—"

"Some were," Edie insisted. "That's what I read."

"Cursed," Bonita murmured again. "They were cursed . . ."

"The people?" Edie asked. Maybe that was how the woman explained mental illness, not as a disease but as a curse? Maybe it was easier for her to understand that way.

"You need to leave," Evelyn said.

"Really?" Edie asked. "Why don't you want me asking you about the hall?" Rosemary must have asked about it, and they'd seemed to embrace her—quite literally.

"The place is cursed," Evelyn said. "You shouldn't even talk about it. And you need to stay away from it."

"Why?" Edie asked. "What happens there?"

"People disappear . . ." Bonita murmured the reply.

"And some are never seen again," Evelyn added with a glance at her sister.

Excitement coursed through Edie. This was the story. A damn big story . . . and sure, it might prove dangerous. But that had never stopped her before, and it wouldn't stop her now.

Chapter Fifteen

Hands reached out of the darkness, holding her down—
pulling her legs apart, hurting her. She cried out, but a hand
covered her mouth. So many hands . . .

So much pain . . .

A cry burning her throat, tears burning her eyes,
Rosemary jerked awake. And the scream tore free of her
lips and echoed off the walls of the rose room.

Her heart raced. Sweat beaded on her brow. Usually
when Rosemary awoke from the nightmare, she tried to
block it from her mind—tried to forget it. But this time
she reached into her memory, searching for details.

Had she seen Whit's face then, in the darkness . . . ?

Had it been his hands holding her down? Was he the
man hurting her?

He swore that it hadn't been him, that he'd never
touched her that way. Dare she believe him?

God help her, she wanted to. She wanted to believe that
it hadn't been him, so she hadn't been wrong to have
that crush on him so long ago.

But if he wasn't Genevieve's father, who was?

Genevieve . . .

She had to find her, had to make sure that she was all

right. She was all that mattered now—not that nightmare, not how she'd come into the world.

Only Genevieve mattered . . .

Evelyn's door creaked open and moments later a shadow fell across her bed. "Bonita?" she asked—even though she knew.

Her sister didn't often come into her room, but she knew why she had. She'd heard it, too.

"She's screaming," Bonita said, her voice tremulous with fear. "Like *they* screamed . . ."

Evelyn didn't know who they were—specifically—but she knew Bonita was talking about the past. Her past . . .

What she remembered of it . . .

Unfortunately, she remembered too much—sometimes— when a scream like Rosemary's jarred her memory.

"Is somebody hurting her?" Bonita asked.

Evelyn pulled back her blankets and patted the mattress beside her. "No, nobody's hurting her. It's just us here."

Bonita settled onto the bed beside her. "Just us?"

"Yes," Evelyn assured her. "She must be having a bad dream. That must be why she screamed."

"Nightmares," Bonita said, and she trembled in the bed next to Evelyn. "Nightmares . . ."

Bonita had them, too, and often screamed in her sleep like Rosemary did. Evelyn knew why—because of Bainesworth Manor, because of what they'd done to Bonita while she was there. Why did Rosemary scream? What monsters haunted her dreams?

Were they old monsters—like Bonita's? From her past? Or were they new ones brought on by not being able to see her child? Brought on by the curse of Bainesworth Manor?

Rosemary shouldn't go back. But until she found her daughter, she would keep returning so she would learn what Evelyn didn't want to tell her. She would find out that he'd called—that Dr. Elijah Cooke wanted to see her again.

Evelyn shivered, and Bonita tucked the blankets around her shoulders like she was covering up her beloved doll. "You're cold," she murmured.

No. She was scared.

For all of them . . .

Rosemary Tulle was reopening all their old wounds, bringing back all their nightmares and bringing danger to their door. Evelyn hadn't been able to protect Bonita all those years ago when their parents had sent her off to Bainesworth Manor.

Would Evelyn be able to protect her now? From the past? And from the curse haunting them anew?

She glared at him. Hell, that was the only way she looked at him now—on the rare occasions when she actually looked at him at all. "I could have driven myself to work," Holly said.

An image of Rosemary Tulle's crumpled car sprang to Deacon's mind. He shook his head. "No, the roads are too slippery."

"You're driving," she said.

"I'm an experienced driver," he said, "with special training for defensive driving."

She snorted again. "Like there's any reason to have to drive defensively on an island."

"You'd be surprised," he murmured.

Somebody was after Rosemary Tulle. The fender bender

on the bridge had been no accident. He'd already suspected as much before confirming his suspicion the night before. After dropping Rosemary at the boardinghouse, he'd inspected what was left of her rental car. The brake line hadn't been frayed or damaged in that previous crash. It had been neatly cut.

Somebody had sabotaged Rosemary's car. And it must have happened when she'd been at the manor.

The gate to the employee driveway opened as they approached. He hated that Holly worked here, which was probably the reason she'd applied and the reason that Cooke had hired her. Elijah was a sadistic bastard—just like the rest of his damn family.

And Holly . . .

She hated him. If it didn't hurt so damn much, he probably would have been relieved that at least they had one thing in common.

"Don't pick me up," she said, reaching for the door handle before he'd even stopped the SUV. "I can get a ride home."

"No," he said. "Not from this place . . ." He didn't trust anyone who worked here.

"Stop it," she said. "Stop blaming the hall for what happened." She glared at him again—hard. "When we both know whose fault it really is."

He knew; she'd rather blame him. For once he glared back at her. "You don't know as much as you think you do," he said. "You're young and you trust the wrong people. That's why you'll wait for me to come get you after work. Or you won't ever be coming back."

"You told me to get a job," she reminded him.

"Not here," he said. "And you know it . . ."

A slight smile curved her lips even as her dark eyes

glimmered with hatred. "It doesn't bother me to be here," she said, "because I don't have a guilty conscience." She threw open the passenger's door and stepped out.

When he turned the key off and stepped out, she whirled back toward him and gasped. "What are you doing? You're not coming in!"

Maybe she thought he was going to make good on his threat to make her quit. Or get her fired . . .

"I have police business here," he told her.

"Yeah, right . . ." she murmured as she turned toward the employee entrance.

"Holly!" he said, his voice sharp enough that she whirled back to face him.

"A woman was nearly killed leaving here yesterday. Somebody here is responsible for that."

Her brow puckered. "What are you blaming them for now? That she wasn't healed? Sometimes people are too screwed up to help." Her face flushed now—with embarrassment or anger. When she glared at him again, he determined which. "Other people have screwed them up too much!"

He sighed. She was young. So damn young . . .

Like Rosemary's daughter, the missing Genevieve . . .

"Hey!" he shouted.

She flinched like he'd slapped her, which made him flinch with regret. He lowered his voice and asked, "Do you know anything about Genevieve Walcott?"

"Is that who almost died after leaving here?" she asked.

He shook his head. "No." At least he didn't think so. "The person looking for her got hurt. Genevieve supposedly ran away from here."

Holly shrugged. "I don't know. I don't interact with the guests. I'm just a dishwasher."

"You could do dishes at the diner," he said. But he knew why she chose to work here—to punish him.

"Dad . . ." She turned away then and pushed open the door to the employee entrance. It wasn't locked.

Genevieve could have slipped out that way. But then how had she managed to get through the gates without anyone seeing her leave? Especially when cameras were everywhere?

Deacon pushed open the door behind Holly, who turned away from the timeclock to glare at him. "Dad, you're not supposed to come in this way."

He did a lot of things he wasn't supposed to do—which was probably why he wouldn't be reelected. He wasn't going to worry about that now, though. All he was worried about was doing his job—for however much longer he had it—and protecting his daughter and Rosemary Tulle.

"Don't worry about it," he told her.

"You're going to get me fired," she said. "I'm already late."

He chuckled. "Cooke isn't going to fire you." Not when he knew how much Deacon hated her working there. Cooke . . .

That was whom he wanted to see. No. Not wanted. Had to see . . .

It would have been easier going in the front doors than walking from the back of the enormous hall. But he didn't get far down the hall before a familiar-looking security guard greeted him.

"Sheriff, what are you doing here?" his deputy asked. But instead of wearing his uniform, he was wearing a suit.

Deacon wasn't surprised to see him here; he knew his deputy had two jobs and one allegiance. To his twisted family . . .

"I need your security footage from yesterday," he said.

"Do you have a warrant?" Warren asked.

"Soon," the sheriff said. He'd left voicemails to a prosecutor and a judge but had yet to hear back. Maybe they'd called Elijah first. If that was the case, he might never see that footage.

"Then you won't have long to wait before we hand it over," a deep voice chimed in.

Deacon turned to find Elijah standing behind him. Unfortunately, he was not alone. Elijah's cousin David stood next to him. He was still taller and broader than his younger cousin, like he'd been in school, but not as tall or broad as he'd seemed back then to Deacon.

After sparing him just a brief glance, Deacon ignored David and focused on Elijah. "Rosemary Tulle nearly died after leaving here yesterday," he said.

Elijah's long body tensed. "What?"

"Someone cut the brake line on her car," he said. He glanced back at David again, gauging his reaction. Back in school, he'd always done Elijah's dirty work for him. Of course, Elijah could have assigned the task to the youngest Cooke, since Warren had been curiously unavailable despite being on duty yesterday. "She rolled it and was lucky to have survived the crash."

Elijah gasped. "Is she all right?"

"I said she was lucky to survive," Deacon reminded him.

Elijah persisted, "How badly was she hurt?"

Deacon sighed. "Concussion, bumps and bruises . . ."

"Nothing broken?" Warren asked. "Doesn't sound like it was all that bad."

"Whoever cut the line wouldn't be up on murder charges," Deacon conceded. "But there's enough of a case for attempted murder."

Warren snorted. "Doesn't sound like you have a case at all or you'd already have that warrant, Sheriff."

Building a case was never easy on the island, especially when this damn family closed ranks on him. Unfortunately, Warren had already been working as a rookie deputy when Deacon had been elected sheriff nearly four years ago. Not that he hadn't had cause to fire him since . . .

"Why would anyone try to kill Rosemary?" Elijah asked—with a familiarity that had Deacon's guts tightening.

"Because they don't want her finding out what happened to her daughter," Deacon suggested.

Elijah shook his head. "Nothing happened to her."

"So she's here?"

"You obviously know she's not," Elijah said.

"Rosemary told me what you claim," he said. "The minute I showed up at the wreck all she wanted was for me to find Genevieve."

"Genevieve?" David repeated the name as if he wasn't familiar with it.

But Deacon wasn't fooled. He'd learned long ago to never trust this man. Hell, he'd learned back when they'd all been just boys.

"She's a young guest who left of her own accord," Elijah explained to his cousin. "She must have had a friend pick her up from the hall."

"Why was she being held against her will?" Deacon asked.

"Of course she wasn't being held here against her will," Elijah said. "Her parents dropped her off for a stay—"

"And she didn't want to stay," Deacon interjected. "Just like all those other girls whose parents forced them to stay here. They were right to want to leave."

A muscle twitched in Elijah's cheek as he clenched his jaw. It was David who spoke for him. "That was a long time ago, Howell," he said. "That had nothing to do with any of us."

Deacon narrowed his eyes. "I'm not so sure . . ."

"Not with me," David insisted.

That much was true. David and Warren were related to Elijah through the shrink's father's family. It was through his mother that Elijah was a Bainesworth.

"And you have nothing to do with Genevieve Walcott either?" Deacon asked his old nemesis.

David shook his head. "Don't know her. Never met her."

"What about you?" Deacon asked his deputy. He was younger than the rest of them—closer to Genevieve's age.

Warren shook his head, too.

Elijah glanced at his cousins' faces then, as if he was trying to gauge if the men were telling the truth. Or did he know that one of them was lying?

"So you have no idea where she is?"

Warren shook his head.

"And you?" he asked Elijah.

"As I told you, she left of her own accord," Elijah said. "Her parents chose not to file a missing person's report because she's nearly eighteen. They're not concerned about her."

"Rosemary is concerned," Deacon pointed out. So concerned that her search for her daughter was probably going to get her killed . . .

"Rosemary isn't legally Genevieve's parent," Elijah said.

"I could only release information after Genevieve's legal parents authorized me to do so."

Deacon snorted. "You're all by the book now? That's why you wouldn't tell Rosemary what was going on? Or were you just wanting to cover your own ass?"

"You'd know about covering your own ass, Sheriff," David said, and he glared at Deacon in the same hateful way that Holly had.

"I don't have anything to hide," Deacon said, and he stared hard at the Cooke men. "I doubt any of you can say the same."

But what were they hiding this time?

Chapter Sixteen

Rosemary stood alone in Dr. Cooke's office just a couple of days after her interview. This time he hadn't been waiting for her when she'd arrived. In fact she wasn't sure where he was, just as she wasn't sure where he'd gone the day he'd finally told her what happened to Genevieve. To hide her daughter's belongings? Or dispose of them?

She couldn't believe that Genevieve had run away and not contacted her to at least let her know she was all right.

"Are you all right?" Dr. Cooke asked.

She whirled away from the windows she'd been staring out to see that he stood behind her. When had he come in? How long had he been watching her? She glanced around the darkly paneled room, looking for security cameras, because he could have been watching her the entire time.

"I'm fine," she said.

"Sorry to keep you waiting," he said.

"Sorry to keep you waiting," she replied. "I didn't get the messages you'd left for me at the boardinghouse." Evelyn hadn't told her that he'd called; she only learned about the calls when she'd replaced the cell phone lost in the crash.

He smiled, but it did not warm the iciness of his eyes. "I totally understand," he said.

She doubted that—unless he knew how afraid her landladies were of the hall, unless he knew how scared they were that she would be hurt. Because she knew their concerns, she wasn't angry with them for keeping his messages from her. It wasn't as if she would have been able to come out the day before anyway—not with how sore she'd been. She also hadn't had a replacement vehicle from the rental company yet. Fortunately, she'd had the insurance the sheriff had joked about; otherwise the rental company might not have given her another loaner.

Dr. Cooke's smile slid down into a slight frown. "I heard about your unfortunate accident."

It had been unfortunate for her—even more unfortunate for whoever had been trying to get rid of her when they'd cut that brake line—because she wasn't going anywhere. It hadn't been an accident, though, but she suspected he knew that.

"The sheriff asked for surveillance footage from the parking lot where you were parked," he said. "I hope you don't think someone sabotaged your vehicle while you were here for your interview."

Was that why he'd called her in for an interview? To set her up?

"Did you give him the footage?" she asked.

He sighed. "Unfortunately, by the time he'd produced a warrant, the footage he wanted had been recorded over."

Cold sank deeper into her flesh until she was chilled to the bone. Something must have been on that footage. Him? Was that where he'd gone when he'd disappeared during their interview? Maybe he hadn't been getting rid of Genevieve's things. Maybe he'd been cutting her brake line in order to get rid of her.

"I'm sorry we couldn't help the sheriff's investigation," he said. "But I'm sure he's mistaken about someone tampering with your brake line. He tends to see conspiracies where there are none."

She narrowed her eyes to study his handsome face. "Sounds like you and Sheriff Howell have a history."

That slight smile curved his lips again. "The sheriff and I went to elementary school together here on the island. He was quite the bully then." His broad shoulders lifted in a shrug. "Some things never change."

"It's hard to imagine you as the victim of a bully," she said. He was tall and broad, but more than physical strength, he had the power of the intelligence glowing in his eerie light-colored eyes.

"Anyone can be a victim," he said, and he studied her thoughtfully, almost as if he knew about her past, about her nightmares.

"Yes," she agreed. "And anyone can be a survivor."

"Fortunately, you seem to be," he said. "The sheriff says you've survived two accidents."

She opened her mouth to deny that anything about the wrecks had been accidental, but another question slipped out instead. "Why did you ask me to come back here?" If it had been to set her up again, he was too smart to admit it. "Do you have more information about Genevieve?"

He shook his head. "I'm afraid I don't know any more than I did the last time we spoke," he said. "You haven't heard from her?"

"No." After replacing her phone, she'd checked her voicemail. Unlike him, Genevieve had left her no messages. There had been no missed calls that could have been her.

"I'm sorry," he said. "I had hoped you would have heard from her by now. I know you're worried."

Terrified was more like it, but she just nodded. "Yes, I am."

"She's a smart girl," he said. "I'm sure she's fine."

Rosemary didn't believe that Genevieve had been getting into the trouble Abigail claimed she had. Genevieve had been sheltered; Rosemary's mother had seen to that, so that Genevieve would not embarrass her like Rosemary had. So that she wouldn't be wild and take unnecessary risks. Running away was a risk she wouldn't have taken . . . unless she'd been running for her life.

"I hope so, too," she told Dr. Cooke. Hope was all she had of ever seeing Genevieve again—unless she could find some leads to her whereabouts, some reason that she might have run away. "Is that why you asked me here?" she wondered. "Just to find out if I'd heard from her?"

He shook his head and gestured toward one of the chairs in front of his desk. "Please, take a seat," he urged her. "Would you like anything? Coffee? Tea?"

"Your receptionist already offered," she said. "No, thanks."

He settled into the chair behind his desk and smiled at her again, that smile that didn't warm his cold eyes. "Are you planning on staying on the island?" he asked. "Or will you be returning home to look for Genevieve?"

"I'm not leaving," she said.

"But more than likely she's back home—staying with whatever friend picked her up," he said.

"If that was the case, I would have heard from her," Rosemary insisted.

He sighed. "Teenagers—especially angry teenagers—

often strike out at all the adults in their lives. She may not reach out to you for a while."

"Do you have a teenager?" she asked. The sheriff had one, and the two men were the same age.

"No, I'm just speaking from professional experience, not personal," he admitted.

She couldn't imagine a teenage girl striking out at him. His good looks would have them falling all over him to get closer, not farther away.

"Of course, teenage girls aren't my area of expertise," he said. "Not that I have much time for counseling at all anymore with acting as director of Halcyon Hall."

"I'm sure you're very busy," she acknowledged. So why was he wasting his time with her?

His smile curved slightly higher, as if he'd read her mind. "You can help me with that," he said.

She stiffened. He wanted her to stop bothering him. "I'm not leaving," she began.

"Good," he interrupted. "I'd like for you to stay. I'd like for you to come on staff as our newest counselor."

"What?" she asked, shocked. "You're offering me a job?"

"On one condition," he said.

She suspected he wanted her to stop her investigation but asked anyway, "What is that?"

"That you take the job for the right reason," he said. "That you truly want to help people. That's why the hall is here—to help."

A chill chased down her spine, but she resisted the urge to shiver. Instead she smiled. "I'm here to help, too."

Her daughter . . .

As if he'd read her mind, he chuckled. "I need your help with our current and future guests, not our previous ones." The smile slid away from his handsome face. "No one can change the past, Ms. Tulle. No matter how much they might like to . . ."

She wanted to ask what he wished he could change, because it was obvious there was something, but his door rattled with a knock.

"I'm sorry," he said. "I told her not to interrupt—"

"It's Dr. Chase," her old mentor spoke through the door.

Cooke must have pressed a button or something because the door suddenly opened. Gordon rushed toward her. "Thank goodness you came, Rosemary," he said. "After what happened last time you were here, I was afraid you might not come back."

She smiled. "Me too. I was lucky I survived. The car was not as fortunate."

He sucked in a breath. "Oh, my goodness. The roads are just not very well maintained on the island. The limited crews can't keep up with weather conditions."

Her accident had had nothing to do with weather conditions, but she refrained from telling him that. She was more interested in what Dr. Cooke had been saying, so she turned back toward him. "If you're serious," she said, "I will accept your job offer."

Gordon clapped. "That's fabulous," he said. "I'm so happy that you'll be here to help. There are some patients—"

"Guests," Dr. Cooke corrected him. "We have guests at the hall—not patients."

Obviously, he was trying to distance himself from the specter of the psychiatric hospital the manor had once been. No matter how much he tried, she doubted that would ever happen.

"I would love to get your input on some of these guests," Gordon said, his eyes twinkling with amusement.

"Before she can see any guests, she'll need to sign a contract," Dr. Cooke reminded him.

She didn't just want to see the guests to ask about their problems; she wanted to ask them about Genevieve, too. She stood up and approached his desk. "Where is it?" she asked. "I'll sign."

"You don't want to read it over first?" he asked. "You don't want to negotiate?"

She shook her head. "I just want to get started."

Gordon clapped again. "Good! That's excellent."

"You looked over the contract before you signed," Cooke reminded him. "You negotiated."

Dr. Chase smiled. "Rosemary isn't as mercenary as I am. I'm sure she'll be happy with whatever you offer her."

Because she wasn't here for the money.

Dr. Cooke must have told him that she was really Genevieve's mother. Gordon stared at her as if he was trying to peer inside her soul. Of course, he'd always looked at her that way—as a friend of her father's and later as her professor.

But then she hadn't believed he'd really seen it. Now he did.

Because Genevieve was her soul.

"I'm sure it's fine," she told Dr. Cooke. But she was cautious enough to take a moment to read it over while the two men talked of other things, of the weather, of the chef's latest culinary creation . . .

Fortunately, the contract held a trial period during which either party could terminate it. So if Genevieve showed up, Rosemary would be able to leave. She *had* to show up.

Rosemary picked up a pen from the desk and the conversation ceased between the men. The sound of the pen point scrawling across the paper was the only sound in the room . . . until Dr. Chase released a shaky sigh.

"So we've got her now," he said. "And we're not going to let her leave." He clapped his hands together with glee.

Maybe a little too much glee for Rosemary's peace of mind. But she had always enjoyed her father's friend's enthusiasm for life and for his work. Despite his age, he had a timeless vitality to him, which was probably why he always gravitated toward younger people. He was the reason why she'd chosen to pursue her own career in psychology.

A grimace briefly contorted Dr. Cooke's handsome face. "She will be free to leave if she chooses," he said almost defensively.

"Let's hope she chooses to stay then," Dr. Chase remarked. "Let me show you around the old place, Rosemary."

"It's not old," Cooke said with another grimace, and there was definitely a defensive tone to his suddenly sharp voice.

Unabashed at his boss's not so subtle rebuke, Dr. Chase chuckled. "Elijah would like to forget what this place once was," he said, as he guided Rosemary toward the door with a hand on her back, "but his efforts are futile. Nobody else will ever let him forget."

Rosemary waited until the door closed, shutting Dr. Cooke alone in his office while they walked down the hall. Then she asked, "Was it as bad as everyone says it was?"

Dr. Chase shrugged. "Its legend has taken on a life of its own."

"I've met someone who was here," she said, "back then. She has nightmares about it." Nightmares were the least of the problems that Bainesworth Manor had caused Bonita—at least according to her sister. But Evelyn must have been a child when her sister had been a patient at the asylum, though. Maybe she was only romanticizing how her sister had been before her stay.

Dr. Chase squeezed her hand. "She's not the only one who has nightmares." He was staring at her now, at the circles that she hadn't quite been able to conceal beneath her eyes. "I think I know what yours are about now."

She sighed. "I've always known."

"You were so young, Rosemary. Why didn't you tell me?" he asked, his voice cracking with concern. "Why didn't you come to me all those years ago?"

She shook her head. "My mother . . ."

He sighed. "Your mother. She wouldn't have wanted anyone to know." He grimaced. "Probably especially me."

"Probably," she acknowledged. Her mother hadn't appreciated his checking up on them as much as Rosemary had.

"Who's the father?" he asked.

"I thought I knew . . ." She sucked in a breath. But dare she believe Whit as much as she wanted to? "But that night . . . it's all a blur."

"A nightmare," he said.

"It doesn't matter now," she said. "I need to find Genevieve. You can talk to me about her now. You can tell me if you really think she ran away."

"She did," Dr. Chase said. "She hated it here."

Rosemary couldn't deny that; she'd heard the hatred in that voicemail Genevieve had left her. But she'd heard more than that. "She was afraid to be here," Rosemary said. "Do you know why?"

From what she'd seen of the place, it was quite luxurious with marble and hardwood floors, coffered ceilings, and expensive furnishings. And all the leaded glass windows would have let in much light if the dark clouds hovering over the island ever let any sunshine through.

He shook his head. "There are people who feed into the legend, into the old stories. It's why some of them come here to stay—for the ghosts. Maybe one of them got to her."

"She didn't talk to you?"

He shook his head again. "I think she blamed me for her being here."

"Oh, no . . . that's why . . ."

He nodded. "I suggested the hall when your mother called to ask my opinion about another facility. I thought this would be better for Genevieve because I would be here. But she felt like I betrayed her." He squeezed Rosemary's hand. "She felt like you betrayed her, too. That's probably why you haven't heard from her."

"How do you know I haven't?" she asked.

"You wouldn't be here if you had," he said. "And you wouldn't have those dark circles—unless your nightmares are causing those. I know you're worried about her, Rosemary, but you need to worry about yourself. You need to put the past behind you once and for all."

"I have—I—"

"You have not," he said. "Or you'd be able to sleep at night. You need to know the truth. I can help you . . . if you'll let me."

"Dr. Cooke hired me to help the guests," she reminded him. "Not for you to help me."

Gordon grinned. "He's a better man than anyone will give him credit for. He did this to help you as much as for you to help his guests. Maybe more so." His brow furrowed. "Actually he would probably be able to help you more than I would . . . with those nightmares . . ."

Ignoring his persistence, she brought the subject back

to what was most important to her. "So you don't think he has anything to do with Genevieve's disappearance?"

"She ran away, Rosemary."

"Then why did someone mess with my car while I was here for my interview?"

He shrugged. "Are you sure it was really messed with?"

"The sheriff said—"

"The sheriff has a personal vendetta against Elijah," he said. "He'll say or do anything to implicate him and this place in a crime. He even tried blaming them for his wife's death."

"What?"

"She came here to get away from him, from his abuse," he said. "But she still felt so hopeless that she wound up killing herself." His brow furrowed. "Or at least the sheriff claims it was a suicide. From the bruises on her wrists, I have my doubts."

"You really think he could be responsible? That he could be a killer?" She'd trusted this man to help her—despite all the times he'd refused. Dare she trust anyone on this island?

Even Dr. Chase?

Someone else flitted into her mind with his chiseled features and warm green eyes: Whit. Could she trust him? He'd showed up on the island though—just about the time her brake line had been cut. Despite Dr. Chase's suspicions about the sheriff, Rosemary believed someone must have cut the line. Why else would she have so abruptly lost her ability to brake the car?

It must have happened here. How would Whit have gotten inside the gates that she'd struggled for days to get inside?

No. Perhaps Whittaker Lawrence was the only person

she could trust. Something she wouldn't have believed until she'd come to the island, until she'd begun to face her nightmare.

Maybe Dr. Chase was right; she needed to know the truth. For her sake and for Genevieve's.

"How would you help me find out what really happened that night?" she asked.

He stilled and stared at her. "Uh . . . you'd consider it?"

"Yes."

"Hypnosis," he said. "That would be the best way to bring you back to when the nightmare started, to find out what it really means."

The thought of returning to that night made her feel physically ill. But then she went back so often already. "I don't know. . . ." she murmured. "I don't know if I'd like to do that."

At least not alone . . .

Not with just the doctor to guide her through the nightmare. She needed someone else, someone who would be there for her. And for the first time she realized how alone she actually was. She always shut down every relationship before it could become too close, too important, too intimate. She shut down every chance she had of being hurt. Again . . .

"Rosemary . . ."

She shook her head. "I'll think about it," she promised.

"You can trust me," he said, as if he'd read her mind.

She smiled. "I want to focus on my new job," she said, "on the guests. Tell me about the current ones." Because when she was focused on other people's problems, she could forget about her own.

At least for a little while . . .

She could forget the nightmares. But she couldn't forget

that Genevieve was missing. But maybe when she talked to some of these guests, they would be able to provide clues as to what had happened to her daughter.

"What the hell were you thinking?"

Elijah turned toward Jamie. Or Bode as he preferred to be called now that he was a big boy. To Elijah, he would always be the annoying chubby little kid that had followed him around—until Elijah had finally gotten off the island.

Bode had convinced him to return, to help him salvage the manor and their family name. Yet neither of them used the family name. They wanted to distance themselves as much from it as Elijah once had the island. He never should have come back.

Bode planted his big hands on Elijah's desk and leaned over it. "What the hell were you thinking?"

"I wonder that myself," he murmured.

Bode's brow furrowed with confusion. "So why'd you do it? Why did you hire her?"

He chuckled. "Oh, you're talking about Rosemary Tulle."

"Damn right I am," Bode said. "What the hell did you think I was talking about?"

"The manor," Elijah said. Despite all the renovations David had done, he still saw it when he looked around—he saw the ruins it had once been. Stone walls crumbling, plaster rotting . . . holes in the ceiling . . .

The air thick with the smell of decay and sadness. Such profound sadness . . .

"I am talking about the hall," Bode said, "and how your recent hire is going to put at risk everything we've worked so hard to build."

"Why?" Elijah asked. "Do you have something to hide?"

Bode's face flushed. "What are you asking me?"

"For the truth," Elijah said.

"The truth about what?" Bode asked. "I—I don't know anything about that girl."

Elijah arched an eyebrow. "Really? She was young. She was beautiful. That's your type."

"Was?" Bode asked, arching a dark brow of his own over eyes that weren't quite as pale as Elijah's but were still a silvery gray. "Why are you talking about her in the past tense? What are you hiding, big brother?"

Elijah shook his head. "If I was hiding something, why would I have hired Rosemary Tulle?"

Bode shrugged. "I don't know why you do anything that you do," he replied. "Masochism? Punishing yourself?" He shrugged again. "I don't know."

"Rosemary will help the guests," Elijah insisted. "She's highly qualified and recommended. The hall isn't all about the physical appearance of our guests."

Bode tensed. "You think that's all I'm about? The superficial?"

Elijah had no idea what his brother was really about; sometimes it was as if they barely knew each other.

"I'm not," Bode said. "Looking good makes a person feel good. Being healthy physically affects mental and emotional health as well."

"Is that from your book?" Elijah asked.

Bode snorted. "Yeah, I wouldn't expect you to know that. You haven't read any of them. You have no idea what I'm about. . . ." His mouth twisted into a grimace of disgust.

"I didn't realize you were still trying to impress me," Elijah said.

"Fuck you," Bode said. "You know I'm the reason that

we get any guests at all to this godforsaken place. My books. My television appearances. Without me, we wouldn't have attracted one guest."

"Fuck you," Elijah said. "Without me and David, this place would still be a pile of moldy stones. You have no idea what it takes to run a facility like this. No idea about business at all."

"I know not to hire someone who keeps reporting us to the sheriff who already has it out for us," Bode said. "So that makes me a hell of a lot smarter than you are, big brother." He turned then and headed toward the door.

Elijah didn't press the button, though, he didn't open the door—until Bode turned back and flipped him off.

"What are you scared of, little brother?" he asked— because there was fear beneath the anger and contempt. Real fear.

Bode sighed, and his broad shoulders slumped slightly. "I'm afraid of you destroying everything we're trying to do here."

Elijah pressed the button then and when the office door opened, it revealed Rosemary Tulle standing in the doorway. Had she been listening in the hallway? If so, she had probably gotten a hell of an earful.

Bode just nodded at her in passing. They had probably met earlier when Gordon had taken her on a tour of the facility. If not, Elijah didn't call him back to introduce them himself. It was clear his brother wasn't going to welcome her.

Why?

If he had nothing to hide, it shouldn't matter how many times she brought the sheriff out to investigate Genevieve's disappearance. So what was Bode hiding? Or whom?

Chapter Seventeen

"I hear them at night. . . ."

"Who?" Rosemary asked as she glanced around the sunshine-filled conservatory. "Who do you hear?" Was this the lead she'd been looking for? The clue to where Genevieve could be, to what had really happened to her?

The day before, when she'd eavesdropped on the conversation between the hall director and the fitness expert, she'd been left with more questions than answers. They were brothers?

Clearly, they didn't like or trust each other. Why not?

What were they both hiding?

Genevieve?

"The girls . . ." Morgana Drake leaned across the small table between her and Rosemary and pitched her voice to a soft whisper as if she didn't want them to hear her now. Morgana hadn't been a girl for quite a while. She was probably older than the Pierce sisters though it was hard to tell with her hair dyed a bright red and all the makeup she wore. She appeared quite the eccentric. "I hear the girls crying. . . ."

"What girls?" Rosemary asked. Had there been more than one? More than Genevieve upset with having to stay here? After touring the facilities and spending some time there, Rosemary couldn't help but wonder why. The hall was luxurious with a warm indoor pool, sauna and hot tubs along with a well-equipped gym, movie rooms, and dining room. Rosemary loved this room, the English-style conservatory that seemed to fill with sunshine despite the clouds that hung over the island.

"The girls, you know," Morgana continued in her whisper that vibrated with excitement. "The crazy girls that were imprisoned here at the manor."

"Committed," Rosemary corrected her. "And they weren't crazy." She hated that word, hated how freely it was tossed around as a derogatory label. "But that all happened in the past. Is that what you're talking about?"

"Yes," she said. "It's why I came to this place, to talk to the restless spirits."

"Oh . . ." The word slipped through Rosemary's lips but hopefully her disappointment hadn't slipped out with it. But maybe she should have been relieved that the woman hadn't heard Genevieve crying.

"I'm a medium," Morgana explained. "I talk to the dead."

"Why did you ask to speak to me then?" Until Rosemary had been hired, Morgana hadn't asked for any counseling services since her arrival—months ago—at the hall. Neither of the psychiatrists had a file on her, and on her application to stay, she had stated her reason as relaxation.

"I thought maybe you could help them," Morgana said, her dark eyes bright with excitement.

"Me?" Rosemary asked. "Why didn't you ask Dr. Chase or Dr. Cooke?"

The woman shivered despite the warmth of the sun shining through all the conservatory glass. "Oh, no, neither of them could help. They're not to be trusted." She leaned closer and placed her hand, with its bulging veins and dark spots, over Rosemary's. "At all . . ."

"Why not?" Rosemary asked, and she pitched her voice to a whisper, too. Maybe the woman actually knew something—something that Rosemary needed to be aware of.

"They don't care," Morgana replied. "They don't care about the dead . . . or the living . . ."

"They're both doctors," Rosemary reminded her. "They chose that profession so they could help people."

Morgana shook her head and one of her bright curls fell across her face. She reached up to push it away, taking her hand from Rosemary's. "They have no souls," Morgana said with another shake of her head. "So how could they reach lost souls?"

"How can I?" Rosemary asked.

Morgana curved her brightly painted lips into a wide smile. "You are an old soul. You have empathy, like me. You'll be able to hear them, too."

Rosemary forced a smile. "I haven't before," she told the woman. "I don't have your ability."

"You'll hear them here," Morgana assured her. "You can't help but hear them. The spirits are loud and restless within these walls—with the manor's horrible history of abuse and pain."

"That's in the past," Rosemary said. "It's nothing to do with the present." At least she hoped like hell it didn't have anything to do with it.

"The spirits can't leave," Morgana said. "Not until they find peace."

"What about you?" Rosemary asked. "Can you leave?" She hadn't been committed; nobody had. The place was a voluntary treatment center, almost more of a spa now than the psychiatric hospital it had once been. But then Genevieve hadn't been able to leave on her own.

Morgana shook her head. "No. I can't leave."

Rosemary leaned forward now and asked with concern. "Why not? Is someone keeping you here?"

Morgana glanced around the conservatory that was empty but for them and the multitude of plants filling the space. "They are . . ."

"Who's they?" Rosemary asked. The brothers . . . ?

"The spirits," Morgana replied, her voice sharp with impatience. "I have to stay to help them cross over."

Rosemary nodded and held in a sigh of disappointment. Morgana wasn't going to be able to help her any more than Rosemary would be able to help the spirits Morgana claimed to hear.

"You don't believe me," Morgana said.

"I don't doubt that you believe it," she said. "I know there are a lot of rumors and stories going around—"

"It's cursed," Morgana interjected. "That's why they can't leave, why they can't cross over. They came here and they're cursed now."

"Why did you come here then?" Rosemary asked. "If that's how you feel about it?"

Despite her age Morgana moved with such suddenness that she knocked over her chair when she jumped up. "I told you. I have to help them. I thought you might help but I can see now that you have no more soul than those other doctors have."

Rosemary jumped up, too, but before she could say anything else, or even reach out to the woman, Morgana rushed out of the conservatory, nearly knocking down another woman who stood in the doorway. As the younger woman stepped aside, she collided with a tall, potted tree and lost her balance. Unable to help Morgana, Rosemary rushed over to the other woman who lay sprawled across the stone floor, her long golden brown hair splayed out around her.

"Are you okay?" she asked her.

Maybe she was dazed because the woman, with wide, heavily lashed eyes, stared up at her for a moment before taking Rosemary's hand. She was so slight that Rosemary easily pulled her up. "I'm fine," the woman replied, "this is not my first run-in with Morgana."

"Has she hurt you before?" Rosemary asked.

The woman shook her head. "No. She's harmless. Crazy but harmless."

Rosemary must have flinched at the insensitive term because the woman chuckled.

"I'm sorry," she said, her voice husky. "You must be the new shrink."

"And you are?"

The woman's lips curved slightly. "I'd tell you . . . but . . ."

"I'm sworn to secrecy," Rosemary said. "I've signed a contract."

The woman's smile widened, revealing a slight gap between her front teeth. "It doesn't matter," she said. "I'm nobody . . ."

Rosemary tilted her head and studied that face. There was something faintly familiar about it—at least around her mouth with its bow-shaped lips. The woman's heavily lashed eyes were green with gold flecks, like the faint gold streaks in her brown hair.

"I doubt you're nobody," Rosemary said.

And the woman chuckled again. The husky voice struck a chord in Rosemary's memory, too.

"In fact you seem vaguely familiar to me."

"Maybe Morgana's right," the woman replied. "And your old soul met my old soul somewhere before." Amusement twinkled in her green eyes.

"You were listening for a while," Rosemary said.

The woman shrugged her slight shoulders. A big sweater hung on her, dwarfing her tiny frame. Beneath it, she wore leggings that had dirt stuck to them from where she'd fallen over the plant.

"I can guess what she said. She's always going on about the spirits crying out. . . ."

"You haven't heard anything . . . have you?" Rosemary asked. Maybe it wasn't spirits that Morgana had heard. Maybe it had been someone alive and scared . . .

The woman laughed. "Looking to catch me in your butterfly net, too?" She shook her head. "I'm not here to get my head shrunk or to help spirits cross over."

"Why are you here?" Rosemary wondered.

"To rest," the woman replied with a heavy sigh. Dark circles rimmed her green eyes, and those slim shoulders slumped as if it took too much effort to hold them up, to hold up her head even.

"Have you seen the doctor?" Rosemary asked.

"I know what's wrong with me," the woman replied. "Exhaustion." She studied Rosemary. "What about you? Why are you here?"

"I'm the new shrink, remember?"

She snorted. "Yeah, but why are you *here*?"

"I'm looking for someone," she admitted. "Someone who was staying here until just last week. A girl named Genevieve."

The woman shook her head. "The only girl I've seen around here is the one who works on the weekends." She glanced around, as if looking for the girl, and as if on cue, a dark-haired teenager appeared in the doorway. Those lips curved slightly again. "Her . . ."

"That's not Genevieve," Rosemary said. She turned back toward the woman. "I'm also here to help," she said. "If you ever want to talk, that doesn't mean you're crazy."

"Oh, we're all crazy," the woman replied. "Some more than others . . ."

Was she talking about herself or Morgana now? Before Rosemary could ask, she turned away—toward the door. "You can stay," Rosemary told her. "I won't bother you."

"Not you . . ." the woman murmured. She glanced at the teenager as she hurried past her and into the hall.

The teenage girl stared after her, dark eyes wide with awe. "Do you think I scared her off?" she asked Rosemary. "Am I being creepy?"

"Creepy seems to be what this place does best," Rosemary murmured. "No, if anyone scared her off it was me."

The girl looked at Rosemary now. "What did you say to her?"

"Nothing really," Rosemary said.

"What did she say to you?"

"Nothing really," Rosemary replied again. "She wouldn't even tell me her name."

"You don't know who she is?"

Rosemary shook her head. "I'm afraid not."

"She's famous," the teenager murmured with awe.

She must have been to have elicited such adoration from the girl. "She said she was nobody."

"So she told you!" the girl exclaimed. "She admitted it."

Rosemary's brow furrowed with confusion. Then she remembered the singer who used that name. Nobody. Whenever she was in public, she wore a cloak with the hood pulled over her head and sunglasses over her eyes. Only her mouth showed. "Oh . . ."

"You've heard of her," the girl said. "My dad has no idea who she is. But he doesn't know anybody that doesn't live on this damn island."

"You live here?" Rosemary asked.

"Not here," the girl replied. "I just work here. I live on the island, though."

Rosemary held out her hand. "I work here now, too. My name is Rosemary."

"Holly," the girl replied.

"Nice to meet you, Holly."

"You too," the girl replied with a smile. Like with the singer, the girl looked vaguely familiar to Rosemary, but it was more something about her deep-set dark eyes that struck a chord.

"I have to confess," Rosemary said, "that the only reason I've heard about Nobody is because my daughter told me about her. Haven't you told your dad?"

Holly shook her head. "I talk to my dad as little as possible." Anger and pain roiled in those dark eyes. "You and your daughter must be close. . . ." she murmured wistfully.

"Not really," Rosemary admitted. "Right now I don't even know where she is. The last time she was seen was here. Maybe you remember her? She's about your age. Genevieve Walcott."

The girl glanced away from her now. "I only work weekends."

"You could have met her then."

"She wasn't here long."

"So you do remember her?"

"I don't know her," Holly said.

"I think you do," Rosemary said.

Holly shook her head. "I just know she wanted out of here. That she would have done anything to get out of here."

"Even run away?" Rosemary asked. "That's what they tell me happened. That she ran away . . ."

Holly nodded. "Yeah. But it isn't easy to run away from a damn island."

She spoke as if from experience.

Rosemary realized why she looked familiar. Holly was the sheriff's daughter, the one he'd admitted ran away.

"Somebody always finds you," Holly murmured. She was obviously talking about her dad.

Who had found Genevieve? And what had he done to her after finding her?

Whit pressed his finger against the button for the intercom, surprised that his skin didn't stick on it as damn cold as it was on the island. Wind hurled snow and ice pellets through the wrought iron gates. The icy blast struck his face and stole away his breath.

"Halcyon Hall, how may we help you?"

"I'm here to see Rosemary Tulle." The sister at the boardinghouse who actually spoke had informed him that Rosemary was working here now. Not that she'd seemed all that happy about it. But she hadn't seemed much more approving of him than she'd been of the hall.

It was as he'd turned to leave that the other sister had spoken again. "Don't go," she'd murmured.

He'd turned back, startled that she'd spoken to him. "I'm sorry?"

"Don't go," she said, her eyes glazed with fear. Or maybe they'd always looked that way. "Don't go."

Her sister had tugged her back from the doorway and

tried to close the door. But the other woman had persisted. "Don't go. It's cursed."

Then the door had slammed in his face.

"Your name?" the disembodied voice asked with an impatience that suggested she might have asked before.

He'd been too damn distracted lately—because of Rosemary, because of his fears for her. Fears the sisters obviously shared.

Even if he'd heard the voice the first time, he would have hesitated over giving his name. Not that it was a scandal to visit an employee of a treatment center.

"Whittaker Lawrence."

"You're not on the list," the woman replied.

"List? What?"

"You're not on the list of visitors."

"Rosemary isn't a resident," he said. "She's a counselor. I just want to talk to her."

"You're not on the list, sir."

"What the hell—" A shadow fell across the drive on the other side of the gates, and he stepped forward. Somebody— or—something had been let inside the damn place.

Just not him . . .

"Hello?" he called out. Branches rustled on one of the pine trees, knocking snow to the already snow-covered driveway. "Is somebody there?" He curled his hands around the wrought iron to peer through it, and the cold metal seared his skin as if it were burning. He jerked his hands away and cursed.

On the other side of the gates, more branches rustled, sending another dusting of snow to the ground. Then the wind kicked up again, blasting him in the face. Sucking in a breath, he whirled away—toward the street.

A car idled on the street behind his vehicle. It wasn't

pointed toward the gates, wasn't trying to get inside like he was. Instead it appeared as if the driver had noticed him and stopped. When he looked through the driver's window, his gaze caught hers, and his breath left his lungs again. She was so damn beautiful.

The driver's window lowered, and she leaned out. "Are you checking in?" she asked him.

"They won't let me in," he said. "My name isn't on some damn list."

She laughed, and the sound had him gasping for breath again. It was as beautiful as her face. "And unless you've made a reservation, you're not getting in for months."

"I don't want to get in now," he said. "I just wanted to see you."

"Why?"

"To make sure you're okay."

"Since you knew where to find me, you must have talked to Evelyn and Bonita."

He nodded. "You should listen to them and stay away from here. It just might be cursed. The name of the island alone suggests that the whole place might be."

Her mouth turned up into a slight smile. "I don't believe in curses."

"Maybe you should, after that crash." Anger gripped him again over someone cutting her brake line, trapping her inside the wreckage of her overturned vehicle. He'd just recently learned something else about the island, about the sheriff, that had brought him back to Bane. Rosemary really couldn't trust *anyone* here, especially not the sheriff.

"It's cold," she said. "You should get back inside your car."

"I should," he agreed, but he remained standing next to hers, staring through that open driver's window at her beautiful face. He asked, "Where are you going? Back to the boardinghouse?"

She sighed. "I should. They worry . . ."

"With good cause," he said.

"They barely know me," she said.

"They know this place," he pointed out. He didn't know if that was just because they lived on the island or if they had a more personal connection to it—like Rosemary did. "Did you find your daughter?"

She shook her head.

"Then why are you still here?" he asked. "Why don't you go home?"

"Not without Genevieve," she said. "Why don't you go home? You've talked to me. You see that I'm fine."

"You're not fine," he said, shaking his head. "I'll follow you back to the boardinghouse."

She tilted her head, studying his face for a long moment.

"You can trust me," he said. "I swear I didn't hurt you, that I would never hurt you." But would he ever be able to make her believe that? "I don't know how to prove it to you—until Genevieve is found, until we can do that DNA test."

"Help me find her," she implored him.

He nodded. "I'm already working on it." When he'd been DA, he'd worked with some great investigators, but he'd found one even better than them, though. "Edie Stone is helping."

Rosemary snorted. "Sure she is."

"Oh, she wants the story," he admitted. But at least he wasn't the focus of the story anymore. The hall was. "She's good. In fact she's already found out something about Sheriff—"

"I know," she said.

"Did he tell you?" he wondered. The sheriff had been quite protective of her, almost possessive.

"No," she admitted. "But there's no proof, just speculation."

"He still should have told you," Whit said.

"Why?"

"You're not involved with him?"

"I barely know him," she said.

He expelled a ragged breath. "Good."

"Why?" she asked.

"I wouldn't want you to trust someone who wasn't worthy of your trust," he said.

"Again?" she asked.

"I didn't betray your trust," he said. Someone else had, though. "You really don't remember any more about that night?"

She shook her head. "I'm not sure I want to."

A horn honked as a car passed Rosemary's on the right. The tires sent a spray of snow and gravel from the shoulder onto the road and onto the passenger side of her car.

"I need to get out of here," she said.

"Am I still invited to follow you back to the boarding-house?" he asked.

She nodded. "If you dare . . ."

"The Pierce sisters don't scare me," he said. But he couldn't deny that the older women were very eccentric.

"It's not them you should be afraid of," she said, her lips curving into a teasing smile.

His heart pounded faster and harder. And he knew she was right. He needed to be afraid of her. Very afraid . . .

* * *

Snow sneaked between his hat and the collar of his coat, sliding down his neck. He shook, but not with cold. He shook with rage as he peered through the pine boughs at the couple on the other side of the gates. She was outside now. But she would be back.

Rosemary Tulle would keep coming back to the estate that should have been his or at least partially his. Bainesworth blood ran through his veins. Maybe the curse did, too, since he couldn't seem to get rid of her no matter how hard he'd tried.

He belonged here. She didn't.

But she would keep coming, keep badgering everyone for answers about Genevieve. She wasn't going to give up.

Until she was dead . . .

Chapter Eighteen

For the first time since she'd given birth to Genevieve and given her up, Rosemary didn't feel alone. The hollow ache of loneliness had finally been filled—with Whit. He hadn't just followed her back to the boardinghouse.

He'd stayed.

And somehow he'd charmed the Pierce sisters. They stopped regarding him with suspicion and interacted with him with the same consideration and care with which they interacted with Rosemary.

Even Bonita . . .

In fact, from the way she'd brought him an extra slice of apple pie after dinner, it was clear that the older Pierce sister had a crush on him. Rosemary couldn't blame her.

He was so good-looking—even more so now that he was older. All those interesting angles and dimples were even more pronounced, sexier, than they'd been when he was younger. And the lines that had been added to his face only spoke of his experience and wisdom.

When she'd first googled him and learned he was a judge, she'd been shocked, but now she could see it, could see how he would look sitting on the bench. Tough but fair . . . was how some of the articles had referred to him.

Others had called him harsh, at least when it came to rapists; she'd thought that was hypocritical then. Now she wondered . . . what had really happened that night, because she believed him.

"It's too late for you to go across the bridge now," Evelyn told him as she cleared the plates from the table. "Bonita will make up a bed for you."

"The green room," Bonita murmured, and she was already rushing out of the dining room. She turned before heading up the stairs, though, and added, "It'll match his eyes."

Rosemary smiled. She had always loved his eyes, too. Even in the nightmare . . . when he stared down at her.

She hadn't been afraid then. It was later . . . in the darkness . . . when she could see nothing but just feel the pain, the degradation . . .

"Are you all right?" he asked her, laying his hand over hers on the tablecloth. His hand was so big it completely covered hers.

Surprised that she didn't mind his touch, she nodded.

"She won't be all right until she finds her daughter," Evelyn said.

Appreciative of her landlady's understanding, Rosemary smiled at her.

"Are you going to stay to help her?" Evelyn asked Whit.

"He just came to check on me," Rosemary said, and she hadn't expected even that from him. She believed he wasn't Genevieve's father.

"I also want to help," he said. "I have no trial currently in session, so I can stay."

Evelyn, her arms full of plates, just nodded and said, "Good."

Rosemary waited until the swinging door to the kitchen closed behind Evelyn before asking him, "Why?"

"Why what?" he asked.

"Why would you help look for Genevieve?" she asked. "She's not yours."

A ragged breath escaped his lips. "Good. I'm glad you know that."

"Then why stay?"

"I know what it's like to lose a child," he said. "A daughter . . ."

She'd discovered that, too, when she'd googled him—that he'd experienced personal tragedy. She turned her hand over beneath his and entwined their fingers. Squeezing, she murmured, "I'm sorry. How old was she?"

He shook his head. "Just hours. That was all she lasted before she passed after her mother."

Pain clutched her heart. "You lost them both at the same time?"

He nodded.

"I'm so sorry," she said.

"I'm the one who's sorry," he said, and his broad shoulders slumped with guilt and loss.

"How long ago?" she asked.

"It's been a while now, nearly eight years," he said. "But the media back home like to keep dredging it up."

"I don't live there," she said. Where she'd grown up had ceased to be home once her dad had died. "I live in Michigan." Lived. She wondered now if she would ever go back. "And I never kept track of you . . . after that night . . ." She'd wanted to forget all about him.

She realized now that had never been possible.

There was no forgetting Whittaker Lawrence.

His handsome face twisted into a grimace of pain, probably over reliving his loss. Instead he said, "I hate that you thought I could have hurt you."

"I don't remember much of that night," she admitted. "And when I never saw you afterward . . ."

"Your mother threatened me and told me to stay away," he told her, as he had the other day.

Frustration nagged at Rosemary. "I don't remember her being there that night. I don't remember so damn much. . . ."

"You said earlier that you're not sure you want to remember," he said. "But do you think it might help?"

"With the nightmares?" She shrugged. "I don't know if it would help or make them worse."

"You have nightmares—even all these years later?"

She nodded.

He squeezed her hand. "I'm so sorry. I thought you would be safe since your parents had come home. I had no idea something might happen to you after I left. If I had, I would have stayed no matter what your mom threatened to do to me," he said, his voice gruff with regret.

"It's not your fault."

It was hers. She'd been so besotted with him, desperate to spend time with him and show him that she was mature enough for him that she'd thrown that stupid party.

Instead of moving their relationship to the next level, as she'd wanted, that night had ended it. It had ended so many things in her life. Her relationship with her mother. And her relationship with her daughter as a daughter . . .

What would Genevieve say when she learned the truth? Or had she, was that why she wouldn't return any of Rosemary's calls?

Was she furious with her?

His fingers skimmed along her jaw. "You spent all these years hating me."

"I don't hate you anymore," she assured him.

Or maybe she just didn't want to be alone again, to feel

that hollow ache of loneliness inside her. She rose from the table, and using their entwined hands, tugged him up with her. "Let me show you to your room," she said.

"I could go back to the mainland," he offered, as if worried that she was still scared of him. "It's not that late."

She shook her head. "It's too late now. Unless . . . do you have someone who wants you home tonight? Your wife died a long time ago. . . ." So he must have moved on.

He shook his head. "Nobody's waiting for me."

He must have loved her very much if he'd never recovered from his loss. But what a loss it had been. . . .

Her heart ached for him.

"What about you . . . ?" he asked.

She shook her head. "Nobody."

He flinched. "You said that quickly. Has there ever been anyone? Anyone important?"

She shook her head again. "No . . . I wouldn't let myself get close to anyone, to trust anyone . . ."

"I'm sorry," he said again, his voice gruff with guilt. "I thought you'd be okay after I left that night."

"I know." And she should have been safe. What the hell had happened?

They passed Bonita on the stairs, heading back down. "The room's all ready," she told them with a bright smile. "Do you want me to show it to you?"

"I'll show him," Rosemary said. "I know where it is." At the top of the stairs, she first pointed out the bathroom before heading down the hall. She pushed open the door that was just before hers. "This is the green room."

He glanced around at the deep green walls that were just a shade darker than the green velvet drapes pulled closed over the windows. He stepped over the threshold and peered around the room. Bonita had turned down the velvet comforter on the four-poster bed.

The room actually looked more comfortable than her rose room. But she said, "You don't have to stay here . . . if you don't want to . . ."

His long body tensed. "Did you change your mind? Don't you want me here now?"

She shook her head. "No. But if you want to leave, I understand. With your plans to run for governor, you don't need to get caught up in my drama."

He gently tugged her inside with him and closed the door. "This time I know you're in danger," he said. "So I don't want to leave you."

"I don't want you to leave," she admitted, but she knew she was fragile right now, worrying about her daughter, about her past, about . . .

"Then I'll stay here," he said, "I know that you still don't trust me."

"I shouldn't," she agreed.

"But you can," he said. "And if you can, you can stay here—with me—and all I'll do is hold you."

Temptation tugged at her. She'd been alone so long.

He kicked off his shoes and shrugged off his suit jacket. When he reached for his tie, she sucked in a breath. But it was all he removed. Still in his shirt and pants, he pulled back the blankets and crawled into bed.

Her pulse racing, she hesitated a long moment . . . before kicking off her shoes and crawling into that bed with him. She settled against his side, her head on his shoulder. When he curled his arm around her, she tensed.

"It's okay," he murmured. "I'm not going to hurt you. I'm just going to hold you." He was true to his word, keeping just that arm wrapped loosely around her as he drifted off to sleep.

Rosemary hadn't slept much since she'd played that voicemail Genevieve had left for her. But the warmth of his body, the steadiness of his breathing, made her feel safe for the first time since she was sixteen. And Rosemary found herself drifting off to sleep as well.

Whit awoke to a scream. The terror in that scream sent a jolt of fear rushing through him.

What happened?

Where was he?

Disoriented and dazed, he had no time to react before a fist struck him, hands and feet flailing around in the dark. "What? What's wrong?" he murmured.

Then he remembered: the nightmares . . .

"Rosemary, it's me," he said. "It's Whit."

Maybe that was what had frightened her so much, though, realizing that she'd spent the night in his bed. And it had been most of the night as faint light filtered through the heavy drapes pulled across the bedroom window.

"Whit?" she whispered in the dark.

He didn't know whether confirming it would upset her more, but he said, "Yes, it's me. You're safe. I won't hurt you." His heart wrenched with pain over her thinking for so long that he had hurt her.

Her hands, which had been tight fists against his chest, clutched at his shoulders instead, as she clung to him. "I'm sorry," she said. "I'm sorry . . ."

He slid his arms around her, holding her close to his chest where his heart beat fast and frantically for her. For her fear. "Rosemary . . ." He wanted to say more, but he didn't know how to help her. "I wish I could do something to end this nightmare for you."

"You are," she said, as her breath escaped in a shaky sigh and her body melted against his. "Just by holding me, by being here . . . I've felt so alone for so long."

"So have I," he admitted.

Her arms tightened around him. "I'm sure you have," she said. "And I'm sorry that you went through that, that you lost so much."

His wife and daughter hadn't been his first loss, though. Rosemary had been.

"I'm sorry that I wasn't there for you," he said, "that I dropped out of your life as abruptly as I did."

"You said it wasn't your choice. My mother threatened you."

"Yes, but I shouldn't have let her intimidate me. I should have stood up to her." He'd felt so ineffectual back then, so much like he hadn't belonged anywhere. Certainly not in that prep school with all those wealthy kids who'd known their fathers. Rosemary had been the only person who'd ever accepted him for him.

"You were a kid," she reminded him. "And my mother can be pretty damn intimidating."

"Yes, she can." But he should have been stronger—for Rosemary. He couldn't imagine how she must have felt when he just stopped having any contact with her—when she thought . . .

"I wish there was a way we could figure out what happened that night," he said, "after your mother threw me and the other kids out."

"Everybody else left, too?" she asked.

He nodded. "I made some of them leave," he said. Those sons of bitches who'd confessed to drugging her drink so that she would sleep with the maid's bastard kid. "And some more ran out when they saw your mother's car heading up the driveway. The few that were left were tossed out with me, or so I thought."

"It really wasn't you," she murmured.

"Didn't you talk to anyone after that night?" he asked.

She shook her head. "My mother pulled me out of school. She blamed everybody—including me—for my going bad. I was sent off to a boarding school until I started showing—then she brought me back to be home-schooled until the baby came." Emotion cracked her voice. "Until Genevieve came . . ."

"You'll find her," he said. He only hoped that when they did, the girl was alive. Rosemary couldn't lose her child twice.

She shook her head. "I'm not so sure. I don't know why I haven't heard from her."

"Do you think she found out?" he wondered. "That she learned you're her mother?"

"And she's mad at me for lying to her?" She shrugged. "It's possible. But I would think that she would at least give me a chance to explain or ask me questions." She sighed. "Questions I don't have the answers to."

"Like who her father is," Whit replied.

"There is a way that I can find out," she said. "A psychiatrist at the hall, an old professor of mine, suggested hypnosis."

Nerves knotted his stomach muscles. "Are you sure that's a good idea?"

"No," she admitted. "I didn't want to do it. I didn't want to relive that night—alone."

"I'll go with you," he offered. His campaign manager would probably go ballistic if he knew how involved Whit was getting with the hall and Rosemary Tulle. But Whit was determined to do the right thing for her this time. "I want to be there."

Her breath shuddered out with relief. "Thank you . . ." Then she leaned forward and brushed her mouth across his.

He wanted to kiss her back—really kiss her, but he didn't want to scare her with his passion or violate the trust she'd given him. He just stroked her cheek with fingers that shook slightly and smiled. "Thank you," he said, "for believing me . . ."

She had no reason to—nothing but his word. And she'd taken him at it. But he wondered if she still had doubts. . . .

She jumped up from the bed. "I should get back to my room before Bonita realizes I stayed here."

He chuckled at that and at how stealthily she cracked open the door and checked the hall before leaving him. Moments later he heard her talking to someone, but he heard only her voice so she must have been on the phone. He took a moment to check his own messages. He hadn't heard his phone ring, but he had a voicemail from the investigative reporter. When he listened to it, he felt sick and his concern for Rosemary increased.

While he wanted to be with her, he also needed to regroup before he saw her again, so he did the same thing she had, checking the hall before he hurried across it to the bathroom. He took a long shower, hoping the steam would get some of the wrinkles from his shirt. But when he returned to his room, he found an ironing board and iron in the closet. He was standing in his pants and undershirt, ironing his dress shirt when his door opened.

"It's set up," Rosemary told him as she stepped inside his room. She'd changed into jeans and a black sweater, maybe wanting to be comfortable for what was to come. "Dr. Cooke is going to do it."

He tensed and hesitated, wondering if he should tell her what Edie had learned.

"Did you change your mind?" she asked. "Don't you want to do this?"

"No," he said. "I want to know as much as you do." Maybe more. If one of his former prep school classmates had hurt her, Whit would deliver a sentence no matter how long ago the statute of limitations had expired.

She nodded. "Then let's do this before I change my mind."

He would tell her about Edie's call after she was hypnotized. He didn't want her postponing it for any reason. Maybe it would even help her, not just with the nightmares from her past but with her current nightmare of not knowing where her daughter was. Maybe it would provide a clue that he and the investigative reporter hadn't been able to find. He turned off the iron and put on his warm shirt. After buttoning it up and putting on his tie and suit jacket, he said, "I'm ready."

"I don't want to wrinkle your shirt again," she said as she slid her arms around his waist and hugged him against her. "But I want you to know how much I appreciate you staying here. I don't know how I'd do this alone."

"Just like you've done everything else," he said as he patted her back, his hand sliding over the softness of her sweater. "You're very strong, Rosemary."

"I hope so," she said. "I hope so. . . ."

Obviously, despite the drugs those idiots had slipped into her drink, she remembered enough about what had happened that it caused her to have nightmares. She knew it was going to be painful, and he didn't want to put her through more pain.

"Maybe this isn't the best—"

She pulled back and pressed her fingers over his lips. "Don't. Don't give me any doubts now."

He nodded. "Okay, let's go."

Despite the sisters' objections, they refused breakfast and headed straight for the hall. Rosemary drove through another gate in the stone wall. It was as high as the visitors' gates and just as formidable.

"Why the wall?" he murmured. "To keep people out or . . ."

"To keep people in," she finished for him. "When it was an asylum, it was probably to keep the people inside."

"Why'd they bother renovating the place with the reputation it has?"

"Not renovating it would have been a waste of beautiful property on a beautiful island."

He didn't see the beauty in the snow-covered trees and icy winding drive. Even when the renovated main building came into view, the huge stone structure looked more like a prison than a treatment center. "They could have done a better job," he murmured.

"It really is beautiful."

She was the beautiful one. Inside and out.

"Yes . . ." he murmured, staring at her.

She glanced over at him and smiled. "The place. I think it's beautiful."

He chuckled and teased, "How long have you been suffering from delusions?"

"Hey, I'm the counselor," she said. "You're the judge."

"I was a DA, which is a counselor," he said. "And a lot of times I've felt like a shrink." Like now.

She had pulled into a parking spot and turned off the car. Her hands gripped the steering wheel tightly, and her entire body was tense with nerves.

He covered one of her hands on the wheel and squeezed. "I'll be right here. I'll be with you the entire time. I won't leave you alone again." Not like last time . . .

"Thank you," she said.

He wasn't sure she would thank him when this was all over—when she knew the truth. She might blame him as much as she already had—as much as he'd been blaming himself.

She knew.

She'd heard the rumors. Deacon realized it the moment his gaze met Rosemary's, when she and the judge entered the foyer of the hall, and she quickly looked away from him. Holly couldn't bear to look at him either.

Hell, maybe Holly was the one who'd told her—since they worked together now. Or maybe the judge had dug up the dirt on Deacon. Surprisingly, Deacon hadn't been able to find any on Whittaker Lawrence.

Lawrence must have heard the rumors, too, and from the hard, disapproving glare he directed at Deacon, he'd accepted those rumors as fact. Fortunately, not everybody had.

Some people knew him too well to believe him capable of such violence. Too bad his daughter wasn't one of those people.

Despite her suspicions, Rosemary approached him, but the judge stuck close to her—too close. Why didn't she have suspicions about Lawrence anymore? What had he done to change her mind?

"Have you found out anything more about Genevieve's disappearance?" she asked Deacon.

He shook his head. "She's probably just holed up with one of her friends."

The judge shook his head. "No, she's not. She's not with any of them."

Rosemary turned toward him, her eyes wide with shock. "How do you know who her friends are? I don't even know."

Deacon could relate. He didn't know many of Holly's friends anymore. He only hoped that she still had some.

"I don't know who her friends are," Whittaker replied. "But instead of trying to get rid of Edie Stone, I put her and her sources to good use."

"Teenagers are not sources," Deacon said. "I'm sure they wouldn't tell her the truth even if she paid them for it."

"Their phones told her the truth," Lawrence said. "Somehow she got access to their text records and voice-mails. Nobody heard from Genevieve since shortly after her . . . adoptive parents checked her into this place."

Deacon grimaced. The last thing he wanted was to co-ordinate his investigation with a reporter, but he wanted to help Rosemary, too. And Genevieve . . .

Maybe he'd at least be able to help one teenager—if it wasn't already too late. "I'll need copies of these text messages," he told Lawrence. "I need to establish a timeline of when she disappeared."

"Dr. Cooke told me it was just a couple of days before I showed up on the island," Rosemary said.

He snorted.

"You don't trust this Dr. Cooke?" Lawrence asked.

Deacon shook his head. "Not as far as I can throw him." That wouldn't be very far now. Not like when they were kids.

"Maybe you shouldn't have him hypnotize you," Lawrence said to Rosemary.

Deacon felt a jab of panic. "You're not going to get hyp-notized. That's not going to help you find Genevieve."

"Maybe it will," Rosemary said. She turned back toward Lawrence. "Dr. Cooke is the director of the hall. My boss."

Whittaker flinched.

Deacon felt his pain.

"Rosemary . . ."

Elijah's deep voice grated on Deacon's already frayed nerves. But he whirled toward him and said, "You're supposed to be meeting with me."

"You don't have an appointment," Elijah said. "Rosemary does."

Deacon shook his head and looked at Rosemary. "No, not him. Don't trust him." His wife had and then he'd messed with her mind, messed her up even more than she'd been.

Whittaker met his gaze over Rosemary's head, concern darkening his green eyes. "Rosemary, maybe we shouldn't—"

"We shouldn't have any discussion out here," Elijah said with a pointed glance at Deacon. "This conversation should be had privately, Mr. Lawrence."

Whittaker's eyes widened now with surprise—probably that the guy knew his name. But before he could say anything more, Elijah turned back toward Rosemary.

"Are you ready?" he asked her.

She nodded and followed as he headed back toward his office.

"Don't . . ." Deacon murmured. Nobody at this place ever helped anyone—they only hurt them more.

But she was already walking away with the doctor, already letting him lead her down a dark path. He could only hope it wouldn't lead her to the same place it had led his wife—to her death.

Chapter Nineteen

The door to Dr. Cooke's office automatically opened, and he stepped inside. But before she could follow him across the threshold, Whit caught her arm and held her back in the hall. "Are you sure about this?" he asked, his handsome face tense with concern.

"No." She wasn't sure about anything. "Why didn't you tell me about having that reporter investigate my daughter? Why didn't you tell me that she'd found Genevieve's friends, that she'd contacted them?" Panic tightened its grasp on her heart. They hadn't heard from her. She wasn't with any of them.

"I just found out this morning, and I didn't want to distract you from this," he said. "But now I think I should have. Maybe the sheriff is right—this is a bad idea."

"Have you changed your mind?" Dr. Cooke asked as he turned back toward the open door. "Would you rather not do this?"

He sounded almost hopeful. But then he was a busy man. She knew that since she worked at the hall, too.

"I'm sorry," she said. "I don't want to waste your time."

He shook his head. "It's not a waste of my time," he said. "Not if it will help you . . ."

"But will it?" Whit asked. "Will it help you?"

Frustration bubbled up inside her—frustration over her inability to find Genevieve, frustration over the nightmares, frustration over letting the past rule her life for nearly two decades. "Yes!" she said. "I need to know what happened."

Maybe knowing who Genevieve's father was would help her daughter, too. Maybe he'd found his child. Rosemary's stomach churned at the thought of her daughter being with the man who'd hurt her. It would explain why Genevieve hadn't contacted her—why nobody knew where the teenager was . . .

"I need to do this," she said.

Whit nodded, then reached for her hand. Entwining their fingers together, he walked through the doorway to Dr. Cooke's office with her just as he would walk back into the past with her.

"Are you absolutely sure you want to do this?" the psychiatrist asked again. But he wasn't looking at Rosemary now; he was focused on Whit. And there was the same suspicion on his face that was on Whit's.

Whit nodded. "I want to be here for Rosemary."

"You were part of her past, of that night," Dr. Cooke said. She hadn't told him that; maybe Dr. Chase had. Or the sheriff, not that they were exactly friends. "It might be hard to relive."

"Not as hard for me as it will be for her," Whit said. "That's why I want to be here. I *need* to be here." His voice was gruff with guilt.

She squeezed his hand. "Knowing the truth will make it better," she said. She hoped.

"Then let's get started," Dr. Cooke said. He reached into his pocket and must have hit some kind of remote-control switch because one of the panels on the walls slid aside to reveal another room.

"There's the couch," Whit murmured.

"This is the therapy room," Dr. Cooke said. "I need to keep it separate from my office to avoid distractions when I'm with a guest." After they stepped inside the space, the panel slid closed again.

So it looked as though the room had no door and no windows. No escape. Panic clawed at her, and she squeezed Whit's hand tighter.

"People feel comfortable here?" Whit asked, skepticism furrowing his brow.

"Yes," Dr. Cooke maintained. He must have touched something else because the room took on a soft glow as if it was infused with sunshine despite having no windows.

Nervous, Rosemary drew in a deep breath that felt like pure oxygen. The room had a special ventilation system with relaxing scents of lavender and jasmine. Her racing heart began to slow its frenetic pace.

"Have a seat," he told her, gesturing toward that couch.

It wasn't the stereotypical leather lounger. This was almost like velvet, soft and warm, and as she settled onto it, she felt as if she was dissolving into it. Instead of reaching for one of the chairs in the room, Whit knelt on the floor beside her—as if unwilling to let her go for even a moment. Or maybe it was because she grasped his hand so tightly, afraid to let him go even for a moment.

"Relax," Dr. Cooke said—to them both.

She heard his voice but when she glanced around, she couldn't find him. It was as if the light had swallowed him. He was only a voice now.

Was she traveling backward through a real-life version of *The Wizard of Oz*? Her journey had started when she'd seen the man behind the curtain and now he'd pulled the curtain closed? Dr. Cooke had never seemed like just a man to her, though.

"Are you really sure about this?" Whit whispered, his mouth close to her ear.

Her breath escaped in a long sigh and she nodded. "Yes . . ." Her heart rate slowed even more. Without saying much of anything at all, Dr. Cooke had already begun to hypnotize her, or so it seemed to her. She felt disconnected from everything but Whit. She could feel his hand on hers, holding on to her. But it was as if he were rope tethering her within the hemisphere while she floated above him, above herself even.

Then she realized that Dr. Cooke had been speaking the entire time, softly, his voice like white noise that only her subconscious heard. And to which it responded.

She slipped back more than eighteen years to that night, to the giddiness of throwing a forbidden party while her parents were gone. To impressing the older guy on whom she'd had such a huge crush. "Whit . . ." she murmured.

"I'm here," he said, and the years had slipped away from him, from his voice, from his face. He was eighteen again.

And she was sixteen.

Her lips curved into a smile. "You're so cute," she murmured, then giggled. Her head was so light that she felt funny. Everything was funny. She giggled again.

How much had she had to drink?

Some friends of Whit's had made trash can punch, throwing in everything from Bobby's liquor cabinet. Her mom was going to be so mad. Fear flickered through her as she considered the consequences of what she'd done.

But maybe she could find somebody with a fake ID, somebody who would replace what they used. How much had they used?

Music echoed throughout the space. Then light . . . flashing, light bright in her face, until she closed her eyes. Then she drifted again, into the darkness, in Whit's arms.

He carried her now, climbing up the stairs to her bedroom. This was it. What she'd wanted . . .

But that fear gripped her again. "Please . . ." she murmured. "No . . ."

Soft lips brushed across hers and then she was alone, the room spinning around her. She groaned, wanting to die. Embarrassment heated her body. Then water suddenly jolted her, and bright lights. Somebody had pushed her into the shower, rushing water over her head and her naked body. She shivered and cursed.

Then she was back in the dark. But she wasn't alone.

"You stupid little bitch," her mother berated her. "You stupid little bitch."

Tears leaked from her eyes. "I'm sorry . . ."

"You're going to be . . ."

Then big hands gripped her, holding her down onto the bed. Other hands pulled her legs apart. And pain ripped through her as a penis was shoved inside her.

"It's hurting her." That was Bobby's voice, Bobby inside her.

She screamed and screamed.

A hand slapped her face. "The little bitch can be useful for once. And she won't even know. That kid said she was drugged. So she can give us the child we want."

That was her mother's voice. Her mother's rationalization for having her own daughter raped.

Bile rose in her throat, choking her.

"She's—"

"I don't care," her mother said. "Just do it!"

Grunting and groaning and then sticky heat filling her where she burned, where she hurt. So much pain. She screamed again and again.

But still those hands held her down, gripping her shoulders. Pulling her close. She swung her hands out, trying to fight them off.

"Rosemary!" Whit shouted her name, and his hands soothed down her back as she trembled in his arms. "What is it? What happened? Who was it?"

She shuddered against him. "My mother. My mother had my stepfather rape me." Her voice shook with the horror of it, the horror she'd endured.

"No wonder you blocked it," Dr. Cooke said.

She saw him now, standing in the room. He was real. Just like Whit was real. Now so was the nightmare. She understood completely why she'd been haunted for so long. The reality was even worse, even sicker, than she could have ever imagined.

Whit's muscular body shook with fury. "How could they . . ." His voice cracked with his anger and disgust. "How could they do that to you? I should have stayed even if she'd called the damn cops. I shouldn't have left you!"

She reached up and clasped his face in her hands. "She's my mother. Why wouldn't you think she'd keep me safe?"

Instead she'd betrayed her in a way no woman should ever betray another, let alone one's daughter.

"She's a monster," Whit said. "And him . . . you need to call the police. You need to report them."

"Your Honor, you know the law," Dr. Cooke told him. "You know the statute of limitations has expired."

Whit cursed.

Punishing anyone was the least of her concerns right now. She couldn't even think. Couldn't breathe. Despite the oxygen blowing into the room, she needed air—nearly gasped for it as panic pressed down on her lungs, squeezing her chest.

"Rosemary," Whit said, and he tightened his grasp around her.

But she pushed against his shoulders. "I can't breathe," she said. "I need to get out of here." She jumped up from the couch.

"You need to talk," Dr. Cooke said. "You need to tell us what you're feeling."

"Disgust!" she yelled. "Absolute disgust. And horror. I handed my baby—my sweet innocent baby—over to my rapists! I trusted my child to the monsters that destroyed my childhood. How the hell do you think I feel?"

Whit's guilt was nothing compared to hers—though she could see it weighing heavily on him. "It wasn't your fault," he tried to tell her. "You didn't know—"

"I remembered now," she said. "I couldn't have brought out those memories if they weren't there. If I hadn't always known . . ." And instead of facing the truth, she'd blamed Whit.

Of course, her mother had helped her do that, had always claimed that he'd raped her. That she'd been a fool to trust him. She'd been a fool to trust her mother and

Bobby. That bile rose in her throat again. She glanced at the couch, surprised she hadn't thrown up like she had in that nightmare.

But it wasn't a dream. It was a memory—a memory of what had really happened. Not her mother's lies . . .

Anger chased away the guilt. She was so damn angry. "Let me out!" she yelled at Dr. Cooke. She was angry with him, too, angry with him for bringing out the memory she'd rather think she didn't have, that she had completely blacked out and not known what had happened. That would have been better than the reality. Anything would have been better than knowing the truth.

No . . .

Not blaming Whit. She should never have blamed him. But he had left her that night. Her anger turned on him now. "I need to be alone!" she told him, holding her hands out as if to hold him back.

But he wasn't reaching for her. He was probably as disgusted as she was. She turned toward Dr. Cooke. "Let me the hell out of this room right now or I will tell the sheriff you've held me against my will just like you held Genevieve."

Genevieve. Had she found out the truth somehow? Did she know her mother had given her up to monsters? Had they hurt her like they'd hurt Rosemary?

"Rosemary, you're distraught right now," Dr. Cooke said in that maddening soothing tone that had lured her back to that nightmare. "You need to calm down. I can administer a sedative—"

"Fuck off!" she yelled. "Let me out of here or I swear I will press charges!"

"Rosemary," Whit said, and now he used that same fake calm voice with her as if she was some wounded wild animal he didn't want attacking him while he tried to help it. "You need to listen to the doctor. I can leave, if you'd rather talk to him alone."

"I want to be alone," she said. "I need to process . . ." But there was no way to process what she'd learned, no way to deal with the horror of her reality, of Genevieve's reality.

Was that why the girl had run away?

Rosemary wanted to run now, too. Needed to run . . .

She rushed over to the wall and began pounding on it. There had to be another switch somewhere, something that would open the panel that had let them inside the windowless, doorless room.

"I have to let her out," Dr. Cooke murmured, and he pressed a button to open that panel.

"No!" Whit said. But before he could reach for her, she was out of that room. Fortunately Dr. Cooke had opened his office door, too, and she was able to run out in the hall. Once she started running, she didn't stop—not until she was outside.

Then the snow slowed her down as her boots sank through the crunchy surface into the cold, fluffy depths. Fortunately, her boots were high enough that the snow didn't go over the tops of them, and it wasn't snowing now. She was so hot with anger that she didn't feel the cold even though she wore only a sweater with her jeans. She'd left her coat back in the office. The wind was strong enough that it tangled her hair around her face, and blinded, she nearly tripped. But she kept walking.

She couldn't go back to the hall now.

She couldn't see anyone—talk to anyone—not with what she knew, not with the disgust she felt not just with her family but with herself. How could she have let them get away with it? How could she have given them her daughter?

Would Genevieve ever forgive her if she learned the truth? Would she ever learn the truth?

Where was she?

That was all that mattered. She was all that mattered— not how she'd come into the world but in how she might have gone out of it.

Rosemary gasped as the errant thought struck her like a blow. Just as she hadn't wanted to examine her nightmare for the truth, she hadn't wanted to consider one of the reasons why she might not have heard from Genevieve: She could be dead.

Rosemary doubled over as if someone had punched her in the gut. The pain was unbearable, even worse than in her nightmare. This pain gripped her heart so tightly it could barely beat; she could barely breathe.

No.

Genevieve could not be gone.

She couldn't . . .

Tears overflowed her eyes and rolled down her face. Finally she felt the cold as it nearly froze those tears on her skin that the wind chafed and burned. It penetrated her clothes, chilling her flesh as much as the thought of Genevieve being dead chilled her soul.

Maybe she'd never really run away from the hall. Maybe she was still here—somewhere on the property. Rosemary had wandered farther from the hall than she'd ever been— even that first day when she'd looked around while someone had cut her brake line. Or so the sheriff suspected.

Why would someone want to hurt her? Or worse?

So she would stop looking for Genevieve?

Who didn't want her daughter found?

Her mother and Bobby didn't seem particularly anxious to find Genevieve. Just the thought of them had bile rising up the back of Rosemary's throat as disgust and nausea overwhelmed her.

Had Genevieve learned the truth? Were Abigail and Bobby Walcott behind Rosemary's daughter's disappearance?

She reached into her pocket and pulled out her cell phone. She needed to call them, but the thought had her choking on more bile. Her stomach churned with dread. But for Genevieve, she had to swallow it—the disgust, the horror of it all.

Her fingers trembling with cold and nerves, she punched in the contact for her mother. Of course the call went directly to voicemail. Just the sound of her mother's voice had Rosemary choking on a wave of revulsion. To leave a message, she had to clear her throat.

"I know!" she shouted. "I know what you and Bobby did to me, you sick bitch! I know what you did, and if you don't want everyone else to know, you will help me find Genevieve and then you'll never have any contact with her or with me again!"

She disconnected the call and wrapped her cold fingers around the cell, barely resisting the urge to hurl it across the snow. She glanced around now, uncertain of where she was. How far had she walked from the hall?

She turned back but didn't catch even a glimpse of the stone structure. Only shrubs and pine trees surrounded her, the boughs bowing beneath the weight of snow. One of the trees shuddered like she had leaving that message, and snow showered to the ground.

Where was she?

And was she alone? With the snow off the branches, the

tree cast a strange shadow across the ground—an almost human shadow.

"Hello?"

Whit had probably followed her. He'd been so worried about her and so guilt-ridden. A sharp pang of guilt stabbed her heart for how she'd lashed out at him and at Dr. Cooke. She would be lucky if she had a job after the way she'd acted.

And Whit . . .

She would be lucky if he had followed her, if he wanted anything to do with her after what he'd learned about her and her sick family.

"Whit?" she called out as tree branches moved again. It could have been the wind but for that strange shadow. "Are you there?"

Nobody answered her.

Whit hadn't followed her, but somebody had. Somebody who wouldn't answer her. Whoever it was stood between her and the direction of the hall. Scared of confronting him, she turned away and hurried along the path she'd found in the snow.

It wasn't a real path. Not a trail or a sidewalk, just a line of animal tracks across the snow. She glanced down at the imprints. Those weren't deer tracks but big paw prints. Like dogs or the coyotes she'd heard that very first day she'd arrived on the island. She heard nothing howling now but the wind as it whipped up around her, blowing snow at her.

She needed to get back to the hall, but as she looked over her shoulder, the shadow moved through the trees behind her. Maybe it wasn't even human.

Maybe it was something else chasing her across the snow, something predatory. But then she knew now how predatory humans could be. She quickened her step, nearly falling as her boots slipped. She had to hurry. She couldn't let whatever that was catch her.

Fear had her heart racing, her lungs straining for breath along with the cold. She was so damn cold, not just her skin and flesh chilled but her very soul. She ran blindly because of the wind tangling her hair across her face. She ran until she stumbled over some rocks.

Then her breath caught, painfully, coldly, in her throat as she gasped. She'd reached the edge of the property, a steep drop off to the rocky shore below.

Ice jammed up against those rocks and several yards out into the ocean. Despite the cold, waves rose up and broke over the ice—sending spray up so high that Rosemary felt the dampness of it against her frozen skin. She jerked back, from the edge of that steep drop. But before she could turn around and head back toward the hall, strong hands slammed into her back—shoving her over the edge and down the rocky slope.

A scream tore free from her mouth as she fell. But she doubted that anyone would hear it—that anyone would be able to help her.

Where was she?

She had been gone a long time. He should have followed her. But when Whit had started out of the windowless room after her, the doctor had caught his arm, physically holding him back.

"Let her have some time," Dr. Cooke had advised.

Whit had tried to shake off Dr. Cooke's grasp, but the man was strong. "She shouldn't be alone right now—not when she's so distraught."

He'd watched his wife and daughter die, but he'd never seen anyone in as much pain as Rosemary had been in—was still in. Now she was off somewhere alone. At least he'd been there for Deborah and Isabella. He'd never been there for Rosemary—not like he should have been. He shouldn't have left her alone that night.

"I need to find her," he'd insisted to Dr. Cooke. "I need to talk to her."

But the shrink hadn't released him. "Maybe you should talk to me first."

Whit had snorted. "I don't need to process anything."

"What about your guilt?" Dr. Cooke asked.

"It's nothing new to me," Whit assured him. "I can handle it. I'm not so sure that Rosemary can handle what she learned."

"She always knew," Dr. Cooke insisted. "The memory was there. I couldn't have brought it out if it wasn't. She had just suppressed it."

"So she's feeling guilty now, too," Whit acknowledged. "That she gave her baby to those monsters."

Dr. Cooke nodded.

He knew guilt well. He'd felt guilty over how he came into the world, over the pain it had caused his mother. And he'd felt guilty over Deborah dying giving birth to his child. But he'd experienced nothing like the guilt and horror he'd seen on Rosemary's face. "I can't imagine how she's feeling. . . ."

"I can," Dr. Cooke murmured.

"What?" Whit asked.

The doctor shook his head and released his grasp on Whit's arm. "I have things I need to take care of." But he didn't head toward his desk; instead he headed to the door that was open to the hall.

Whit rushed out after him, not wanting to get trapped in that strange office. "I'm going to look for her," he insisted. "Where would she have gone?"

"She likes the conservatory," he said, and gestured in the opposite direction from the reception area—the opposite direction in which he was heading.

"Are you leaving?" Whit asked.

Dr. Cooke turned back toward him. "If she needs me, the receptionist can reach me."

Whit hoped Rosemary wouldn't need the shrink or anyone else. Not even him—since he'd already failed her when it had mattered most. And now . . .

He shouldn't have let her run out of the office on her own. He should have made sure that she wasn't alone. He headed down the hall in the direction Dr. Cooke had pointed. The corridor was dark, with tall mahogany doors lining it, except for the light that glowed at the end of it— kind of like the light in Cooke's secret room.

No. This light glowed like real sunshine. It must have been from the conservatory. He rushed down the hall toward that light and the glass-walled room for which the double doors stood open—almost as if someone had pushed through them in a hurry.

He peered around the potted trees and plants, but while there were other women in the room, none of them was Rosemary. One woman was very slight—so small that she could have been a teenager if not for the dark circles beneath her eyes and the faint lines around her mouth. The other woman would not have been mistaken as a teenager for several decades. Her face was heavily lined beneath heavily applied makeup, and her red hair curled every which way.

She stood at a set of patio doors, looking out over the

snow-covered estate. She must have spied his reflection in the glass because she whirled around at his approach. "Do you hear them?" she asked.

"Who?" Whit asked as he glanced around the room again.

The other woman said nothing as she bent over a book at the table at which she sat. She seemed intent on ignoring them both, or maybe she was more intent that they ignore her—because it was almost as if she was making herself smaller, slouching deep in her chair.

"I don't hear anything," Whit said.

The older woman's brow furrowed. "I swear I heard them . . . screaming."

"Who?" he asked.

"The girls," she replied.

"Girls?" he repeated. Maybe Genevieve hadn't been the only teenager staying at the hall. "Do you mean the teenager that was staying here? The one that Dr. Cooke claims ran away?"

"No . . ."

The older woman hadn't answered him. The younger one had—without even looking up.

"What?" he asked.

She sighed and raised her head. "She's talking about ghosts," she explained. "Not real people."

"They are real to me," the older woman replied defensively. "I am here to help them find peace." She focused on Whit. "I'm a medium."

"Oh . . ." he murmured—at a loss as to what else he could say to her since he did not believe in ghosts. If it was possible for someone to actually come back from the dead to haunt the living, he would have had a lot of ghosts haunting him. "I'm looking for someone alive," he told the elderly redhead. Then he turned toward the younger woman. "Rosemary Tulle. Do you know her?"

"The new lady shrink?" she asked.

He nodded. "Have you seen her?"

She sighed again—a long, ragged-sounding one. "She tore through here a while ago looking like she needed a shrink herself. Why was she so upset?" She held up a hand. "No. Forget I asked. It's none of my business."

"It's this place," the redhead said. "It affects us sensitive beings, like Rosemary. That's why she ran off. She probably heard them, too. That's the direction she headed—where the cries are coming from now."

Whit's blood chilled. "Where?" he asked. "Where did she go?"

The woman gestured out across the property, and as she did the wind whipped up, blowing snow and ice at the glass so that it rattled. He didn't care. He pushed open the French doors leading out onto what was probably a patio outside the conservatory, but snow covered it now.

He sucked in a breath at the cold as that wind caught him in the face with a blast of ice and snow.

"You need your coat," the other woman said; she'd joined the redhead at the patio doors.

"Rosemary didn't have hers either," the redhead remarked.

Whit and the other woman cursed.

"I didn't notice," the younger woman said. "Or I would have stopped her. Wait!"

But Whit was forcing his face back toward the wind and the faint sound that carried on it.

"You hear them, too," the elderly woman said. "You hear the girls crying."

He only heard one cry—a faint one—and it wasn't

coming from a girl. He would bet that it was Rosemary out there somewhere screaming. Panic clutched his heart and stole away his breath more than the cold wind. And in that panic he rushed off—in the direction from which the scream echoed.

He only hoped he could find her in time, but the wind was blowing so hard now that it was blowing the snow across whatever tracks she might have left for him to follow. He had nothing to lead him to her—but the sound of her voice—and even that seemed distorted, as if coming from a long distance away. He shouldn't have left her alone—even for a moment—because now he might not make it in time. As her screams grew louder, he could hear the terror in them.

She wasn't just upset like she'd been earlier. She was in danger.

All he had to do was wait. She couldn't hold on much longer. Her bare hands had to be frozen and ready to slip off the big rock from which she clung. If only she would shut the hell up . . .

Someone was going to hear her screaming and rush to her rescue like had happened before, and she would escape death again—like she'd escaped before. She couldn't keep escaping.

She had to die.

He closed his gloved hands around a rock, ready to hurl it down at her—down to where she clung to that rock on the steep slope below him. But if he leaned too far over, she would see him, and if he didn't knock her down to the rocky shore, if he didn't kill her . . .

She would be able to identify him. And then all his

plans for the future, for staking claim to what was his, would be ruined.

If her screaming drew people to the cliff, then someone else would see him, someone who knew who he was. Anger coursing through him, he hurled the rock over the edge. But he wasn't close enough to see if he struck her.

But at least she finally stopped screaming.

Hopeful that she'd slipped to her death, he ran off—just as the sound of running footsteps echoed around him. Whoever was rushing to her rescue was going to be too late, too damn late to save her.

Chapter Twenty

That rock hadn't just come tumbling over the side of the cliff any more than she had come tumbling over it. Someone had thrown it—just as someone had thrown her off it. As she'd fallen though, Rosemary had spread her arms out, grasping at anything to stop her. And she'd caught the rough edge of another rock.

Despite her fingers being nearly frozen and numb, she clutched at the rock as she dangled just below the edge of that cliff. Her feet flailed for purchase, for anything to help as she struggled to maintain her grip and ease the unbearable tension in her arms and shoulders. She forced the toes of her boots between some crevices in the rocky cliff, but the rocks were so icy that one of her boots slipped free. All around her the wind howled, hurling snow and ice at her, as if it was trying to help whoever had pushed her.

She'd been screaming since she'd first felt those hands on her back. But after the rock soared over the edge and nearly struck her, she held back the next scream that burned her throat. She wanted her attacker to think he'd gotten rid of her and to leave. But nobody else would come if she kept quiet. Nobody would know where she was.

So she released the next scream, but the force of it had

her grip slipping from the rock. She gasped and readjusted her hand and foot holds, but her body trembled from the exertion. If someone didn't come soon . . .

She wasn't going to be able to hold on much longer. So she screamed louder, but the wind tore her cry from her lips and hurled it into the ocean like it was nearly hurling her. Her body shaking with cold and fear, her fingers started to slip again. She wasn't going to make it.

"Rosemary!"

The voice—Whit's voice—jolted her, and one of her feet slipped again. And her grasp on the rock loosened more, her fingers sliding across the rough surface. Before she fell though, another hand shot down and strong fingers closed around her wrist.

"Hang on!" he shouted as he dangled over the side.

If she fell, he would probably go with her . . . tumble over the edge and onto the rocky shore, too. Tears burned her eyes and her face, but she fought them back. She had to be strong for herself and for Whit.

She had to climb up, or he would slip over the edge. Only his legs must have been on the ground on top of the cliff. As she peered up at him, a dark shadow fell across him. Had her attacker come back?

Was he going to push Whit off the cliff, too?

She screamed, and her grasp slipped completely off the rock. Whit's arm jerked as he held her dangling over the rocky shore. Only his grasp on her wrist kept her from dropping all those yards down to the jagged boulders, down to her death.

But he wouldn't be able to hold on to her long, not without falling himself.

"Let me go," she said. "You're going to fall."

"I've got him," another voice chimed in. So the shadow looming over him wasn't intent on hurting him but on helping him. And he must have pulled back on Whit because Whit was pulling her up. Her body bounced off the side of the cliff, and she flinched as sharp rocks jabbed at her.

But then, finally, she was up, and grasped tightly in Whit's arms as he laid back on the snow. And that shadow loomed over them both.

"What the hell were you thinking?" the sheriff shouted the question. But she wasn't sure to whom he was talking.

Her?

Or Whit?

He'd risked his life to save hers—even after how horribly she'd lashed out at him for something that had not been his fault. Nothing had been his fault, and she'd spent nearly two decades hating him for no reason. Guilt twisted her heart in her chest, and she clung to him—not just for warmth and comfort but for . . .

What?

She had no right for anything from him—not after she'd doubted him. No. She hadn't just doubted him; she'd blamed him. So now she leaped to his defense. "He saved my life," she said. And she would never be able to repay him for risking his in the process.

"Yeah, he did," Sheriff Howell agreed. "But he wouldn't have had to if you hadn't been trying to end yours! What the hell were you thinking? Why would you give up now?"

"Give up?" she asked. "You think I jumped?" Her body trembled not with cold or shock but fury. Anger coursed through her. "I would never do something like that."

But Whit was looking at her, too, with suspicion, and

he softly murmured, "After Cooke hypnotized you, you were very upset. . . ."

"Not upset enough to end my life," she said. Maybe her mother's and her stepfather's but not her own.

"Then how did you *fall*?" the sheriff asked, his voice thick with skepticism.

"I didn't fall," she said. "I was pushed. Somebody pushed me."

"Did you see who it was?" the sheriff asked.

"She's freezing," Whit said. His big body shook beneath hers, so he was freezing, too. But then he was lying flat on his back in the snow. "We need to get her inside. Now." His arms still wrapped tightly around her, he sat up and then stood, lifting her with him. He didn't wait for the sheriff's agreement; he just started walking toward the hall.

She should have argued with him, should have wriggled free of his arms. But she was frozen with fear—over nearly losing her life. Over Whit nearly losing his . . .

All she wanted was to keep clinging to him, to never let him go. But she also wanted her attacker found. And even more than finding him, she wanted Genevieve found. So she forced her head from the crook between Whit's neck and broad shoulder and peered at the sheriff. "You need to search the grounds."

"I will," he replied. "I'll look around to see if I can find whoever *pushed* you."

"No!" she said. "Not for him. Look for Genevieve. Look for her."

"So someone didn't just try to kill you?" the sheriff asked.

Why was he so certain that she'd jumped? Then she remembered. "I am not your wife. I didn't try to kill myself."

"Rumor is that isn't what his wife did either," Whit murmured.

Deacon cursed. "More information your investigative reporter gave you, Lawrence?"

A twinge of jealousy struck Rosemary's heart as she remembered the blond reporter hanging around Whit.

But he shook his head. "She's not mine. But she has been good at finding information, information you can't."

"She can't find the facts," the sheriff replied. "Like most reporters, it sounds like she just looks for the unsubstantiated rumors to make up a scandal."

Whit sighed. "Usually I'd agree with you . . ."

"Stop arguing," Rosemary implored them. "Find Genevieve." While everyone claimed she'd run away, Rosemary had a sick feeling in the pit of her stomach that she had never left this place, that she was here—somewhere.

But was she alive?

"What do you think I'm doing here?" the sheriff asked. "I was trying to get Cooke to let me search the grounds for her."

A ragged sigh slipped through Rosemary's lips. "Good."

"He didn't agree to a search," the sheriff warned her.

Whit cursed and whirled around, with her in his arms, toward the lawman. "Why the hell not?"

"That's what I would like to know," the sheriff said.

He clearly suspected that Dr. Cooke had something to do with Genevieve's disappearance. Rosemary wasn't as convinced of her boss's guilt, though.

"Privacy," Rosemary said with another sigh. "He promises all the guests the utmost privacy." Knowing how famous at least one of them was, she understood. If the paparazzi found out that the singer was staying at the treatment center, they would swarm the place. While the gates had kept out Rosemary, she doubted they would keep out all the press that would show up on the island.

"I might know a judge or two," Whit sardonically remarked. "I'll make sure you get a warrant."

"Good," the sheriff said. "Then I'll be able to bring in a search party. We'll find her."

Hopefully, alive . . .

"Here's your fucking warrant," Deacon Howell said as he shoved a paper in Elijah's face the minute he stepped inside the foyer.

"There's no need to be crude," Elijah admonished his old school nemesis. But the sheriff wasn't just an old nemesis. He harbored a fresh grudge against Elijah—over his wife.

Was that what this was about?

"There would have been no need for this warrant if you'd agreed to do the right thing," Deacon said.

"Let you waste your time?" Elijah asked. "Because that's all you'll be doing if you search the entire property."

As well as endangering the privacy of Elijah's guests. But they weren't just his guests; they were Bode's as well. He would have to warn his little brother about the search warrant. He had a feeling that it might affect him more than it would Elijah.

Bode was the one who seemed as if he was hiding something. But what? A teenage girl?

"It's my time to waste," Deacon replied.

"Then I must be much busier than you are," Elijah said. "Because I have no time to waste." He had to track down Bode. Their family couldn't weather any more scandal and neither could the treatment center. Elijah had to make sure that nothing would be found during the sheriff's search. "I'll leave you to it," he said. But instead of heading back to his office, he stepped outside.

He'd seen Bode leave earlier—shortly after Rosemary had run out after being hypnotized. And his little brother had yet to return.

Where the hell was he?

Once the doors closed behind him, he pulled out his cell and punched in his brother's contact.

"Hey," Bode answered.

All the times he'd called earlier it had gone to voicemail. Now Bode's voice was live and echoing from the phone as he stood just feet in front of him. "What's going on?" he asked. "Why's the sheriff hanging around today?"

"Is that why you left earlier?" Elijah asked, as he shoved his phone back into his pocket. "Because you're avoiding him?"

Bode's brow furrowed. "Why? I'm not the one he hates."

"No, you're not."

Bode never got blamed for anything—because he never took responsibility for anything. Well, he hadn't until recently, but then he'd been given no choice.

"What the hell were you doing?" Elijah asked. "I've been trying to get a hold of you for hours."

His brother sighed and stepped farther away from the doors to the foyer—and the sheriff. "I was taking care of something before he found out about it."

Elijah's stomach lurched with dread. "God, no."

Not that girl. Not that poor girl. Rosemary had already dealt with enough today. If something had happened to her daughter . . .

"It was just some drugs," Bode said.

"What drugs?" Elijah asked. "Yours?"

Bode shook his head. "No. I caught one of the grounds-keeper's crew selling some to a guest, so I fired him." He lifted his hand to his jaw, and blood oozed from his swollen knuckles.

"You beat him up?" Elijah groaned. "The guy might press charges." There was no way they were going to avoid a scandal now.

Bode snorted. "And face charges for peddling narcotics? I don't think even Teddy Bowers is that stupid."

"How the hell does a groundskeeper get his hands on narcotics?" Elijah wondered. He needed to get back inside—needed to check the drug supply cabinet.

Bode shrugged. "I don't know. And he wouldn't tell me." He cupped his swollen hand in his undamaged one. "No matter how much I tried to persuade him."

"You should have let me handle it," Elijah said.

"Why? Because you're such a people person?"

"Because I'm the director," Elijah said. "I'm the one in charge."

"And you never let anyone forget that," Bode said. "I could handle this on my own. And I did."

What else had he handled on his own? Genevieve Walcott?

Chapter Twenty-One

He was wasting his time. At least searching the hall had been a waste of time . . .

Deacon hadn't found a damn incriminating thing inside the place. The warrant didn't extend to records or to the private rooms, and as if everyone had been warned that he was coming, the guests had locked themselves up inside their suites. Judge Lawrence must have called in some favors to get the warrant, in an area outside his jurisdiction, so quickly. But maybe someone he'd called had tipped off the hall.

So the sheriff hadn't even been able to question anyone. Yet.

With Lawrence's help, he would get material witness warrants if necessary and make the guests talk to him. Not that he wanted to go to the judge again for anything . . .

But he had to find Genevieve. And he damn well wanted to find her alive—or Rosemary might do what he suspected she'd tried earlier. She might jump—just as his wife had jumped months ago.

He flinched as he remembered that moment he'd looked over the cliff. She hadn't been dangling off the side like

Whittaker Lawrence had found Rosemary. She hadn't been screaming for help.

Deacon had been too late to save her. Her body had lain, broken, on the rocky shore. But he'd lost her long before that day; he'd been too late long before then, long before she'd jumped.

Had Rosemary?

She stood now in the foyer next to Whittaker, who kept an arm protectively or possessively wrapped around her shoulders. Her face was chafed red from the wind and cold, her sweater torn in a few places from her ordeal earlier that day.

"What are you doing here yet?" he asked. "I thought you would go home." He glared at her male companion. "Or to the hospital." Maybe a mental hospital—a real one, not this weird treatment center.

"I knew Whit was getting you that search warrant," she said, "and I want to help you look for her."

"Since you work here, you must have already checked out this building," he said. "You know I didn't find any sign of her in here."

"Out there then," she said. "I want to help you search the grounds."

"We all do," Lawrence chimed in.

Deacon shook his head. "It's too dangerous. Surely, you both have to realize that. You could have fallen to your deaths earlier today."

"I didn't fall," Rosemary replied, her body stiff with defensiveness.

His wife had gotten like that, too—every time he'd confronted her. About her cheating, about her mental state, about how she'd treated Holly . . .

Maybe he had pushed her—just like nearly everybody believed he had. He just hadn't done it physically.

"Somebody shoved me," she insisted.

He nodded. "All the more reason you can't be out there searching," he said. "I put together my own team. Deputies and locals who know the island, who've helped me search before." Like the day they'd all searched for his wife.

He only hoped they wouldn't find Genevieve like they had found her. Too damn late . . .

At least Whittaker Lawrence had managed to save Rosemary earlier. But if Deacon hadn't been heading to his vehicle and overheard the screams, they might have both tumbled down to their deaths. He'd searched that area after they'd left for the hospital, but the wind and snow had hidden any signs of a struggle if there had been one.

So who knew if she'd really been shoved? Even Rosemary herself admitted she hadn't seen anyone. But her brake line had been cut. And her car had been hit . . .

Had someone else been responsible for those things, though? Or had she staged everything with the intention of getting him to investigate her daughter's disappearance?

He didn't trust her. Hell, he didn't trust anyone. Not anymore . . .

"With the snow and the wind chill, I'm not sure how long we'll be able to search," he said. "So you should return to the boardinghouse." He didn't want her here in case he did find something.

In case he did find a body . . .

"I'm not leaving," Rosemary said.

The judge slid an arm around her shoulders. "Then I'm staying, too."

He could have argued with them, could have threatened them with a charge of interfering with an investigation.

But hell, Lawrence was a judge, so he held his silence, just shrugged and walked out the open foyer doors to join the team that had gathered in the parking lot.

Margaret had put together a grid of the property. He assigned each searcher four of the grids, including himself—and he knew which ones to take, the ones where he'd found Whit and Rosemary earlier and the one where he'd found his wife. Because maybe Genevieve hadn't been running away from the hall. Maybe she'd been running away from everything—just as his wife had been.

He assigned Warren the ones closest to the hall, the ones where he'd already searched himself. He had good reason not to trust that deputy—since his last name was Cooke.

Before his team headed out, each one picked up a walkie-talkie. "Keep in touch," he advised. "We don't want to lose anyone else out there." With the way the wind and snow had picked up, it was a possibility. He could have postponed the search but knowing now that none of her friends had heard from Genevieve had an urgency racing through him. This was the last place she'd been seen.

The last place anyone had seen her.

Searching the property was probably the best chance of finding her. The areas he was searching didn't offer any shelter for someone to hide and survive, though. The ravines on the property and the cliffs on the ocean side offered no protection from the elements.

He'd dressed for the weather in a heavy snowsuit with a ski mask pulled over his head. Despite his precautions the wind cut through him, chilled him. He should have postponed the search, but he wanted to help Rosemary. Hell, he'd been interested in her, but it was clear that if she'd ever had any interest in him, she didn't now. Those damn rumors . . .

They'd destroyed his life. He was certain to lose the next election. But he'd already lost something far more important than his job: He'd lost his daughter. She lived with him—when she wasn't running away to one of her friends. But she hated him.

Fortunately, he'd always found her alive. He had to find Genevieve the same way—for her mother's sake as well as for hers. But if he found her out there, on the cliffs or in the ravines, he wasn't going to find her the way he wanted to. . . .

As he headed down the steep bank of the ravine, his boots sank deep into the snow. The wind had blown so much into the ravine that it was deeper here than anywhere else. If there was a body beneath this, he probably wouldn't find it until spring, which was a couple of months away yet. Rosemary couldn't wait a couple of months.

A cry rang out suddenly. His blood chilled. Unlike earlier, this cry wasn't human. It was the forlorn cry of a coyote. Usually they ran from humans, but it had been so cold that food would have been scarce. So he drew his weapon . . . just in case.

In a pack, they got brave—just like humans. Another cry echoed the first, as if they were circling him. One shot would probably send them running. But it might bring others running toward him, and he didn't need human help. He could handle some damn coyotes on his own.

He continued trudging through the snow. The bottom of the ravine had the deepest snowfall, so deep that he had to use his free hand to grab pine boughs and pull himself out of it. Branches snapped and broke off. But his weren't the only broken branches. Some other ones had been snapped off, too, leaving sharp ends protruding from the trunk. The broken off pieces were gone now, buried beneath the snow—probably along with whatever or whoever had caused them to snap off.

Had someone come running through here? Running away from what? The manor? Or from someone?

The coyotes howled now. What the hell were they doing out already? It wasn't dark yet. He glanced around, looking for them, yet could see nothing. They must have been hiding in the trees and brush. But as he looked, he noticed the blood sprayed across the snow above him.

Son of a bitch . . .

He'd found something.

Maybe it was just a deer. Maybe that was why the coyotes were howling. Maybe they were trying to scare him away from their fresh kill. But as he approached, he saw no hooves, no fur . . .

There was hair though. Long, tangled blond hair.

Son of a bitch . . .

He'd found a body. It was only partially exposed from the snow with dirt and dead leaves caked on it, too, as if it had been buried. Maybe the coyotes had dragged it out of a shallow grave. Dread gripping him, he approached slowly. His grip tightened on his gun as a snarl emanated from somewhere close.

Oh, hell . . .

He was going to need help anyway—to get the body out of the ravine. To process the scene . . .

So he raised his barrel into the air and fired. The shot was ear-piercing and echoed throughout the ravine. A yip echoed it, too, and branches rustled as the coyotes scattered, abandoning their kill.

But no, it couldn't be their kill, or it wouldn't have been buried like it must have been. Like she must have been . . .

He stepped closer to the body, which lay facedown. The dirty and torn material left on it appeared to be some kind of gown, like a hospital gown. Even though he knew he shouldn't contaminate the scene, he reached out with a gloved hand and rolled the body slightly.

Bile rose up the back of his throat as revulsion gripped him. The face was gone. Hell, the flesh was gone from everything that had been exposed from the snow and dirt. The coyotes had picked it nearly to the bone.

He gagged and swallowed hard, fighting to not throw up. Not that he had to worry much about contaminating the scene; the coyotes had already done that. He wasn't sure the coroner would even be able to determine cause of death with the condition of the corpse.

As for identity . . .

It had to be Genevieve Walcott. Nobody else had been reported missing on the island. Not since the last time he'd chased down his teenage runaway. Genevieve had probably just been running away as well and must have fallen. Tumbling down the steep slope could have been why her body was covered in so much dirt and leaves. Maybe she hadn't been buried, just hurt in the fall.

Or worse . . .

And the dirt, leaves, and snow had covered her until the hungry coyotes had found and partially uncovered her.

Panic pressed down on Rosemary's heart and lungs. "What was that?" she asked again about the noise they'd heard moments before. If she'd been in the city, she would have guessed that a car had misfired. Or something else . . .

"Gunshot," Whit said, his brow furrowing beneath a lock of dark blond hair. He continued to pace the conservatory like Rosemary had before exhaustion, more from panic than her earlier close call, had weighed too heavily on her and she'd dropped into one of the chairs around the table.

"Why would one of the searchers fire a weapon?" Rosemary asked. "Do you think they were attacked by whoever pushed me earlier?"

"A hunter could have fired it."

"Is it hunting season?" Rosemary asked. "And if so, why would someone be shooting at animals so close to people searching the area?"

Whit cursed, and Rosemary knew she was right. A hunter hadn't fired that shot; he or she wouldn't have risked a human life over a kill unless they were a killer. She stood up. "I'm going to check with the deputy in the lobby."

She had to find out what that noise had been, so she rushed out of the conservatory and down the hall. Whit followed her, as if he didn't trust her out of his sight now.

The female deputy glanced over at her, then quickly looked away.

Panic pressed harder on Rosemary's chest. "What?" she asked. "What is it?"

The deputy shook her head.

"We heard a shot," Whit said. He must have noticed the woman's reaction to Rosemary, too, because he slid his arm around her—offering her comfort she hoped like hell she didn't need.

"Did they find her?" she asked the woman.

The deputy lowered her chin nearly to her chest, as if

desperately trying to avoid meeting Rosemary's gaze. "I can't tell you about the investigation, Ms. Tulle. You'll have to wait for the sheriff."

You'll want *to wait for the sheriff.* . . .

That was what she meant. "He has something to tell me," she surmised. "He found something."

If Genevieve had been found alive, wouldn't the woman have been able to share that—wouldn't she have looked happier or relieved instead of just sorry? The panic was crushing now, so much so that she could barely draw a breath into her lungs. As she had earlier in the hypnosis room, she felt as though she was suffocating. She needed air. Wriggling free of Whit's one-armed embrace, she rushed toward the foyer doors, which opened to a blast of cold wind.

It struck her face like a bucket of ice water. She blinked against the chill and the swirling flakes of snow. As her vision cleared, she noticed the van that had just pulled into the parking lot.

BANE MEDICAL EXAMINER was emblazoned across the side panel. Not an ambulance. The body they'd found was dead.

"Damn it!" a deep voice remarked.

It wasn't Whit even though he'd followed her out. She felt his presence behind her. The man who spoke to her stood in front of her. She wouldn't have recognized him beneath his snow-encrusted ski mask if he hadn't spoken.

"Did you find her?" Rosemary asked, her heart pounding madly as she waited for his response.

"I don't know," the sheriff said.

"But you found something," Whit surmised, and once again his arm slid around Rosemary.

She barely felt it now. She was frozen with dread. With fear . . .

She felt as if she was dangling from that cliff all over again. And whatever the sheriff said would send her spiraling down to the rocky shore.

"I found a body," he said. "A female. I can't confirm her identity."

"Let me see her," Rosemary said.

He shook his head. "No. You can't . . . not like this . . ."

Her stomach pitched with dread. "Like what?"

His throat moved as if he was struggling to swallow. Then he had to clear it with a cough before replying, "Coyotes got ahold of the body."

Her legs trembled and nearly folded beneath her. If not for Whit wrapped nearly around her, she might have slipped to the ground. She locked her knees and steadied herself, though. "I have a photo of her."

"You showed me," the sheriff reminded her. She had done that when he'd gone to the hospital with her. "And I have a copy of her driver's license picture. I can't identify her either. It's going to take DNA testing. I'll need to contact your parents to get something of hers."

"Me," Rosemary said. "Compare her DNA to mine. If it's Genevieve, there'll be a familial match."

He nodded. "Okay. But it's going to take a while to run the test and have confirmation. It's not like on TV—it's not that fast."

She nodded now. "I know."

"But I wouldn't get your hopes up that it won't match," he warned her. "Nobody else has been reported missing on the island."

"And if she was alive, she would have called me," Rosemary murmured. If she'd been able . . .

But she hadn't been able if she'd already been dead. Rosemary had been too late to save her. She waited for the devastation of loss . . . but maybe she was just too numb right now to feel anything else.

"Do you know what happened?" Whit asked. "What the cause of death is?"

The sheriff shook his head. "Coroner will have to determine that, too, if he can."

"You couldn't tell from the scene?" the judge persisted.

The sheriff shook his head again. "Not much of a scene. Too much snow. Too much . . ." He grimaced, then glanced apologetically at Rosemary. "It could have just been an accident. She fell running away."

She shook her head. "But if it was just an accident, why is someone trying to get rid of me? First they nearly ran me off the road. Then my brakes. And today . . ."

And if Genevieve was already dead, why was someone trying to stop Rosemary from looking for her?

The sheriff said nothing. Did he doubt that those things had really happened?

"You told me the brake line was cut," she reminded him. "You found the evidence."

"But I don't know who cut it."

"Are you implying that I did?" she asked.

He sighed. "I don't know what to think . . ."

"It's easier to think this death was an accident," Rosemary said. "But your daughter told me that running away on this island is no use. Someone always finds you. I want to know who found Genevieve."

But if she'd been found, why would she have been left somewhere on the property? Rosemary had too many questions—the biggest was if her daughter was really dead. She wouldn't—she couldn't—accept that she was. Not yet . . .

She was gone. The loss hit him hard every time he walked through the door to the cottage he used on the property. She'd been gone long enough that he should have been used to her absence.

It wasn't even as if he missed her all that much. It was what she'd left behind that made Bode ache with her loss—because of what she was missing.

He needed to go up to the hall, help out Elijah with all the police who were searching the property. At least he'd gotten rid of the damn groundskeeper before the sheriff had arrived. Why hadn't their security officer caught Teddy Bowers before now, though? Why hadn't good old Cousin Warren figured out what was going on right under his nose?

Could he have been the one supplying the kid with the drugs to sell? Bode needed to deal with him, too. But Warren was probably out assisting his other boss with the search. Bode should be helping, too, but before he dealt with all that, he needed a moment alone. He didn't have very many of them anymore.

But he wasn't very far inside his front door before he realized he wasn't alone. A strange scent caught his attention. Before he could identify it, something swung out and struck him. Pain radiated throughout his skull and everything went black.

Had she come back?

But that wasn't possible . . .

Was it?

Chapter Twenty-Two

It had damn well not been an accident. No matter what the sheriff claimed, Whit didn't believe that any more than Rosemary had. If it was, why had someone gone after Rosemary? Like the sheriff, he'd had his doubts earlier about her fall off the cliff. But remembering the brake line and her other accident convinced him that someone was trying to stop her from looking for her daughter. The logical reason was so that a crime wouldn't be discovered and the killer caught.

In the downstairs powder room of the boardinghouse, Whit splashed some cold water on his face to cool off his anger over the senseless death of a girl he'd never met. But she was a part of Rosemary, so he felt like he knew her. He imagined she'd been like her mother had been as a girl, the girl that he had fallen for so long ago. Genevieve had been too young to die—way too young.

Regret that he'd never met her added to the pain gripping him. If he hadn't been such a coward all those years ago when he'd let Mrs. Walcott's threats chase him away, he might have been a part of her life. Or she might never have had a life . . . if he hadn't left that night.

At least there was that . . . at least Genevieve would be

spared from ever learning how she'd been conceived. Because that was a pain and guilt he always carried. But that was nothing in comparison to what Rosemary was suffering. He needed to be with her, but when he stepped into the hall, he found her waiting for him.

"Are you okay?" she asked with concern.

"I should be asking you that," he said.

"You have," she said. "Ever since that session in Dr. Cooke's office." She sighed. "Was that only this morning?"

He nodded. "I can't believe it either. So much has happened. . . ." So much since that moment she'd stormed into his office . . .

"Yes," she said.

In awe, he studied her. "How are you still standing?" he wondered. "You've been through so much."

She shrugged.

"Let me take you home," he said.

She gestured at the foyer. "You did. You brought me back here."

"This isn't home."

Her lips curved into a slight smile. "It is for now."

He shook his head. "There's nothing here for you now."

"I don't know that," she said. "I don't know that the body the sheriff found is Genevieve."

Whit opened his mouth, then closed it, uncertain of what to say. He didn't want to push her, not with as fragile as she had to be right now—after the day she'd had. All he could do was murmur her name. "Rosemary . . ."

"I know," she assured him. "It probably is her—since nobody else had been reported missing. But if I hadn't kept at the sheriff and the hall, Genevieve wouldn't have been reported missing either. So maybe somebody else slipped through the cracks."

"Cracks?" he asked. "More like negligence, on the part of the hall and the local authorities." The body should have been recovered long before the coyotes had found and desecrated it. He grimaced thinking of what the sheriff must have seen.

Fortunately, he hadn't allowed Rosemary to look at it—even after it had been brought up from the ravine in a black body bag. The bag had looked just about empty and the medical examiner and his assistant had carried it as if it had weighed very little.

"I don't know what really happened," Rosemary said, "and I'm not leaving until I find out."

"It's too dangerous for you to stay," he said. His anger surged back as he remembered her dangling from that cliff. If she had slipped . . .

Her broken body would have been zipped into one of the coroner's bags, too.

He stepped closer to her and lowered his voice so that the Pierce sisters wouldn't overhear him before saying, "Someone's been trying to kill you." He didn't want to worry the older ladies any more than they already were.

Rosemary shrugged. "Kill me? Or scare me off?" she asked. "And the only reason to do that was because of what the sheriff found today, to keep anyone from finding that body. But now that she's been found, I'm safe." Tears glistened in her eyes. "I feel guilty even saying that."

"You didn't hurt that girl," he said. "Maybe nobody did. Maybe it was an accident like the sheriff suggested."

"The sheriff wants to think everything's an accident," she said.

"Well, that would make his job easier," Whit pointed out.

"But if it was an accident, nobody would care that the

body was found, they wouldn't have been trying to scare me off."

"Unless they wanted to avoid a scandal," he said. "Seems like the hall has the most to lose. You need to stay away from that place. It's too dangerous for you to go back there, for you to even stay here on the island."

"If that's Genevieve . . ." Her voice cracked with emotion, but she drew in a deep breath and steadied it before continuing, "I won't stop until I find out what happened to her." She sighed. "And if it's not Genevieve . . ."

"Then she's out there somewhere," he said.

"Dead or alive?" she asked.

He closed his arms around her. He couldn't leave her now—not like this. She was still upset, just trying very hard to be strong. For herself? Or for him? "We'll find out," he said. "We'll just have to wait for the DNA results to come back."

She shook her head. "Not we. Just me."

"It could take a while," he warned her—even though he intended to make some calls like he had for that warrant. "You'll want to be home."

She shook her head. "I gave up my job when I took the one at the hall. And I can give up my apartment any time. My lease has been month to month for the past year. That's not home."

"Then come home with me," he suggested.

Her eyes widened, and she sucked in a breath. "Whit . . ."

Heat rushed to his face. "I know it's soon—"

"Too soon," she said. "We barely know each other."

"I know you."

"You know the girl I was nearly two decades ago," she said. "And you feel bad because of what we learned today.

That wasn't your fault. I wasn't your responsibility then and I'm not now."

"I cared about you then," he said. "And I still do." He lifted his hand to her face and ran his fingertips along her jaw. Her skin was cool, chilled yet from all her time outside, and so damn silky. "I can stay a while longer. . . ."

But he would have to leave her here eventually. Alone and vulnerable . . .

And that scared him—not just for her sake but for his. He didn't want to lose Rosemary again.

Despite the fire burning high in the hearth, Rosemary couldn't get warm. The chill had penetrated too deeply into her flesh, into her bones. But not her heart . . .

That held hope yet—hope that that body wasn't Genevieve's. And hope that Whit cared about her. It wasn't fair to want him involved though. He'd already lost so much; he couldn't lose his career, too, over her.

"Are you okay?" he asked.

She jumped, startled that she was no longer alone. Not that she had been alone for long; he'd barely left her side since they'd returned from the hall. She turned to find him in the parlor with her. He'd removed his suit jacket and rolled up the sleeves of his dress shirt—probably because he'd insisted on helping the sisters with the dinner dishes.

She should have, too, but he'd insisted she warm herself by the fire he'd built. He joined her at the fire now, sliding his arm around her to offer comfort. She felt more than that as a wave of gratitude rushed over her. And desire . . .

She cared about him. So much . . .

She wrapped her arms around his lean waist and rose on tiptoe to press her mouth to his. He tasted like the tea the sisters had served after dinner, tart with lemon and ginger but also sweet from the snickerdoodles that had accompanied the tea. Bonita had, no doubt, made sure he had some more when he'd helped with the dishes. Her lips curved into a smile against his.

He kissed her back, gently, as if afraid that she might break.

She lifted her fingers to his jaw, to which light stubble clung. But even the faint stubble had her flinching. Her fingers were scraped and chafed from clinging to that rock. If Whit hadn't showed up when he had, she would have died . . . like the girl in the ravine.

"Thank you," she murmured.

He pulled back. "For what?"

"You saved my life earlier today," she said. All these years she'd thought she'd been wrong to crush on and idolize him when they were kids, but she'd had every reason to fall for him then. Even more reasons now . . .

But she couldn't. For his sake as much as hers. With his campaign for governor starting, he couldn't afford to get sucked into her drama. "You need to leave," she said.

"Not without you," he said.

"I'll be fine," she said. "Now that the body's been found, there's no reason for anyone to try to stop a search of the property." Unless that body wasn't Genevieve's and even though her mind had doubts, her heart ached to believe that her daughter was still alive. She couldn't give up yet—not when she'd given her up too easily before.

He sighed, his breath stirring her hair. "If the person didn't want the body to be found, it was probably because the girl didn't die of an accident. She was killed—just like someone has tried to kill you. You need to leave with me."

She shook her head. "I can't. I have an obligation—"

"You can quit that job at the hall," he said.

"An obligation to Genevieve," she said. "If that body is hers, I need to find out what has happened to her. And if it isn't, then I need to find her. And I have to stay at the hall in order to do that." Before he could argue with her, she laid her hand on his chest, over his heart, which thumped heavily beneath her palm. "And you need to return to your life, to the bench, and to the campaign you'll be starting soon."

"But—"

She pressed her fingers over his lips. "You've already done more than you should have. You've no obligation to me. We haven't seen each other for nearly two decades."

"That was a mistake," he said. "Your mother—"

"I don't want to talk about her," she said. "Even if that night had never happened, we might have lost touch with each other. We were just kids back then."

"We're not kids anymore," he said. "And what we have—"

"Is guilt. You feel guilty over leaving me that night," she said. "But you had no choice."

"Then," he said. "I had no choice. But now—"

"You have no choice now either," she said. "You have a life and obligations, and so do I." She couldn't see any way to combine those lives and obligations. Not now. Probably not ever . . .

He stopped arguing, so he must have come to the same conclusion she had. They had no future together.

Just as Genevieve had no future . . . if that body was hers. And if it wasn't, where the hell was she?

* * *

The years slipped away every time he stepped inside this house, making him feel like a scared little kid again. Hell, everything about this place had scared him. The ruins of the manor . . .

The dilapidated state of this ivy-covered brick house that had once belonged to the caretaker.

He was most afraid of the man who lived here: James Bainesworth. But Elijah's fear was of becoming anything like him. James Bainesworth was his grandfather.

A door creaked open, and a gust of cold air blew into the foyer and through Elijah. Bode walked in, shaking snow from his hair. When he moved his head, he flinched, though.

"What's wrong?" Elijah asked him. "Hangover?"

Bode grimaced and glared at him. "I don't drink, and you know it. Do you also know that somebody hit me over the head earlier today—when I went back to my place to grab something?"

Elijah shook his head. "Of course I didn't know that. Did you call the police?"

"They were a little busy," Bode said. "And the last thing we need is them hanging around any more than they're already going to be."

"But don't you want to know who hit you?"

Bode shrugged. "Probably that groundskeeper I fired."

"You didn't show him off the property after firing him?"

"He had to get his stuff from the bunk cabin he was staying in," Bode explained. "But once I regained consciousness I went looking for him. He was gone then."

"Regained consciousness?" Concern rushing over him, Elijah stepped closer to his brother. "Are you okay? Did you go to the hospital and get checked for a concussion?"

"I'm fine," Bode said. "Or as fine as I can be with the police crawling all over the property."

"The sheriff found a body," Elijah reminded him. He'd called to tell him, and Bode had insisted they needed to come here—to Grandfather's house.

"Found?" Bode asked. "Are you sure? Was anyone with him?"

Elijah furrowed his brow. "You think he planted it?"

"You know Deacon Howell better than I do," Bode said. He was almost ten years younger than Elijah and Deacon, and that decade felt like an entire generation on the island. "He seems to have a habit of finding bodies here."

Elijah sighed. "The other one was his wife."

"Exactly."

"I don't know," he admitted. "I don't know what to think."

Bode narrowed his eyes again with the same suspicion he'd showed earlier. Could he have thought—for even a moment—that Elijah would have struck him over the head? But then Elijah didn't entirely trust him either. He suspected Bode knew more about Genevieve Walcott than he'd admitted.

"I don't know either," Bode said. "I just know that we need to tell him." He pointed toward the staircase that wound up to the second story.

Elijah shook his head. "No. We don't. The hall has nothing to do with him." Elijah intended to keep it that way—after what their grandfather had done at the manor.

Bode snorted. "Everything has to do with him. And you don't think he'll find out? You don't think he has that nurse of his spying on us? You don't think he already knows everything that happens here? His body might be failing him, but his mind is as sharp as ever."

His brother was right. But maybe it would have been more merciful for Grandfather's mind to fail him rather than his body, though. Then he'd be able to forget what he'd done. Not that it seemed to bother him. He left his guilt for the rest of his family to bear.

"He's ready to see you now," a deep voice called down from the top of the stairs. The burly, middle-aged guy looked more like a bodybuilder than a nurse. Elijah wondered who had hired him—Bode or Grandfather?

"You're here," Bode remarked to the man as he climbed the stairs.

"Of course," the nurse replied.

Bode snorted. "You weren't here earlier today when I checked on him."

Apparently, Bode spent far more time with their grandfather than he did. Elijah waited for a pang of guilt, but it was only unease. Why did his brother spend so much time here? With such a . . .

"Your grandfather had sent me on an errand for him," the man explained.

"He sends you off on a lot of errands," Bode remarked, and his eyes narrowed with suspicion again as he stared at the male nurse.

The man was not intimidated. Technically he didn't work for the hall, though. Maybe that was why he wasn't intimidated, or maybe it was because he was older than Bode, even older than Elijah, and a lot bigger than both of them. He just shrugged. "You know your grandfather can be demanding."

And exhausting . . .

Every meeting with the elderly man exhausted Elijah. As he joined his brother at the top of the steps, he noticed the dark circles rimming the nurse's eyes. So he suggested, "Maybe we should hire another nurse."

Both the nurse and Bode responded with a resounding, "No!"

Bode turned toward Elijah. "Theo is the only nurse Grandfather hasn't run off. Unless you want to take care of him . . ."

Elijah glared at his brother, who must have been more aware than he'd realized of Elijah's feelings for the Bainesworth patriarch.

"Where the hell are they?" a voice boomed from the doorway near the stairwell.

The nurse stepped back and so did Bode, allowing Elijah to enter first. He didn't want to; he never wanted to, but just like with every other visit he'd made here, he forced himself to step into his grandfather's room—into his grandfather's presence. But for the faint glow of a lamp, the room was dark with heavy drapes at the windows and heavy wood on the walls and floor and even the coffered ceiling. But the darkness wasn't limited to just the room; it radiated from the man as well. Despite his age and physical frailty, he was still pretty damn intimidating. His big body was folded into a wheelchair, his shoulders and head bowed as if he carried a heavy burden.

And he did. Or he should . . .

But as he had so many times before, Elijah wondered if his grandfather felt anything at all. But contempt. It was in his eyes—eyes as pale a gray as Elijah's—when he looked at his grandsons.

"You can spare me a visit?" he asked, his thin lips curling.

"I was here earlier today," Bode said.

"I'm not talking to you," Grandfather said, his gaze

sharp on Elijah's face. "I'm talking to *Dr. Cooke*." The contempt was in his voice now, too, which was strong and deep despite his age. The son of a bitch was ninety-two years old. But he never forgot or forgave a damn thing.

Hating that he felt like a little kid again making excuses, he said, "I have been busy, Grandfather."

The old man snorted dismissively.

"He has," Bode said, surprisingly coming to his defense. "There's been a lot going on up at the hall."

The old man nodded. "I know."

Of course he did. Bode was right about him having the nurse spy on them. Or maybe James Bainesworth saw it all firsthand from that bedroom window. The carpet was worn in that spot from the wheels of his chair, as if it was often parked there.

"Then do you know what was found today?" Elijah asked. Maybe they didn't even have to tell him.

But the gray-haired head shook now.

Although Elijah couldn't help but wonder if he knew and just wanted to hear it aloud.

Before Elijah could determine that, though, Bode said, "Grandfather, the sheriff found a body on the property."

The old man arched a gray brow over one of his pale gray eyes and murmured, "Just one?"

Chapter Twenty-Three

"So you weren't going to tell me they found a body?" Edie Stone asked the minute Whit stepped out of his chambers, an overnight bag dangling from his hand.

"I'm sorry, Your Honor," his clerk said. "I should have warned you she was here."

Whit glared at the young man. "You think?" He had no doubts now about where the reporter had been getting her information. Either the young man had a crush on her, or Edie had paid him. He turned back toward her. "I don't have time to talk to you now."

"Just when you want information from me?" she asked. "Not when I want information from you?"

He glanced at his red-faced clerk as he headed toward the door to the hall. "I don't think you need to talk to me to get information from me."

"Should I talk to Rosemary Tulle?" she asked.

He stopped at the door and cursed. "No. You should not." She was going through enough. It had been a week since the body had been found and the DNA results hadn't come back yet. Not even the coroner's report. He'd been reaching out to everybody he knew to rush the findings, and unfortunately he'd had Dwight place those calls for him. "She doesn't know any more than you or I do."

And that had to be killing her, not knowing if her daughter was dead or alive. But if she was alive, where was she?

"Rosemary's not your story anyway," he insisted. "That creepy treatment center is. They were covering up the fact that her daughter had gone missing. And then a body turns up on their property. You need to investigate them."

"I would," Edie said. "If anyone would talk to me. But I'm not on some damn list. I can't even get their PR person to return my calls about an interview. It's impenetrable."

Whit groaned. "I wish it was, but Rosemary got inside. She's working there."

"Even after her daughter was found?" Edie asked.

"Nobody's confirmed that the body is her daughter," Whit said, and inwardly groaned at the information he was giving up himself now. Edie Stone was a damn good reporter. "So she's staying until she finds out." Against his fervent wish that she leave Halcyon Hall and Bane Island far behind her.

Edie clapped her hands together. "Then she can get me inside," she said. "She can get me access to this Dr. Cooke, so I can interview him about all the shady stuff that's happened at the hall. This is the second body that's been found there since the place has reopened."

He nodded. "The sheriff's wife . . ."

Maybe the sheriff hadn't had anything to do with that. Maybe there was a serial killer running around Bane Island. His heart hammering with fear for Rosemary, Whit headed toward the door again. He had to get back to her— had to make sure that she was safe. Hell, he never should have left her. Just as he shouldn't have left her that night nearly two decades ago.

Edie rushed out after him. "Want me to drive?"

"No," he said.

Her lips curved into a mocking smile. "We're heading to the same place."

The same place for different reasons. "What do you get out of this?" he asked. "Out of exploiting people's pain?"

She shook her head. "That's not what I'm doing."

"What are you doing?" he asked.

"The same thing you do," she said. "I'm looking for justice."

He narrowed his eyes and studied her face. For some reason he believed her, or at least he believed that was what she believed. Then he wondered, if like Rosemary, she'd been hurt before and the justice she wanted wasn't just for other people but for herself.

"We'll drive separately," he told her. "There's someplace I need to stop first." Someplace he'd wanted to go since he'd learned the truth about what had happened to Rosemary that night.

"You never should have trusted me," Gordon Chase said, his head bent so far forward with shame that his chin touched his upper chest. He slumped over in the chair across the table from her, sunlight shining off the bald spot on the top of his head. "I feel just terrible, Rosemary."

She glanced around the conservatory to make sure they were alone before asking, "What are you talking about?" She leaned closer to him. "You didn't hurt me."

"But I was supposed to look out for you," he said. "I promised your father that I would."

"My father died from a sudden heart attack," she reminded him. "How could he have asked you for that promise? He had no idea that he was going to die."

He nodded. "He didn't ask me. But that day we all stood around his casket, I promised him then. I know he heard and believed me. I let him down." His voice was gruff with emotion. "I let you down."

"No, you didn't," she assured him. "You couldn't have known what my mother was capable of, of the sick extreme she would go to for Bobby. To give him a child." She shuddered as she thought of it, of the sacrifice her mother had made of *her*.

"She didn't do it for him," Gordon said. "She did it for herself, so that she could get her hands on more of the trust her parents had left to support her children. You were getting older. In a couple of years, you would have inherited it all and left her none. But having another child gave her a claim on it."

The bile rushed up the back of Rosemary's throat again as her stomach pitched. She was sick over what had happened to her, but now she considered what might have happened to Genevieve.

"That child is seventeen, almost eighteen," she murmured. In just a few months she would have inherited whatever was left of the trust because Rosemary had turned over her share as part of the agreement for Abigail raising her daughter. "That bitch . . ."

Abigail had played her. Genevieve might not have been as easily manipulated into turning over the trust. Had Abigail gotten rid of her grandchild to avoid giving up the money? Would she inherit it if that body turned out to be Genevieve's?

"I was never a fan of your mother's," Gordon admitted. "But I had no idea what she was truly capable of."

"Neither did I," Rosemary said. Now that she knew she intended to investigate fully. The statute of limitations had expired for what they'd done to her, but there was no statute of limitations for murder.

Could they have killed Genevieve after years of raising her like their daughter? Well, technically she was Bobby's daughter. Since they'd had no conscience over raping Rosemary, murder probably wasn't that big a stretch for them.

She shuddered. "It's all so sick and twisted." But she hoped like hell that Genevieve had not become their latest victim.

"I'm sorry," Gordon said again.

"As I told you, it's not your fault." But just like Whit had, her father's old friend kept blaming himself for not protecting her. "She was my mother. There was nothing you could have done."

"Was?" Gordon asked.

"After what she did, I can't consider her that anymore." She had yet to discover the truth about what they'd done to Genevieve. Maybe the sheriff would be able to question them. Just the thought of trying to talk to them herself had panic pressing on her lungs, like those hands had pressed her down to the mattress. She closed her eyes as nausea overwhelmed her.

"Are you all right?" Dr. Chase asked.

She shook her head. "No, I'm not."

"I'm sorry," he said again. "Here I am dumping all my guilt on you when you already have a burden of your own."

Guilt. That weighed more heavily on her than the disgust. She'd put her baby in so much danger . . .

* * *

I know what you did. . . .

What did he know? How much? That was the reason why Abigail Walcott let Whittaker Lawrence back into the house she'd banned him from so many years ago. She needed to know what he knew.

"So you decided not to call the cops on me?" Whittaker said as he stepped into the foyer.

She glared at him as he reminded her of the threat she'd made years ago and just recently, when he'd called from the intercom at the gates for her to let him in. "I'll call the police on you. . . ."

"Good," he'd told her. "I know what you did. . . ."

He did. The disgust was in his eyes as he glared back at her.

"Don't believe Rosemary's lies," she advised him.

He shook his head. "She's not lying."

She sucked in a breath and raised her chin. "She can't prove anything." That was what she'd been telling Bobby. Glass clinked from within the den; he must have been pouring himself another drink. The last thing she needed was for him to get drunk and start running his mouth. Because nobody knew everything yet . . .

"I think she can prove it," he said.

"But as a former district attorney and a judge, you know there's nothing she can do about it now," she said. "It's too late."

"I intend to change that," he warned her. "And I think there might be something else that you can be prosecuted for . . . something within the statute of limitations."

She lifted her chin, refusing to be intimidated by the

bastard son of a maid. While he was too damn tall for her to look down her nose at him, she tried. "For what?"

"Murder," he said.

A chill raced down her spine. "You're crazy. Who do you think I killed?"

"Your granddaughter," he said.

She shook her head. "You are crazy. And if you don't leave right now, I will call the police."

"Good. Then they can arrest you both."

"I had nothing to do with anyone's death."

"You put her in that place," he said. "You put her in danger. That makes you culpable, too. Depraved indifference. Manslaughter. If the body that was found is Genevieve's, I will bring charges against you. And if those charges don't stick, we'll file civil suits—take away the estate, the cars, and every last damn dime you have."

Her heart began to beat fast with fear that he could, that he would. "If you try to bring me down, I'll bring you down, too," she threatened. "I'll tell every tabloid about how you seduced an underage girl."

"Then I'll sue you for slander," he calmly replied.

He wasn't the boy she'd intimidated so easily in the past. He was a man now—a self-righteous one bent on avenging an old girlfriend. He was a threat.

He stepped around her, as if she wasn't even there. He must have heard the glass clinking, too, because he headed toward the den. "You son of a bitch!" he yelled when he saw Bobby.

Her husband let out an embarrassing squeak of fear before dropping his glass to the floor. He backed up with his hands in front of him to ward off the younger man. As if he could stop the much taller and stronger-looking Whittaker Lawrence . . .

"I'm calling the police!" she yelled as the judge advanced on her husband.

Whittaker pulled his arm back anyway, his hand curled into a fist. Bobby's hands in front of his face did nothing to deflect the blow that dropped him to the floor. When Whittaker whirled around, she shrank back.

"Are you going to hit me, too?" she asked.

"I'd like nothing more," he said. "But I have more class than that, more class than you."

She shook her head. "You know nothing. . . ." Not yet . . . and if that body was Genevieve's, no one might ever learn the truth.

Chapter Twenty-Four

Where is she?

Evelyn's heart pounded fast as panic rushed over her. Where had she gone?

Not Rosemary. She knew where her boarder had gone, where she always was this past week—at that damned cursed manor.

"Bonita!" she yelled as she pushed open the back door and stepped onto the icy driveway. A blast of cold air struck her face. "Bonita!" She grabbed her coat from the back door and saw her sister's parka swinging from the hook next to hers. She grabbed it, too, and tucked it under her arm as she headed back outside.

She'd gone off without her coat this time, leaving Evelyn no time to call the sheriff. By the time he got here, her sister would be frozen somewhere—probably like that body he'd found. Was that Rosemary's daughter?

Would Evelyn find her sister like that?

"Bonita!" she screamed for her. Her feet slipped on the slick driveway and she splayed her arms out to balance herself. That was when she noticed the door to the carriage house stood ajar.

Why would Bonita have gone in there? Small footprints

led across the drive and over the threshold into the building. Evelyn pushed the door fully open but not much light filtered around her. She could only see the looming shadow of her father's old truck.

"Bonita?" she called out again. She had to be in here. But why?

Her breath hung in the air in front of her, freezing in the cold. The carriage house wasn't insulated, so it was nearly as cold as it was outside. "Bonita!"

A shadow moved inside the cab of the truck. Rushing toward it, Evelyn pulled open the door. Bonita sat on the old bench seat, fiddling with the ignition.

"What are you doing?" she asked her.

"I'm going to get my baby."

"Your baby's inside," Evelyn assured her. She'd found the doll tucked into her sister's bed; she just hadn't been able to find her sister.

Bonita shook her head. "No. They kept my baby."

Evelyn tensed as she remembered the question Rosemary had recently asked her. Could Bonita be talking about something else, something other than that doll, when she went into a panic over her baby?

"Who kept your baby?" she asked.

"They did—the people at the manor," she said. "They took my baby. They kept my baby!" Her slight body shook with sobs of heartbreak and loss.

And for the first time Evelyn wondered . . .

Had her parents committed her sister to that godawful place because she'd been pregnant? And if she had been, what had happened to the child?

* * *

"Miss Tulle," the receptionist said as she stepped inside the conservatory. "I've been looking all over for you."

"I'm sorry. Does a guest need me?"

The young woman shook her head. "No, there's a reporter trying to get in the gates to talk to you," she said, with a faint sneer of disapproval. The receptionist clearly wasn't convinced Dr. Cooke's hiring her had been a good idea. Since the body had been discovered, Rosemary hadn't seen much of her boss. Maybe he regretted hiring her now. Or maybe he was just embarrassed for her, over the memories he'd brought out of her subconscious when he'd hypnotized her.

"She's not on the list," Rosemary said. "So why didn't you just turn her away?"

The woman glanced around at the other women in the conservatory and lowered her voice to whisper her reply. "She knows about the body. . . ."

"Then she should talk to Dr. Cooke," Rosemary said. "Or Amanda Plasky . . ." She'd only met the publicist once, but the woman was fiercely protective of the hall and of Dr. Cooke.

"She wants to talk to you," the receptionist persisted.

"Is it Edie Lawrence?"

She nodded.

The reporter had found out information for Whit; maybe she'd learned what they hadn't yet. The identity of the body. "Please let her in."

"Are you sure?" she asked. "You shouldn't be talking about the body. The sheriff has yet to identify the remains and determine how she died."

That body could be her daughter, and she'd already waited too long to find out.

"Let her in," Rosemary insisted.

A short while later Edie joined her in the conservatory.

"Thanks for agreeing to see me," Edie said. "I didn't think they were going to let me through those damn gates."

"I know the feeling," Rosemary remarked. "But now that I work here, I understand the need to protect the privacy of the guests. You're not going to violate that, are you?"

"I have no interest in your patients," Edie said. "I'm here to see you and only you."

A smile tugged at Rosemary's lips. "So you're only going to violate my privacy?"

"I'm not going to do an article about you," Edie said.

"Still working on your interview about Whit?" Rosemary asked. She hoped not; she didn't want him drawn into the mess that was her current situation. "He's a wonderful man. An honest man." A twinge of regret struck her heart over how she'd hated him for so long, so unfairly.

Edie shrugged. "If he is, he's one of the few. Too bad . . ."

"What's too bad?" she asked.

"That he's gotten drawn into all of this," Edie said. "Young girls, dead bodies . . ." She shuddered but it was as if a delicious chill had passed through her. "He's bound to get tainted with it all."

That was the last thing she wanted. She narrowed her eyes on Edie's face. "Then make certain that he doesn't get drawn into it."

"I won't include him in my coverage but other reporters might," Edie said. "They love to bring up his tragic past." She glanced around the conservatory. "He's kind of like this place, with its tragic past."

Maybe that was why Rosemary was drawn to them both. "I know about his wife and daughter." At least she knew that they'd died; she didn't know how, though. And she felt another twinge of guilt for not asking more questions. She asked Edie.

"Cancer." Edie answered.

"Both of them?"

"The wife found out she had it when she was pregnant, refused treatment so it wouldn't hurt the baby." She sighed. "But she got so sick so fast that they had to take the baby early anyway. Too early . . ."

Tears stung Rosemary's eyes. "That's terrible."

Edie nodded. "Yeah, he's been through hell once. Looks like he's going to be dragged through it again."

Rosemary shook her head. "No. I'll make sure that won't happen. With your help . . ."

"You want me to keep this quiet?"

Rosemary shook her head. "Not at all. I want you to investigate."

Edie snorted. "You're probably going to get fired," she warned her. "The director of this place will go crazy."

"I don't want you to investigate this place," Rosemary clarified. "I want the real villains investigated."

Edie arched that brow again. "Who's that?"

"My parents."

Edie sucked in a breath of shock. Rosemary's heart warmed with appreciation for Whit keeping her secret, but appreciation was all she could ever feel for him. He'd lost too much already; she couldn't cost him his career as well.

While he'd kept her secret, Rosemary had no such qualms. She told Edie everything. When she was done, Edie reached across the table and grabbed her hand. "I'm sorry," she murmured. "So very sorry . . ."

Rosemary chuckled. "It's funny that the people who have no reason to say it keep apologizing to me, and the people who owe me the apology won't even accept my phone calls."

"They're bastards," Edie said.

"They are," Rosemary agreed. "I need to know if they're killers, too. I need to know if they killed Genevieve to keep her from inheriting that trust." But she was still holding on to hope that the body the sheriff had found wasn't her daughter's.

"Your trust."

She'd told her everything. "I gave it up," she reminded her.

"For your daughter," Edie said. "Not for those greedy bastards."

"Please," Rosemary implored her. "Please help me find out if they're responsible. We all deserve to know the truth." Whit should have told her all of it about his wife.

He hadn't chosen to do that with her. The intimacy she'd felt with him, revealing her deepest darkest nightmares, had all just been one-sided. He wasn't as willing to let her into his life—into his heart—as she had been him. Now she understood why.

He really wasn't willing to risk his career to get more serious with her. He was only helping her out of obligation and guilt over the past, just as he probably felt guilty about his wife.

"It might not be her body that was found here," Edie said as she reached across and squeezed her hand again, offering her hope.

Rosemary smiled in appreciation. "That's what I'm hoping, too. But whoever she is, she deserves justice."

Edie nodded. "I'll do a thorough investigation," she promised. "Into your parents and the hall and the sheriff, too."

"Not Whit," Rosemary said. "Please leave him out of it." And from now on she would make certain that he stayed out of it.

"Whit who?" Edie asked with a wink as she stood up. Her body fairly vibrated with excitement. The reporter was determined to find out the truth about everything.

As she walked away though, a chill rushed over Rosemary. "Please be careful," she called after her.

Edie chuckled. "I've reported from war zones. I'm not in any danger here."

Maybe that was what that woman had thought whose body the sheriff had found. But if that body was Genevieve's, she had seemed to know—because she'd wanted so badly to get out of Halcyon Hall. If only Rosemary had gotten to her sooner . . .

Deacon stepped back to let the blond woman pass him in the doorway to the hall. He sure as hell didn't want to stop her from leaving. He was pretty damn surprised she'd been allowed inside the gates. He dipped his head down to avoid meeting her gaze, but she didn't even look at him, just rushed out the door and across the parking lot to a Jeep. Only when she'd jumped inside did she glance back at the building. Before she could change her mind about leaving, he stepped inside and let the doors close behind him, locking her out.

"Sheriff?" Elijah called out to him, his voice sharp with impatience as if he'd been trying to get his attention.

He waited a minute longer, watching the Jeep back out of the lot and head down the driveway, before turning toward Cooke.

"I thought you wanted to see me," Elijah said.

"I wanted to make sure *she* was gone before we talked," Deacon explained.

"She?"

"The reporter," Deacon said as he jerked his thumb toward the doors. "She was just walking out."

Elijah tensed. "I didn't know she was in here. I wouldn't have allowed it." He turned toward the receptionist, whose pretty face flushed pink.

"She didn't ask to see you," she said. "She wanted to see Ms. Tulle, and Ms. Tulle agreed to speak to her."

Elijah clenched his jaw so tightly that a muscle twitched in his cheek. "Do not let her in here again for any reason," he told her. "No matter who authorizes it."

The young woman's lips curved into a slight smile. "Even you?"

He shook his head. "I will never authorize a reporter in the hall."

Her face flushed a deeper red, and the smile slid into a grimace. "I'm sorry, sir. It's just been so busy around here after the sher . . ." She trailed off as she glanced at Deacon.

He finished for her. "After I found the body."

Now the color receded from her face, leaving it so pallid that she might pass out.

"I'm sorry," he murmured with regret. He hadn't meant to upset her, but then if it bothered her that a body had been found on the property, she should have quit. That was why he was here right now, to check out the employees. Thanks to the judge, he had a subpoena for those records. But not even Lawrence had enough influence to get him one for the guest records.

"Do you have that list for me?" he asked Elijah.

"In here," the other man said as he stepped through the doorway into his office.

The door closed behind him automatically—freakishly. Deacon really hated this damn place. He couldn't imagine why Rosemary had chosen to stick around after her daughter had probably been found on the property. But since his daughter worked here, he probably understood better than most what kept Rosemary here. She wanted to find out what had happened to her daughter.

Was that why she'd chosen to talk to that damn reporter?

Because of the rumors, she'd lost her trust in him—if she'd ever had any.

Elijah snapped his fingers. "I lost you again . . . what's going on, Deacon? Did you find out anything yet? Has the body been identified? Has a cause of death been determined?"

He shook his head. "Not yet." But the medical examiner had promised to have a complete report to him soon.

"Then why do you need this?" Elijah asked as he held up a folder. "Why would it matter who has worked here or works here now if the death was just a tragic accident?"

"If Genevieve was running away, like you claim, then why wasn't she wearing any shoes?" Deacon asked. No shoes had been found on the body or at the scene.

Elijah shrugged. "You said coyotes got to the body. Maybe they carried away the shoes."

"And everything else she owned? That body had nothing left with it but scraps of a hospital gown."

Elijah shook his head. "That doesn't make any sense. Genevieve didn't have any medical procedures done while she was at the hall."

"So maybe that body does belong to someone else," he said. "Someone other than Genevieve Walcott."

Elijah flinched. "Is it bad that I hope it does?"

"Even if it is someone else, that doesn't mean that Genevieve is alive," Deacon pointed out. "It could just mean that there's another body out there."

Elijah's face went as pale as the receptionist's had, so pale that his skin was nearly the same light gray of his eyes. His throat moved as if he was choking.

"You okay?" Deacon was concerned enough to ask.

Elijah nodded. "Yes, of—" His voice cracked, and he cleared his throat before continuing, "Of course I am."

Deacon narrowed his eyes. "Really? You seem a little edgy. Like you've seen a ghost. Or maybe one of the skeletons that have been rattling around your closets."

Elijah sneered at him. "I'm not the one who keeps finding bodies, Deacon. Little questionable that you're always the one . . ."

Deacon swallowed a curse, not wanting his old nemesis to know he'd gotten to him. The last thing Deacon wanted to find was a body—least of all his estranged wife's. "I'm good at my job," he said as a warning while he grabbed the folder from Elijah's hand. "I will find out what you're trying to hide."

Elijah shrugged. "I have nothing to hide." He sounded as if he really believed that; Deacon wasn't as convinced of his innocence, though.

"You better hope that's true with that reporter nosing around the island," he warned him.

Elijah shrugged. "She didn't ask to speak to me."

Rosemary . . .

What the hell was she doing talking to that reporter? Anything to find out what had happened to her daughter.

Deacon sighed with understanding. "She's not going to stop until she learns the truth," he warned Elijah.

The doctor cocked his head, sending a lock of black hair falling into his pale eyes. "The reporter?"

"Rosemary Tulle," Deacon replied.

"I hope when she learns it this time that it won't devastate her like it did . . ." He trailed off and shook his head.

And Deacon realized he'd missed something. "What are you talking about?" he asked.

"She learned something recently," Elijah admitted. "Something I'm surprised that she hasn't shared with you, Sheriff. Guess she doesn't trust you either."

Deacon flinched. He'd already determined that was why she was talking to the reporter and not him. But a reporter?

Over a lawman? Over a father of his own teenager? He would do more to find Genevieve than anyone else—unless he already had found her. "I'll talk to her," he said. He was going to damn well make sure he had all the information about this case.

About Genevieve.

And Rosemary.

And Elijah Cooke.

He stopped at the door, waiting for Elijah to open it. He took his damn time, probably as payback for not having Deacon's complete attention earlier. Once the door opened, Deacon paused just inside the threshold and turned back.

"Yeah, I have been the one who found the bodies," he admitted. "So you better hope there aren't any more out there for me to turn up."

Elijah's face grew pale again and he sat on the edge of his desk as if his legs had given out on him.

A chill chased down Deacon's spine, a chill of foreboding. Cooke was definitely hiding something.

More dead bodies?

Chapter Twenty-Five

So many dead bodies had come out of Bainesworth Manor. . . .

The trail of them was what Edie had chosen to follow. Not the Walcotts. Nobody was even sure yet that the most recent body found was Genevieve Walcott's.

She hoped for Rosemary's sake that it wasn't. But Rosemary wasn't the real story here.

She didn't even think that the sheriff was. That was why she'd let him pass her in the doorway without bothering to stop him. No. The story here went back further than his dead wife. Further than the current owners . . .

It went back to the days when the hall had been called Bainesworth Manor. To when all those young girls had been committed there . . .

So many of them hadn't made it out alive.

She sat now in a back room of the library on the island, her laptop flipped open on the table in front of her. Its glow cast more light than the Tiffany lamps that sat in the middle of each table in the room. A sneeze tickled her nose, but she didn't dare to let it escape. The librarian, a gray-haired woman with a stern face, was already regarding her with suspicion. Maybe that was because Edie had asked for all her records about the manor and about the people who'd been committed there.

"Those records are not public information," she'd been frostily informed.

She'd stayed to use the library's free Wi-Fi to search online databases. That was how she'd found the death certificates. But then she found something even stranger . . .

Birth certificates.

Babies had been born in that horrible hospital. Was that why those young girls had been committed—because they'd been pregnant, not mentally ill? But then why the cruel shock treatments and gruesome lobotomies?

Or had those girls gotten pregnant at the manor?

Who the hell would have the answers she sought?

Edie glanced around the library, but she was alone, except for that disapproving-looking older woman. She'd moved closer, pushing a cloth across a table behind the one at which Edie sat, as if she was dusting. But she was staring, not at Edie, but at her laptop screen.

"I found records," she pointed out to the woman.

"Not here," the librarian replied. "Most islanders wish that we could erase that place from our past completely."

"You can't," Edie said. "It's still here. New owners—"

"Not new," the woman abruptly corrected her. "Same people. Grandsons of the old man—of that monster—decided to renovate and get it going again. And don't you know . . . another body turns up . . ." She shuddered. "The second one. They say he's in a wheelchair and too old, but I wonder . . ."

"What? Dr. Bainesworth is still alive?" she asked.

The woman grimly nodded. "He should be in jail."

"For what?" Edie asked. "Some of those practices, although archaic, were accepted back then." Hell, electro-convulsive therapy was used today albeit with anesthesia.

"Not all the practices . . . he took advantage of those girls," she said.

"What do you mean?" Edie asked.

"Let's just say that those two grandsons of his probably aren't really the only Bainesworths left besides him."

Disgust dampened the excitement Edie had experienced earlier. Sure, she was still onto a great story—for her, for her career. But for those women . . . those girls . . .

"How do you know this?" she asked the librarian.

The woman pushed up one of her sleeves, revealing scars from old burns. "I was one of them. . . ."

Had the electrical shock treatments done that to her? Disfigured her?

"Oh, my God, I'm so sorry," she said.

"He wasn't," the woman replied. "He wasn't a bit re-morseful for what he did to us."

"Did you . . ." Edie had to swallow a lump of revulsion. "Did you have a child?"

She shook her head. "No. Thank God. Because any child of a Bainesworth is the spawn of the devil himself."

Edie snapped her laptop shut. She'd come here in search of records, but she'd discovered so much more than any-thing she could have found in old newspapers or online. "I'm sorry," she said again. "I don't want to dredge up the past, but I can't help but think it relates to the present. To what's happening now at the hall . . ."

"To that girl turning up dead," the woman finished for her. "That's why I told you. I recognize you from TV. I know you don't give up until you find the truth."

Edie smiled. "Thank you."

"No more girls should be hurt."

"No, they shouldn't," she agreed. And she couldn't help but think about Rosemary. At least she wasn't alone there. Whit should have arrived by now. But would Rosemary let him stay? Or would she send him away to protect him even though she was the one who needed the protection?

How did she keep coming back here? He knew the why—Genevieve. But how did she force herself to keep returning to the place where her daughter might have been murdered?

Whit shook his head as the gates opened, letting him inside the grounds of Halcyon Hall. When he'd called Rosemary, she'd asked him to come here instead of the boardinghouse. Of course she would be here.

Maybe it was easier for her to keep busy than to sit around and wait for news. Once at the building, he shut off his car and walked through the doors that opened automatically for him. She'd said for him to meet her in her office, but he had to have the receptionist direct him there.

He raised his hand to knock and winced as his bruised knuckles struck the wood. She opened the door before the look must have left his face. "What's wrong?" she asked.

He forced a smile. "You put me on the list."

She laughed, as he'd wanted her to. But the smile quickly slid away from her face. "I shouldn't have. . . ."

"Why not?" he asked.

"Because you shouldn't have come back here," she said.

"I want to see you—be with you . . ." Being away from her for the past week had been one of the hardest things he'd had to do, but he'd had to take over a trial for a judge who'd had to recuse himself. He would have to return

Monday. Until then, he intended to stay close to her, to hold her. But before he could put his arms around her, she turned and walked away—to the windows behind her desk.

Her office wasn't as big as Dr. Cooke's, but it was all dark paneling and coffered ceiling like his outer office was. No wonder she preferred the conservatory.

"What's wrong?" he asked. "Did the sheriff tell you something?" Whit had been promised that the reports would come back soon.

She shook her head. "No. He didn't tell me anything new."

"But you told him something?" he surmised. "What?"

She sighed. "This doesn't concern you."

"What?"

"None of this," she said. "You're not Genevieve's father. I know that now. None of this concerns you."

"You concern me," he said. "I care about you."

"You just feel guilty that you left that night. . . ."

He stalked around her desk then and closed his arms around her. Turning her toward him, he lowered his mouth to hers and kissed her soft lips. When he raised his head long moments later, he asked, "Does that feel like guilt?"

"I can't do this now," she said. "I can't start something with you. I'm out of my mind with worry. So don't force yourself on me now—when I'm most vulnerable."

All the breath left his lungs as if she'd punched him. "Force myself . . ." That was the last thing he would ever do with anyone.

"I get that you feel guilty about our past, about your wife . . ."

He shook his head. But he couldn't deny the guilt about her. About his wife . . .

"Please, go," she implored him.

He jerked his head in a quick nod. She'd already accused

him before of forcing himself on her. But then she hadn't really remembered that night. But to accuse him now . . . "Rosemary . . ."

Tears glistened in her eyes as she stared up at him. "Please, Whit, I can't do this now. I can't . . . I need you to leave. . . ."

A lawyer before a judge, Whit had never been at a loss for words or an argument, but she was too vulnerable now for him to pressure. He forced himself to turn around and walk away from her. But it killed him leaving her alone in that dark office, in that dark place . . .

For years she'd thought he was her rapist. While she knew the truth now, she would probably never completely get over all the nightmares she'd had about him. She'd only contacted him to help her find her daughter. Genevieve was her total focus as well she should be. He couldn't fault that, and he couldn't add to her worries.

Not right now . . .

He kept walking, right out of Halcyon Hall. But he paused in the parking lot, beside his car, and drew in a breath of air so cold it burned his lungs. They were already aching, though, along with his heart.

He wanted to turn back around, to go back to her, to fight for her. But she was too fragile now. He wasn't going to force himself on her, but he wasn't leaving her again. At least he wasn't going far.

He reached for the door handle of his vehicle. As he gripped it, a chill raced over him. The wind had whipped up again, but that chill had nothing to do with the cold. He had an odd sensation that someone was watching him. He glanced toward the hall. Had Rosemary reconsidered?

Was she watching to see if he could turn around and come back to her? No. With as determined as she'd been a while ago, she was probably just making sure that he left. He sighed, and the breath hung like white mist in the air in front of him.

A clanking sound startled him, and he whirled around to peer at the other vehicles parked in the lot. A man stood near a pickup truck, messing with some tools sticking out of the bed. He had a hood pulled over his head and ski mask on under that.

Whit narrowed his eyes with suspicion. He'd seen security footage with so many criminals disguised that same way. What the hell was this guy up to?

He pulled out a shovel and began working on the sidewalk leading up to the hall. The concrete was already pretty clear, but maybe the groundskeeper was worried that the wind had caused drifts. Snow removal was probably the only thing he could do in the winter.

Whit laughed inwardly at himself. He'd spent too many years on the bench, too many years in the courtroom, that he suspected everyone of something. Even Rosemary . . . Why was she so determined to send him away? Had her mother called her after his visit, threatened her in some way? Because he had this feeling that Rosemary wasn't pushing him away for her sake as much as she was for his.

He watched as the blond-haired man drove away from the hall, his car disappearing around a curve in the winding drive. He hadn't stayed. Neither had the sheriff or the reporter. They were all gone now, leaving him a clear shot at the woman.

His pulse raced with excitement as adrenaline rushed through him. He had to be careful, though—had to make sure that he didn't get caught. That nothing could be traced back to him . . .

Because he wasn't done here—at the hall—or on the island. No matter what other people thought or wanted . . .

He wasn't going to leave—wasn't going to just go away. He wasn't giving up his birthright. Not like . . .

No. He forced his mind to stop racing ahead. He wasn't going to deal with *that* yet. First he had to deal with her. And there had never been a better time than now.

He could finally get rid of her and, this time, nobody would be around to rush to her rescue.

Rosemary Tulle's was the next dead body that would be found at Halcyon Hall.

Chapter Twenty-Six

When the shadow fell across the diner table, Deacon glanced up from his plate and groaned.

Whittaker Lawrence slid into the booth across from him. "Nice to see you, too, Sheriff."

"What are you doing here?" Deacon asked.

"I was just about to ask you the same thing," Whit replied. "You don't appear to be doing a lot of investigating."

Deacon poked his fork through the layer of gravy covering the meat on his plate. "I am investigating what the hell the special is supposed to be. . . ." he murmured. "Is that meatloaf or roast beef?"

"You have a bigger mystery than the meat on your plate," Whit pointed out.

Deacon groaned again. "So I'm not supposed to take a minute to eat or sleep?" Maybe it wouldn't be so bad if he lost the election next year. Everybody on the damn island and now even outsiders expected him to work twenty-four seven. They certainly wouldn't get that much time out of Warren, not with his allegiances divided.

"It sure doesn't look like you've taken a minute to sleep," Whit remarked.

Deacon glared at him. "Thanks for noticing." He knew

he looked like hell. He felt like hell, too. He hadn't been sleeping, and he hadn't been eating. He pushed the plate away from him. "What do you want, Lawrence?"

He should have been relieved that it was Lawrence who'd crashed his dinner, though, rather than the reporter. Though she was certainly prettier to look at than the judge.

"I want to know about your investigation," Whit said.

"You know as much as I do," Deacon said. "You've been making calls, I've heard, pushing the DNA results further along the chain." So he probably owed him a sincere thank-you, but it stuck in his throat along with the one bite of the mystery meat he'd taken before the judge had joined him. "They should be back soon."

"So you've just been waiting to hear about those?"

He snorted. "Yup, just been sitting here twiddling my thumbs."

"Really?"

"Whittling, too," he added. "We do a lot of whittling on the island."

Whit snorted now and a chuckle slipped out with it. "I do enjoy whittling myself."

"I'm sure you do," Deacon agreed, a grin tugging at his lips. "Given your name and all . . ."

"Oh . . ." Lawrence nodded. "Yeah, never put that together before."

"Well, I'm pretty good at putting things together," Deacon said. "Take you and Rosemary . . ."

"We're not together," Whit said.

"Then why are you here?"

"I'm worried about her," he said. "About all the things that have happened to her since she arrived on this island."

Deacon sighed and tilted his head, studying the judge's face. The man was good at the guarded expression, at hiding what he was really thinking or feeling. That was the one thing that Deacon had managed to master himself about politics, but that had been more out of self-preservation than playing any game.

"You know nothing happened to her until she made contact with you again after all those years," Deacon mused. "It was on her way back from seeing you that she was nearly run off the bridge. And you were in town that day her brake line was cut. And hell, you were the one holding her off the side of that cliff—"

"On that cliff," Whit interrupted, and his poker face vanished beneath a flushed tide of anger. "I was holding on to her."

"You seem to have let go now," Deacon mused. "You've been pretty scarce this past week." Except for all the calls he'd made and favors he must have cashed in to rush those DNA results.

"That's Rosemary's choice," he admitted. "Not mine . . ."

Deacon groaned—this time in commiseration. He understood now what was going on; he understood too damn well because he'd been there himself. "Well, she's going through a lot right now."

"And she won't let me help her," Whit muttered, his voice gruff with frustration. "So you need to help her, Sheriff."

"She reached out to that reporter you brought here," Deacon said.

Whit flinched. "You need to make sure they both don't get in over their heads."

"I suspect the reporter can handle herself," Deacon said.

"I'm more worried about Rosemary," Whit said.

"Me too," he admitted. After his meeting with Elijah, he'd met with Rosemary and found out more of her family secrets. And he'd thought his family was messed up. He sighed.

"What are you going to do about it?" Whit asked.

"I'm working on it," Deacon assured the judge, and he glanced at his watch. "In fact I have a meeting soon. . . ." He pushed his plate across the table. "It's all yours."

Whit shook his head. "I've had more than enough mystery lately." He was pulling his cell from his pocket as Deacon walked out. No doubt he was going to make more calls, going to apply more pressure to rush those results.

Soon they would know the truth. If that was Genevieve's body Deacon had found . . .

If it wasn't . . . who the hell else had died on the island?

The call had surprised Rosemary. She had not expected to hear from *her*—not after all the voicemails she'd left had gone unanswered. She'd expected even less for her— *for them*—to show up in person in her office. Of course, they had already been on the list, though, from when they'd put Genevieve in the hall.

"You've been making so much trouble for us, and it has to stop. Now," Abigail told her. "You need to call the sheriff and tell him that we had nothing to do with Genevieve taking off."

"Genevieve might be dead," Rosemary said, the words scratching her throat as she forced them out. She didn't want to consider it, but it wasn't just a possibility. It was a probability, or Genevieve would have contacted someone before now. If not Rosemary, then one of her friends. "You already know that, though."

"The sheriff informed us of that when he called," Abigail

admitted, but she sounded unconcerned. "Your friend did as well when he barged onto the estate."

Rosemary forced herself to look at the woman, but Abigail's face was so full of fillers that she couldn't have revealed an emotion if she had actually been feeling one. Since they'd walked into her office at the hall, Rosemary had had trouble looking at them. Bobby had seemed to share her aversion since he kept his head down and stayed near the door, as if ready to bolt. Abigail acted as bold as she always did, as if she had nothing to hide. Or maybe she counted on her plastic face to keep her secrets. "My friend?"

"That bastard—Whittaker Lawrence."

Whit had confronted her mother. She shouldn't have been surprised since he was so determined to protect her—despite the risk to his reputation and his career.

"I can't believe you've forgiven what he did."

"He didn't do anything," Rosemary said. That was why she'd had to send him away. She didn't want his involvement with her to hurt him. "So don't talk about Whit. Talk about Genevieve. Do you care about her at all?"

The woman lifted a slim shoulder in a slight shrug. She was tall but kept herself thin—almost painfully thin. "I don't believe it's her."

"Why?" Rosemary asked. "Have you heard from her?"

The woman pursed her lips and shook her head. "No."

Rosemary turned toward Bobby. "Have you?"

Keeping his head down, he shook it. But now she noticed the red mark on his cheek and the swelling around his eye. Whit had struck him; she was surprised her mother hadn't called the police on him like she'd threatened all those years ago. But now she had even more to hide than she did then.

"Genevieve was furious when we brought her here after

she got suspended from school," Abigail said. "Despite her drinking problem, she thought she was old enough to stay home alone. To care for herself. She is probably just trying to prove that now. And she doesn't want to go back for treatment."

"How is she taking care of herself?" Rosemary asked. "She hasn't contacted any of her friends. Where is she since she isn't with any of them?"

Abigail sighed. "Of course she found someone new. Genevieve is even more boy crazy than you were. I'm sure she found someone to help her get out of here and to take care of her. She's resourceful."

Rosemary hoped that was true. But she couldn't let her mother and Bobby go on acting as if they'd done nothing wrong, as if they had nothing to hide when they'd been hiding the truth from her all these years. "I was not boy crazy," Rosemary said, jumping up from her desk chair. "I know what happened that night. You know I know."

Abigail snorted. "I know that you conjured up some false memory so you would be able to forgive Whittaker Lawrence for what he did to you. It didn't happen the way you claimed in that disturbing voicemail."

Anger coursed through Rosemary now. When they'd first entered her office, she'd stayed behind her desk— keeping it between them for her protection. She stalked around it now. She wasn't afraid anymore. She wasn't the defenseless child she'd been when they'd assaulted her. "You lying bitch!" she yelled at Abigail.

The woman flinched.

And Bobby cringed as if she'd struck him like Whit must have. "You know what you did, and a DNA test will prove it, you sick bastards. And all just to get your hands on my trust fund."

"Who told you that?" Abigail demanded to know. Before Rosemary could answer, she nodded. "Gordon. He's the one who conjured up your memory, too, isn't he?"

Rosemary opened her mouth to deny it, but Abigail rushed on, "He's the one who recommended Genevieve come here—who promised he would take care of her. I should have known better than to trust *him*."

"Why?" Rosemary asked. "Because he would help us learn the truth about you two?"

"Because he can't be trusted around young women," Abigail said. "Why do you think he's no longer teaching? He's been fired from every university he ever worked at over his inappropriate relationships with his students. That's why I hated how much he used to come around you."

"Gordon didn't hypnotize me," Rosemary said. "It was another psychiatrist who brought out the memory of what you two animals did to me."

Abigail shook her head. "Brought out a memory that Gordon probably had him plant. He's trying to take the focus off him—off what he probably did to Genevieve. If anything has really happened to her, he's probably at fault. You've trusted the wrong people, Rosemary, but then you always did that."

Rosemary closed her eyes and focused on that nightmare—the one she'd had all these years, the one she had tried—unsuccessfully—to block from her mind all these years. She opened her eyes and turned toward Bobby. "I know it was you," she said. "You're my rapist. The one who hurt me."

He didn't look at her even now. Instead he turned, pushed open the door, and fled from the room.

"You've broken his heart," Abigail persisted, "making these horrific accusations against him."

Anger surged through Rosemary again so fiercely that her temper snapped. She closed the difference between her and Abigail and swung her hand, slapping the woman so hard that the sound echoed throughout the office.

Abigail sucked in a breath and clasped her hand to her red face. "How dare—"

"Shut the hell up! Stop lying!"

"I'm not—"

"Yes, you are," Rosemary said. "But maybe you don't even know it anymore. You've been lying so long and so hard that maybe you've convinced yourself. Bobby knows the truth. I know the truth. And somewhere, in that black heart of yours, you know the truth. You're an evil bitch. And I never want to see you again."

"Then you'll never see Genevieve again either!"

Pain jabbed Rosemary's heart, poking the bubble of hope she'd been hanging on to that that body wasn't her daughter's. "So you're admitting she's dead? That you killed her?"

Abigail's eyes widened with shock. "Of course not. I don't have any idea what happened to that girl. You're wrong about me, Rosemary. You can research Gordon and learn the truth."

"I might be wrong about him," Rosemary agreed. "But I'm not wrong about you. And if you ever try to keep me from my daughter again, yours will be the next body that gets found. So get the hell out of here."

The woman spun on a heel and headed toward the door. But she stopped with her hand on the jamb and turned back. "I shouldn't be surprised that you've found a way to blame me for this. You've always blamed me for every-thing—even for your father dying. I had nothing to do with that. And if that is Genevieve's body that they found, I had nothing to do with that either."

Shock gripped Rosemary. She had never blamed her mother for her father dying. A heart attack had taken his life. But could she have caused it?

And now that she was conceding the body could be Genevieve's, maybe she was admitting that the girl was dead. Rosemary was glad the sheriff was going to question Abigail; maybe he would be able to get the truth out of her—since Rosemary had never been able.

Her cell phone rang, drawing her attention back to the desk where she'd left it. As she reached down for it, she glanced back at the doorway. Abigail Walcott was gone. Rosemary hoped that she would never see her again. But if she'd been involved in Genevieve's death, she would see her—in court and then in prison.

Her hand shaking, she picked up the phone and clicked the connect button. The connection was so bad that she heard only static.

"Hello?" she called out. "This is Rosemary."

A slap rang out, like the slap that Rosemary had delivered. She sucked in a breath like her mother had. Then the breathy sound of sobs emanated from her phone.

"Who is this?" she asked. "Who's there?"

"Genevieve . . ." the voice murmured. "It's Genevieve."

Relief coursed through Rosemary. Her daughter was alive. But . . .

"Where are you?" Rosemary asked.

More sobs crackled in the phone. Then another slap of skin against skin. Rosemary flinched as if she'd felt the blow, too. "Where are you? What's going on?"

Somebody had her. Somebody was hurting her.

"At the boathouse . . . on the property . . ." Genevieve murmured. "You have to come alone, or he'll kill us both."

"Who?" Rosemary asked. But the phone clicked dead.

And Rosemary knew if she went alone she would probably wind up dead as well. But if she called anyone else to help her, she would risk her daughter's life.

She could not lose Genevieve.

Again . . .

Chapter Twenty-Seven

Where the hell was everyone?

Elijah returned from a visit to his grandfather to find the hall nearly empty but for guests and low-level staff. Dr. Chase was gone. So was Rosemary.

Even his brother was gone. Bode hadn't been with Grandfather either. After his nurse had gone missing, the old man had tried Bode first. He'd made it painfully clear to Elijah that he had been his last choice to call. That hadn't hurt Elijah's feelings. He'd rather not talk to the old man, who reminded him of everything that was wrong with his family.

"What did you mean the other night?" he'd asked him. "When you acted like you were surprised we only found one body?" He hadn't been able to think about anything else after Deacon's visit. No shoes and a hospital gown? What the hell was going on . . . ?

If anyone knew, his grandfather would.

But the old man had shrugged his frail shoulders. "I don't know what you're talking about. A body was found?"

Elijah had held back a snort of derision. The old man wasn't senile. From the glint of light in his pale eyes, he was just messing with Elijah. Now. Had he been messing with them that night—when he'd made that odd comment?

And why hadn't Bode seemed as surprised by the remark as Elijah had been? What the hell did he know?

And where the hell was he?

Elijah had hated helping his grandfather, but there had been no one else. Where the hell had the nurse gone? He hadn't returned before Elijah left, but Grandfather had insisted he was fine alone. He wasn't the one Elijah worried about, though.

The intercom on his desk beeped, and Elijah released a ragged sigh of relief. Finally somebody was calling him back. He pressed the button and asked, "Who is it?"

"That reporter has returned, Dr. Cooke," the receptionist informed him. "She's demanding to talk to you."

He sighed, but it wasn't with relief this time. "I don't want to speak to her."

"She's threatening to call the sheriff if she doesn't see or speak to Ms. Tulle," the receptionist said. "She's worried that she's in danger. And I think she might be right."

His blood chilled now. "Why?"

"The Walcotts were here earlier, visiting with her," the receptionist said, and her voice dropped to a whisper. "I heard them arguing. It sounded as if it had gotten violent."

"And you didn't call the police?" Elijah asked her.

"I didn't think you'd want me to involve them on what must have been a personal matter."

She had every reason to have believed that given how reluctant Elijah always was to talk to the sheriff.

After what they'd learned when he'd hypnotized Rosemary, he was surprised she'd agreed to see them at all. She must have thought they had information about her daughter.

"The Walcotts didn't stay long," the receptionist continued. "Then Ms. Tulle left after they did."

"I didn't think she was here," Elijah said. He'd come back into the hall through the conservatory and had stopped by Rosemary's office on his way to his.

"She's not, but security has informed me that her vehicle is still in the lot."

So she hadn't left the property. . . .

Where the hell was she?

Where the hell was she?

Rosemary had had to stop and ask that young groundskeeper where to find the boathouse. She'd never noticed one before—not even when she'd been dangling over the rocky shore. The property was so vast, though, and encompassed so much of the island and the shore that there was a whole area she never would have thought to explore. Fortunately, the groundskeeper had pointed her in the direction.

So she'd hurried off across the snow-covered land toward a lower area of the island, toward a section of shore that wasn't as rocky as the area where she'd nearly fallen to her death.

She'd felt marginally safer then—until she'd gotten farther and farther from the hall. Then she'd reconsidered her decision to go off alone. But surely the groundskeeper would tell someone where she'd gone . . . if they asked.

Would anyone ask?

She'd sent Whit away. And Gordon . . . Could she trust him or had her mother been right about him? About everything?

No. Abigail was a master manipulator, and she was

just messing with Rosemary's mind as she always had. Rosemary shook her head to clear it and snowflakes dropped from her hair onto her jacket. This time she'd grabbed it and her scarf and her boots before she'd rushed outside.

She was prepared for the cold but not for what she might find. Had that been Genevieve on the phone or someone trying to sound like a scared teenager?

Whoever it was had been scared—very scared. She'd never heard Genevieve sound like that, not even on the voicemail she'd left begging Rosemary to rescue her from Halcyon Hall. But, despite the sobs and fear, the girl on the phone had sounded like Genevieve.

So much like her . . . that Rosemary had been compelled to meet her alone even though she knew she was risking her life. She hurried across the property in the direction the groundskeeper had pointed. Gradually the trees thinned, and the land sloped down toward the ocean, which was frozen along the shore.

Rosemary shivered, and the soles of her boots cracked through the ice-covered snow. The crackling sound echoed, not from her footsteps but from someone else's. Someone was following her. She shoved her hand in her pocket and wrapped her fingers around the pepper spray canister she'd taken out of her purse before she'd left her office. With the canister clasped tightly in her hand, she pulled it from her pocket and whirled around to confront whoever was following her.

But nobody stood here. Only a pine bough moved on a tree some distance behind her. Was there a shadow back there? Was someone hiding behind the pine tree?

"Hello?" she called out.

Maybe someone else had followed her. Someone like Whit . . .

But Whit's car hadn't been in the lot when she'd left. He'd been gone for a while now, probably so long that he'd made it back home. To his home. It would never be hers.

She would never have a life with him. But she wanted a life. She needed to call the sheriff. She reached into her other pocket and pulled out her cell phone. No bars appeared in the corner of the screen, and when she touched the phone icon, nothing happened. She had no signal.

She should have called from her office phone, should have waited until he'd arrived at the hall. But she hadn't wanted to wait because she'd believed that Genevieve needed her. But if Genevieve had been here this entire time, wouldn't someone have found her—especially during that search the sheriff had conducted?

Now that she was out in the cold, it had whipped some sense into her—chilled away the emotion, so that she had to face reality. She'd put herself in danger, and if Genevieve was really alive, she'd put her in danger as well. She held out her phone and tried to press the phone icon again and again.

As she stared down at it, a shadow fell across the snow and across her. As she whirled around, a scream rang out. It wasn't hers. It sounded like . . .

Genevieve . . .

Before she could see her daughter, something struck Rosemary, and the shadow overtook her vision, turning everything black as pain exploded in her skull.

Her last thought was that her mother had been right. She had always trusted the wrong people. She shouldn't have trusted that voice on the phone calling her out— because it had probably called her to her death.

* * *

Whit couldn't do what she wanted; he couldn't just leave her alone on this damn island. And he couldn't leave until he saw who the hell the sheriff was meeting.

The Walcotts . . .

Anger flared as he watched them step out of the limousine onto the sidewalk outside the sheriff's office. He'd seen them just a short while ago, but he'd been so mad then that he hadn't really studied them. Her mother looked the same as she had that night when, nearly two decades ago, she'd shoved him out of her house and out of her daughter's life. Bobby looked older though. His hair had thinned and his once fit body had gotten flabby, and there were new lines and a bruise and swelling on his face. It was clear that they didn't want to be here, but the sheriff had somehow compelled them to show up.

Whatever initial doubts Whit had had about Howell had been allayed and not because the sheriff had tried to allay them but because he hadn't. He hadn't done anything but his job, which clearly meant more to him than he was willing to show. A man who cared that much about representing the law wasn't likely to break it for anyone—not even himself.

And especially not for an obnoxious snob like Abigail Walcott.

They must have realized quickly that Howell would not be easily fooled or manipulated because they weren't inside the office long. The door flew open, and Abigail rushed out with Bobby following closely behind her. The boom of raised voices drifted across the street to where Whit had parked. But he couldn't make out the words—just the outrage.

Howell hadn't arrested them, but he'd clearly rattled them. Maybe he'd threatened them with the same charges Whit had. A grin tugged at Whit's mouth. He was actually beginning to like Deacon Howell.

The couple on the sidewalk climbed into the limousine; it was just pulling away from the curb when a siren rang out and lights began to flash. Was Howell going to arrest them after all?

But his SUV, with light bar flashing on top, sped past the long black car and on down the main street. Instinctively Whit knew where the sheriff was headed. To the hall . . .

To Rosemary.

He wouldn't have turned on the lights and sirens if he just had news for her. This was something else, something more serious. An emergency . . .

As instinctively as he knew where the sheriff was heading, Whit turned the key in the ignition, started his car, and headed after him. The limousine had pulled out between them, but it stopped at the light, its signal on to turn left—toward the bridge. Whit swerved around it and sped through the light. The chauffeur and maybe some other drivers blew their horns. He didn't care. He didn't want to lose the sheriff.

More importantly he didn't want to lose Rosemary.

He only hoped he wasn't already too late. More vehicles, with lights flashing on top of them and sirens blaring, joined in his chase of the sheriff. Had Howell called another search party?

But the volunteers for the last one hadn't showed up with lights flashing. They weren't looking for a dead body this time; they were looking for a live one—or at least one they hoped they would find alive.

The gates stood open to the hall; maybe that was just because the sheriff had sped through them. Or maybe they'd left them open for the others. Whit followed the sheriff's SUV down the winding drive, and those other vehicles followed him.

He stopped in the lot next to a familiar Jeep. Was the reporter the reason the sheriff had come out here with sirens blaring? Was she the one who was missing? Because somebody had to be . . .

But when he jumped out of his car, she rushed up to greet him. "What is it?" she asked him. "What's happened?"

He shook his head and turned toward the sheriff. "What's with all the flashing lights and sirens?"

"Cooke called. Rosemary's missing," Howell said.

He sucked in a breath as pain stabbed his heart. He shouldn't have left her—no matter what she'd said.

"But her car is here," he said, pointing toward it in the lot.

"She's not," Elijah Cooke said as he joined them. "There are tracks leading away from the hall, through the snow." He must have been following those tracks because snow clung to the legs of his dress pants.

"But you didn't find her?" the sheriff asked, his dark eyes narrowed with suspicion as he stared at the psychiatrist.

Cooke shook his head. "I found blood though. That's why I called."

Fear gripped Whit. "Where is it?"

"No body?" Sheriff Howell asked.

Cooke shook his head again. "No. But there are drag marks."

"Any coyote tracks?"

Fear tightened its grip on Whit. He wasn't going to wait

around here while they talked and those wild dogs mauled the woman he . . .

He loved her. He'd always loved her—even all those years ago when he hadn't really known what love was. He'd loved her then. And now he might have lost her. Unconcerned that he wore dress shoes and slacks like the doctor, he headed off across the snow—following the tracks.

A strong hand gripped his arm, pulling him up short. "You're not conducting this search," Sheriff Howell told him.

"You're not stopping me," Whit said. "Not this time."

"No," Howell agreed. "I'm not. I'm going with you." He released Whit's arm then and reached for a walkie-talkie. "I'm following a trail," he said into it. "But I want everybody to be on the lookout for anything suspicious, like someone transporting something, probably in a pickup or SUV. Keep an eye out around the perimeter."

Pickup . . .

Whit remembered the clanging noise from earlier, but that had just been the groundskeeper putting his tools in the box of the truck. That hadn't been Rosemary; she'd been inside the hall then, where he should have stayed with her so that she wouldn't have gone off alone.

"Why the hell did she leave the hall?" he murmured aloud.

"Her parents were here earlier," Cooke said. "They probably upset her."

"Or did you?" Edie asked him.

Whit hadn't realized the reporter was tagging along with them.

The sheriff glanced at her. "You were here earlier today. Did you say something to her?"

"She talked," Edie said. "She told me about this trust fund she'd forfeited."

"I know about that," the sheriff said.

Whit hadn't. She hadn't told him about that. "Why did she shut me out?" he murmured aloud.

Edie's face flushed, and he doubted it was from the cold. "She was probably protecting you."

"Damn it," he said, his earlier suspicion confirmed. Rosemary had pushed him away for his sake.

"Here!" Cooke called out as he hurried a few steps ahead of them to point at blood sprayed across the snow.

Fear clenched Whit's heart so tightly that it felt as if it stopped beating. Blood rushed to his head, making him so dizzy that he nearly stumbled.

Edie caught his arm. "Are you okay?" she asked.

"No . . ." He jerked away from her and walked forward.

But Howell held out his arm, gesturing them back. "This is a crime scene," he said. Glancing at Cooke, he remarked, "That's already been compromised. We have to protect whatever evidence might still be here."

"We have to protect Rosemary," Whit said. He'd wanted to—but she hadn't let him.

"It looks like we're too late," Edie murmured.

"There's no body," the sheriff pointed out. "Just blood and not really a lot of it."

"It looks like a lot," Edie said.

Whit studied the snow and understood what the sheriff meant. The snow around each droplet of blood had changed red as if dyed with the color. Like with dye, it had taken only a few drops to change a lot of snow. He released a shaky breath. "She could be all right then. If she wasn't dragged off . . ."

Howell shook his head and said, "Looks like someone

fell but got back up. How'd you know she ran off?" The sheriff grabbed the shrink's arm then. "Were you the one chasing her?"

"Like your grandfather hurt those girls," Edie added.

Dr. Cooke ignored her as he shoved the sheriff back. "Of course not! I only came out here to look for her after this woman demanded to see her and she wasn't in her office. Then I saw the tracks and just started off. I called you when I found the blood." He gestured at the blood-spattered snow. "When I heard the sirens, I turned back—"

"To stop me from investigating without a warrant?" Howell challenged him.

"To show you where to look," Cooke replied, his voice sharp with impatience. "I want to find Ms. Tulle, too."

"You need to go back to the hall," the sheriff said. "All of you—"

"No!" Whit protested. He wasn't giving up—not again.

"You're just going to mess with whatever evidence there is," the sheriff said, "if we're all trudging around out here."

Clearly, he thought that a crime had been committed this time.

"I'll follow the tracks. I'll find her," the sheriff promised.

But would he find her like he had the last person who'd gone missing? Would he find a body?

Or would he find her alive?

Chapter Twenty-Eight

She was alive. Rosemary had no doubt about it now. That had been Genevieve's voice on the phone—and it had been her screaming at her in warning.

The scream had come too late though. The first blow had already dropped her to the snow. But as she'd been drifting into unconsciousness, she'd heard that scream again, and it had jerked her awake and into action. Though her vision had been blurred, she'd managed to raise her can of pepper spray and direct it at the shadow looming over her.

Then that voice—that voice that had to be Genevieve— screamed at her again. "Run!"

Rosemary didn't want to run—not away from her daughter. She wanted to run toward her. But that urgency in Genevieve's voice had her scrambling up from the snow and running away from that shadow as it rushed toward her again.

Something swung at her, narrowly missing her head again, but swinging so hard that her hair moved and tangled around her face. Blood trailed down her forehead, blinding her nearly as much as the dizziness that threatened.

But she forged ahead, stumbling over the ice-encrusted snow as she tried to run.

Even though the slope to the shore was lower here, it was still strewn with rocks that rose up through the snow. She couldn't maneuver quickly there; she had to get away from the rocks and the frozen water.

Had to get back to the hall . . .

Back to Genevieve . . .

She tilted her head, listening for another scream. She heard nothing but the wind whistling through the pines. She headed toward the trees, but her legs were heavy, leaden as dizziness overwhelmed her. Her vision blurred again and from more than the blood that trickled from the cut on her forehead. She stumbled and tripped, falling into the snow.

But she forced herself up. She had to keep going . . . for Genevieve . . .

She regained her footing and stumbled a few more yards—toward a thick stand of pine trees—before she fell again. She tried to push herself up, but she had no strength left.

Consciousness slipped away from her again. But then she heard another scream . . . and jerked awake. Had the scream been real or just part of her nightmare? The darkness remained as she lay in the shadow not of a tree but of the man looming over her.

She flinched and cried out in fear of the next blow. Curled up on the snow, she wrapped her arms around her head for protection. But a hand grasped her right arm and pulled it down.

"Are you all right?" a deep voice asked.

"Sheriff . . ." she murmured as she blinked back the blood trailing into her eyes and tried to peer up at him.

He reached for something black and metallic, and she flinched again—worrying that it was his gun. Like her mother had said, she trusted the wrong people. But he pressed a button and static emanated from it. "It's the sheriff. I found her." Then he called out behind him. "She's here—she's alive." Then beneath his breath, he murmured, "Thank God . . . I didn't find another body."

Rosemary shuddered.

The sheriff hunched down to reach for her. But then somebody else was there, lifting her up in his strong arms, and she looked into Whit's eyes, which were dark with concern.

"You're bleeding," he said. "You've been hurt." Then, holding her against his chest, he turned toward the sheriff, who'd been joined by Edie and Dr. Cooke. "Did you call an ambulance?"

The sheriff spoke into his walkie-talkie again, asking for paramedics. Rosemary reached out and grasped Deacon Howell's arm. "So you didn't find a body?"

"You're alive," he said, as if assuring her that she was. Or maybe himself . . .

"Genevieve," she said. "She's alive."

"We don't have the DNA back yet," he said.

"No. I heard her. She's alive. . . ." Or she had been. Rosemary looked at the people gathered around her, but they looked away from her—as if they thought she'd lost it. "I heard her," she insisted. "She called me. That's why I'm out here."

"It was a trick," the sheriff said.

She shook her head, and the dizziness overwhelmed her, making her nearly pass out. But then she remembered . . .

"No," she said. "I heard her out here. She screamed at me to run. She distracted him so I could get away. She saved my life." Now Rosemary had to do the same. But when she tried to wriggle away from Whit, the dizziness overwhelmed her again.

"Why were you out here?" Elijah asked.

"I got a phone call. It was her, telling me to meet her in the boathouse," Rosemary said.

Elijah's brow furrowed. "Boathouse? There's no boat-house on the property."

"Yes, there is," Rosemary said. Was the sheriff right to doubt the hall director? "I asked the groundskeeper where it was, and he pointed me in this direction."

Elijah sighed. "Williams has worked here for thirty years. Maybe he remembers where one was years ago. But I don't remember one ever being on the property."

"I couldn't see much of the groundskeeper I talked to," she admitted. Not with his ski mask and his hooded jacket. "But he definitely hasn't worked here or anywhere else for thirty years."

"The guy in the parking lot?" Whit asked. "I saw him, too. He looked younger than thirty."

Dr. Cooke sucked in a breath. "Teddy Bowers. Bode fired him last week. He shouldn't have been anywhere on the property."

"He was," Whit said.

Elijah cursed. "Damn it. Bode was right. The kid is trouble."

"Give me a description," Sheriff Howell ordered. "Of the man and the truck."

She opened her mouth to speak, but Dr. Cooke was already answering him, already giving him more information than she would have been able, especially now with her head pounding so painfully.

"We need to get you to the hospital," Whit murmured as he started walking.

The movement increased the dizziness and the pounding, but Rosemary fought to stay conscious. She wanted to make sure that they found Genevieve—that they saved her daughter. But with each step Whit took, the pounding and the pain intensified. A moan slipped through her lips.

He hastened his step. "I need to get you to that ambulance."

She patted his shoulder, trying to grab it, trying to stop him. She didn't want to go—didn't want to leave Genevieve . . .

Where was her daughter?

The blood kept flowing from the wound on her head, down her face, onto her jacket, into her hair, onto Whit. So much blood . . .

Whit tried to hurry back toward the hall, toward the parking lot. The ambulance had to be there now, had to be waiting to take Rosemary right to the hospital. But the soles of his dress shoes slipped across the icy crust on the snowy ground, slowing his progress. And every time a shoe broke through the crusty surface, he nearly lost it. His socks were soaked, like the legs of his slacks.

The discomfort was nothing in comparison to his fear for Rosemary. Her head wound looked serious. She must have been hit very hard with something—maybe the shovel the groundskeeper had been wielding earlier. Had Whit been that close to her assailant, so close that he could have stopped him then?

Maybe if he'd been less concerned about his hurt feelings

over Rosemary rejecting him, he might have paid more attention to his suspicion about the young man. That noise he'd heard . . . had that been Genevieve?

Was Rosemary right? Was her daughter alive? Or was the head wound making her imagine that she'd heard her? But she'd claimed that she'd heard her on the phone—before the blow to her head.

Her fingers splayed across his shoulder, grasping at the fabric of his coat. "I don't want to leave . . . not until I know if she's all right . . ."

"You have to," he said. Lights flashed across the snow as he drew closer to the parking lot. Lights also glowed in the windows of the hall, but those were the only light as the sun slipped from the sky. "You need stitches and a CT scan." Maybe surgery if she had blood pooling within her skull like it was flowing from the wound.

"I need to know that she got away from him, that she's safe. . . ."

Whit rushed the last few yards to the lot where paramedics were opening the back doors of an ambulance. Before they could bring out the stretcher, he jumped up into the back and laid her on it. "Close the doors," he said. "You need to get her to the hospital right away."

"No!" Her shout echoed throughout the back of the ambulance, and her beautiful face twisted with a grimace of pain.

"You have to go," he said.

"Genevieve—"

"The sheriff will find her," he said. Howell hadn't followed him and Rosemary back to the lot, so he must have been searching for her. "Maybe he already has."

She shook her head, smearing blood across the white sheet on the stretcher. "No . . ."

"Don't listen to her," Whit said. He shouldn't have listened to her earlier. He should have never left her side no matter what she'd said, not when he'd known she was in danger.

She gripped his shoulder and shoved him back. "You stay. You make sure they find her."

"Rosemary . . ." He didn't want to leave her—not alone, not again, not when the man who'd attacked her might try again.

"Please," she murmured. "You're the only one I really trust. Do this for me."

Then he knew that he had to . . . that he had no choice this time. He nodded and turned toward one of the paramedics. "Let me out."

When the doors opened, Edie stood outside them—her face pale. "You ride with her," he told the reporter. "You make sure nobody gets to her."

"Where are you going?" Edie asked as he hopped down from the rig.

"To help them look for Genevieve."

"But Whit, she might be wrong."

He hoped like hell that she wasn't, that she had really heard her daughter. But if she had, that didn't mean that Genevieve was still alive. It just meant that she wasn't the body the sheriff had found last week. Would he find her body now though?

"Where did the sheriff go?" he asked.

"There's a cottage on the property that the grounds-keeper was using before he was fired," she said. "The sheriff and Dr. Cooke went there to find her."

And, obviously, they hadn't let her tag along.

"Get her to the hospital," he said, as he helped her into the back.

"Whit!" Rosemary called out before the doors could close again.

Maybe she didn't want the reporter going with her; he couldn't blame her. But for some reason he was beginning to trust the woman. "What?" he asked.

"I think Teddy Bowers stayed at the boardinghouse, too."

Would he have gone back there—after getting fired? Would he have returned to the house with Genevieve? If so, they would all be in danger. "I'll make sure they're okay," he said.

"Whit . . ." she called out again.

But he closed the doors, making sure she left for the hospital. The sheriff and Cooke led the search here, and they both knew the grounds better than he did. He would check on the sisters. Chances were that they were fine— that the young man wouldn't have stopped there—not once he'd tried for Rosemary again. He'd probably left the property and the island.

So where the hell would he have gone? And would he have brought Genevieve with him if she was still alive?

Hours earlier Bode had started out for his morning run. Due to the wind, he'd stuck closer to the hall and the other buildings on the property. That was when he'd noticed the light on in one of the small cabins that the groundskeeper's helpers used. During the winter, there was only one extra helper on duty, but since Bode had fired Teddy Bowers a week ago and told him to get off the premises, there should have been no lights inside the small cabin.

Maybe Teddy had just left one on when he'd moved out. Hopefully, that was all he'd done . . . though Bode suspected he might have been the one who'd hit him over the head. Who else could it have been?

He slowed his pace and stifled a groan. A woman or two or three might have been holding a grudge against him. Especially . . .

But she'd left him. She hadn't left just him, though.

He glanced at that light again. He should probably shut it off, but as he neared the cabin, he noticed the truck parked near the back of it. It wasn't a Halcyon Hall vehicle although Teddy had had the use of the groundskeeper's SUV until he'd wrecked it. The beat-up old red pickup was the kid's personal vehicle.

So what the hell was it doing here?

Bode drew in a deep breath and headed around the cabin toward the back. As he passed by one of the windows, he glimpsed a shifting of the shadows inside the room. Someone was in there.

But a metallic clank in the pickup drew his attention away from the house. As he walked away though, something tapped at that window. Before he could glance back, Teddy Bowers called out to him. "Bode!"

"What the hell are you doing here?" he asked the kid. "I fired you a week ago."

"I'm moving out."

"I told you to do that when I fired you," Bode said. When he'd regained consciousness, he'd come by and checked the cabin and hadn't seen him there then. Apparently, he should have made more certain that the kid had left, maybe he should have showed him off the damn property himself. He couldn't have trusted Warren to do it. "I gave you a chance, Teddy. I told you I wouldn't call the police. . . ." But he should have—no matter what scandal it might have caused the hall.

At the very least he should have changed the damn security code for the employee gate. Why hadn't he thought of that—especially after he'd been struck over the head in his own damn cottage? Hell, maybe that was why; maybe that blow had rattled his brain.

"I told you that, but you still waited in my place and attacked me," Bode said, shaking his head with disgust.

"What?" Teddy exclaimed. "I didn't—I swear—"

"It had to be you," Bode insisted. He didn't have any other enemies but for a few women and sometimes his own damn brother.

Teddy shook his head. "No, I swear it wasn't. And I'm just here to grab a couple things I left behind. I'm leaving right now."

Bode narrowed his eyes with skepticism. "You better be."

"I—I had some trouble finding another place to stay," Teddy replied.

Bode snorted. "Those old ladies that own the boarding-house always have a room or two open."

"Yeah, yeah, that's where I'm going," he said. "I was just leaving."

Bode nodded. "Make sure that you really are this time."

Teddy nodded. "Yeah, I am. You can get back to your run, Bode."

He seemed really eager to get rid of him and Bode knew why when another noise came from the cabin. This time it wasn't tapping on the glass; it was a scream. He whirled back around, but he wasn't fast enough to avoid the blow.

Metal flashed as Teddy swung a shovel at him. The blow knocked him to the ground. He tried to roll away, but Teddy swung again.

And everything went black.

Chapter Twenty-Nine

Whit would keep his promise to Rosemary to check on the Pierce sisters on his way to the hospital. He'd just make sure they were all right; then he'd make sure Rosemary was all right.

Would she be though? If her daughter wasn't found?

Or had Genevieve already been found? The body in the morgue was probably hers. But then, who had Rosemary heard scream? Had Teddy Bowers faked the voice when he'd called to lure Rosemary out of the hall? Why was a groundskeeper so determined to kill her? It made no sense. But then in his experience as a district attorney and as a judge, crime rarely made sense.

Whit pulled up to the Victorian house, but before turning into the driveway, he glanced at the doors to the carriage house. They were not closed entirely, exposing a familiar red pickup truck parked next to an even older pickup. And his blood chilled.

Rosemary had been right to worry; the groundskeeper had come here. Why?

And was he alone?

Whit hit the emergency call button on his cell phone.

When the dispatcher picked up, he said, "Please connect me with the sheriff."

"Sir, he's out of the office on an emergency call."

"I know—at Halcyon Hall. I found the kid he's looking for. Teddy Bowers." Or at least he'd found his truck. Maybe Bowers had exchanged it for one of the sisters' vehicles, if they owned two. Maybe he wasn't in the house at all. But if he was . . .

Whit couldn't let him hurt either of the sweet ladies.

"Don't approach him," the dispatcher cautioned. "They've found another body at the manor."

Whit cursed. So if Rosemary had heard Genevieve, it might have been the last time.

"Where are you?" the woman asked.

"I'm at the Pierce boardinghouse," he said. "Howell needs to get here ASAP." He didn't wait for the woman's response, just clicked off the phone. He didn't have a gun. But the kid hadn't shot anyone, so he must not have had one either. Whit could handle him. He had to handle him, so that Teddy Bowers didn't hurt anyone else.

Parking the car so that it blocked the driveway, he pushed open the driver's door and slid out. Then he slowly climbed the steps to the front porch, careful to keep his footsteps light. The kid must have seen him drive up because Whit could hear him yelling through the front door. "Shut up, you old hags! Anybody screams this time, and I'm going to kill everybody!"

Whit sucked in a breath. Somebody had screamed, just like Rosemary had said.

"You can't kill us all," a female voice told him. Despite quavering slightly with fear, there was strength in it, too. And youth—it wasn't one of the Pierces. "You can't see to drive yourself. You need one of us to drive you."

"That bitch maced me," he said, "because of you!"

The guy was talking to Genevieve. She was alive. Whit had to make sure she stayed that way. He couldn't wait for the sheriff to show up, not with all of the women in such immediate danger.

"And you," Teddy continued his rant. "I'm your family and you claim you don't even know who I am. . . ."

Who was he talking to now?

"You're not my baby," a woman replied. He'd not heard her speak very often, but he knew it was Bonita. "You're not my baby."

"No, I'm your grandson," Teddy told her. "My dad is your kid—yours and Bainesworth's. You had him at the manor, and they took him away from you and sold him to some desperate couple that couldn't have kids of their own. But he finally found out the truth a year ago and told me. So now I know that property should be mine. But those two legitimate heirs lord it over everybody else. Firing me for making a buck, trying to take everything that's mine."

Genevieve cried out and through the sheer curtains hanging over the tall bay windows in the parlor, Whit could see that the kid had grabbed her arm.

"Just like your damn sister tried taking you away," he said. "Nobody's taking what's mine anymore. Give me the keys to that truck, Grandma! Or I swear I'm going to kill you. I'm going to kill all of you!" With his hand not on Genevieve, he waved around a shovel—probably the same one with which he'd struck Rosemary.

Thinking fast, Whit grabbed one of the rockers off the porch and hurled it through the bay windows. With the explosion of glass, he kicked open the front door and rushed into the foyer. And just as he entered a shot rang out.

He'd been wrong. The kid must have had a gun.

* * *

Rosemary was numb and it wasn't just from the local anesthetic the doctor had injected into her forehead before he'd stitched up her wound. She was numb with shock.

Edie had been waiting when she'd returned from X-ray, and the expression on her face had scared Rosemary more than being attacked had. Then she'd had only herself to worry about—although she had been pretty certain Genevieve was the one who'd screamed the warning at her.

So she'd been worried about her, too. Always . . .

But now she was worried about Whit as well. She shouldn't have sent him off to look for her daughter. He was a judge, not a lawman. She should have insisted he leave the investigation and protection to the professionals. But instead she'd sent him off . . .

To his death?

"What is it? Who's hurt?" Rosemary asked Edie.

"Bode."

Rosemary furrowed her brow and flinched at the pain. The local anesthetic must have worn off. "Bode?"

"Bode James. The famous fitness guy from the hall," Edie added.

"Oh . . ." A pang of guilt struck her that she'd forgotten who he was. "He's hurt? How—what happened?"

"That kid—the groundskeeper—he fired, he attacked Bode, too, like he did you, with a shovel," Edie said. "And then he left him outside in the cold for hours."

Remembering all the time she'd spent out in the snow, Rosemary shivered. "Oh, no, is he okay?"

"He's in another emergency room. I tried talking to his brother, but Cooke wouldn't tell me much," Edie said, her face flushing—probably with anger. "He thought I was just after a story."

"What did the sheriff say?" Rosemary asked.

She looked away, as if unable to meet her eyes before replying, "He had to leave for another call."

Rosemary's stomach dropped. "What?" she asked. "What's going on?"

Edie shrugged. "I don't know for certain. . . ."

"But you suspect . . ." The same thing Rosemary suspected—that the other call involved Whit and maybe Genevieve. "I asked him to check on the Pierce sisters," Rosemary reminded her. "Teddy Bowers had stayed with them before he moved to one of the cabins on the hall property."

"I'll see what more I can find out," Edie said as she rushed out of the room. For Rosemary or for her story?

Rosemary needed to find out for herself. She tried to get up from the bed, but her head spun with dizziness. The doctor, who'd just stepped back into the area, grabbed her and settled her back against the pillows. "You have a concussion. We need to keep you for observation. You could develop a subdural hematoma." She must not have looked suitably worried because he added, "That's very serious. That's bleeding on your brain."

She didn't care about herself—not now—not when her heart was bleeding with fear for her loved ones. For Genevieve . . .

And for Whit . . .

"We're going to move you to the ICU," he said, "so we can keep an eye on you overnight. If you're fine in the morning, you can go home."

Home . . .

The boardinghouse had begun to feel like home, the

Pierce sisters like family. She hoped nothing had happened to them. Tears stung her eyes and her nose, but she squeezed her lids shut to hold them back. She couldn't give in to them now or she might not stop crying. Ever . . .

The doctor must have given her more than anesthesia for her wound because when she opened her eyes again, she was somewhere else. It wasn't exactly a room because it only had three walls; the fourth was glass that looked onto a nurses' station. Or the nurses' station, and a couple of nurses at it, looked onto her.

But they weren't the only ones. Rosemary felt someone else watching her. She was not alone.

Elijah stood next to the hospital bed, staring down at the pale face of the patient. He'd never seen anyone look as lifeless . . . but then he wasn't the sheriff. He didn't find corpses.

Until today . . .

Today when they'd found his brother lying outside the groundskeeper cabin, he'd thought they'd found a corpse. He'd thought Jamie was dead. Jamie . . .

That was whom he'd seen then—his baby brother, not the world-renowned fitness expert, who'd renamed himself Bode. That was whom he saw now as he stared down at the man lying in the hospital bed.

He hadn't regained consciousness yet. Not even when Elijah had left the hospital for the short time that he had. He'd had to return to the hall—not for work—but for *her*.

His niece.

Bode's daughter . . .

He bent his arm, trying to adjust his grip on her. He

couldn't remember the last time he'd held a baby. Maybe never . . .

A pang of guilt struck him that he hadn't been involved in her life before now. What if Bode didn't wake up? Her mother had already deserted her a few months ago. That left Grandfather or him to care for her. Grandfather couldn't really even care for himself anymore. At least not physically . . .

Mentally the old man was as cunning and manipulative as he'd ever been, which made him the last person who should ever raise a child. Elijah had thought that Bode was as well. He'd judged his brother harshly—too harshly—without ever giving him credit for his accomplishments.

Sure, he was famous. But more than that, he was keeping and caring for his daughter with only the help of a nanny he'd hired when the baby's mother had left.

"Tell your daddy to wake up," Elijah told her as he stared down at her face. She was beautiful with perfect pale skin, dark hair, and eyes that were nearly as light as the Bainesworth silver. "Tell him to wake up. . . ."

"Adelaide," a deep voice murmured. "Her name is Adelaide."

Guilt and relief rushed over Elijah, nearly staggering him.

"Don't drop her," Bode said, his voice sharper now with alarm.

That perfect little face crumpled into a scowl and the rosebud lips began to quiver.

"Shhh . . ." Elijah said, and he rocked her.

"Are you shushing me or her?" Bode asked.

"You," Elijah said. "You're scaring her."

Bode's cracked lips curved into a grin. "You're the

one who looks scared. Afraid you were about to become responsible for a baby?"

Elijah opened his mouth, but the sarcastic retort he'd intended to make stuck in his throat. He could only shake his head as emotion overwhelmed him.

"What?" Bode asked.

Elijah shook his head once more but then cleared his throat and admitted, "I was afraid I was going to lose my brother." Bode had looked so lifeless lying on the snow. He'd never seen the vibrant young man look like that. "And my partner," he added.

Bode grinned. "Are you sure you're not the one who was hit on the head? You can't stand me. I've always been the nuisance, the pest, not your pal like your cousin David."

He and David were the same age, so he'd always been close to him, especially because David's parents had been there for him more so than his own had ever been. "You're my brother," Elijah said. "And the hall thing—it was all your idea."

"A bad idea most of the time," Bode murmured as his grin slipped away.

Elijah shook his head. "No. We'll make it work."

Bode nodded, then grimaced. "So my brain isn't too scrambled?"

Elijah shook his head. "Concussion. Bad one. But you probably would have had hypothermia if you weren't so used to working out in all elements." His fitness had saved his life was what the doctor had said. Elijah would share that with him when he was sure that Bode wouldn't gloat too much about it. He had a bigger concern now—the tiny baby in his arms. "What would have happened to her if you weren't okay?"

"She has a mother," Bode said.

"She does?" Elijah wondered aloud.

"I don't know where she is," Bode admitted. "So if nobody was able to find her, Adelaide would become your responsibility."

Elijah glanced down at the baby who stared up at him with nearly the same eyes as her father and as him. She appeared to be comfortable in his arms now, much more comfortable than he was holding her.

"But don't worry," Bode said. "I have a hard head. I'll be fine."

"Like a rock," Elijah agreed. "But about her mother . . ."

Bode's face flushed. "I told you I don't know where she is."

"That wasn't Genevieve Walcott's body that the sheriff found," Elijah said. "What if . . ."

"She left," Bode said. "There was a note. She didn't die."

"But while Adelaide is here, maybe we should have someone swab her cheek for DNA," Elijah suggested. It wouldn't be the only DNA test that was being done. The sheriff had informed him that Teddy Bowers had claimed to be a Bainesworth, that Grandfather had raped one of the Pierce sisters.

It wasn't over. It was never going to be over. . . .

But he pressed his lips together, unwilling to burden his brother with all that information right now. He would explain it all to him later, when he was out of the hospital. He'd tell him then why Teddy had gone after him, that he'd resented not just Bode's firing him but also Bode for having what he'd thought should be his.

"Is that why you brought Adelaide here?" Bode asked. He pushed himself up in the bed and reached for his daughter. "To help identify that damn body?"

Elijah stared down at her again, for a long moment,

before handing her over. "No," he said. "I brought her here for you. I figured you'd wake up for her."

And the doctor had said that the sooner he woke up, the better the outcome for Bode.

"I'd do anything for her," Bode said as he cooed at the baby.

"Then find out if that body is her mother," Elijah said. "Find out the truth for her."

"What is the truth?" Bode asked. "Was that woman murdered?"

Elijah shrugged. "I don't know. . . ."

After that cryptic comment their grandfather had made, he had no idea how many bodies might be on the estate. He was just damned relieved his brother's hadn't been one of them.

Bode was alive and so was he. But they definitely hadn't escaped the curse. Would it ever let them go?

Chapter Thirty

Maybe she was dreaming, but instead of having her usual nightmare, she was having a fairy tale happily ever after. How hard had she been hit on the head? Maybe the doctor had been right to keep her for observation. But it wasn't a medical professional who stood next to her bed, staring down at her; it was Genevieve.

She jerked fully awake, sat up, and reached out for her daughter. Closing her arms tightly around her, she nearly pulled Genevieve into the bed with her. "You're alive! You're really alive."

Genevieve's hands trembled as she patted Rosemary's back. "Yes, yes, I am."

Rosemary pulled back to study her daughter's beautiful face. Genevieve looked exhausted with big dark circles beneath her blue eyes, but those weren't the only marks on her skin. She had bruises, too, and her blond hair was tangled and matted around her face. Rosemary's breath caught. "Oh, my God. Has a doctor seen you?" she asked anxiously. "Have you been examined?"

Genevieve nodded again but grimaced as if repulsed at the thought of even a medical professional touching her. What had she endured the past couple of weeks?

Rosemary's relief in her being alive slipped into concern again. "Are you all right?"

"I'm fine," she said.

"Tell me the truth," Rosemary implored her. "I can see the bruises. . . ."

Genevieve touched her swollen cheek. "This is from today. He really lost it. But he can't hurt me anymore now."

"So he did . . . ?" Rosemary asked, tears stinging her eyes as she considered that her daughter might have been violated the way she had been.

Genevieve shook her head. "It wasn't like that. It was my fault, really. I wanted out of that hall so bad that I sweet-talked Teddy into helping me, but once he got me out . . . he didn't want to let me go. He thought that if I got to know him, or if he got back money or property he had coming, that I would fall in love with him. Like he thought he was in love with me . . ."

"That wasn't your fault," Rosemary assured her. "He's ill. Are you sure he didn't hurt you?"

Genevieve shook her head again. "No. He kept me locked up in a room in this little cabin on the property. It was warm and there was food and water, but he wouldn't let me leave."

Rosemary squeezed her hand. "You must have been so scared."

Genevieve nodded. "But it's over now. How about you? How are you?"

"I have a concussion," Rosemary replied. She squeezed Genevieve's hand. "If not for you screaming, it would have been so much worse. You saved my life." She glanced around then. "What about Whit? How is Whit?"

Genevieve looked up at the glass wall and motioned to

someone standing on the other side. The wall slid open, and Whit joined them. "There's only supposed to be one of us in here at a time," he said.

And he'd had her daughter come in first . . .

Love warmed Rosemary's heart. Love for him and love for her child. "You're all right?" she asked.

He nodded. "I'm fine. And it's all over . . ."

Genevieve had said the same thing. "So he's been caught?" Rosemary asked.

"If not for you macing him, he might have gotten away," Whit said, and he smiled at her with something like pride.

"What happened?" Rosemary asked.

"He stopped at the boardinghouse, like you suspected," he said.

A pang of fear struck her heart. "Are the Pierce sisters okay?"

Whit sighed. "Physically, yes. But . . ." He shook his head. "Teddy told them that he was Bonita's grandson, that his father was Bonita's child who was given up for adoption."

"So she did have a baby," Rosemary murmured. And she'd been looking for him all these years.

"The sheriff's trying to get some warrants for DNA, trying to get the full story," he said.

And she was sure Whit was helping him. While he looked fine—handsome, wonderful—she had to ask, "Are you okay?"

He nodded. "I'm fine."

"He's a hero," Genevieve murmured. "If he hadn't come when he had . . ." Her lips quivered as if she was about to cry.

So Whit had put himself in danger—at Rosemary's

request. She squeezed his hand now. "I'm sorry . . . about everything . . ."

He squeezed her hand gently in return. "You need to talk to Genevieve now. And I want to check in with the sheriff. I'll be back soon." His hand slipped from hers as he stepped away from the bed and from her.

"He'll come back," Genevieve assured her.

A pang of guilt over her selfishness struck Rosemary's heart. She needed to focus on her daughter—on telling her that she was her daughter. But first she had to know how stable she was. "Are you really all right?" she asked.

Genevieve uttered a ragged sigh. "I don't know," she admitted. "I was such an idiot. I thought I was using him to get me out of there. I didn't know that he would hold me hostage."

"Hostage? Did he know about the trust? Was that the money he was after?"

Genevieve's brow furrowed beneath a fall of dirty blond hair. "What trust?"

Rosemary cursed her mother and Bobby. They had definitely stolen it. "Yours," she said. "Mother must have used it all up."

"That?" Genevieve asked. "She said you used it all up."

"That lying bitch . . ." Rosemary murmured.

Genevieve's lips finally curved into a slight smile. "That would be our mother."

"No," Rosemary said. "She's mine. Not yours . . ."

Genevieve's eyes narrowed. "Are you really okay? How hard did you get hit?"

"It's true," Rosemary said. "I'm your mother."

Genevieve shook her head. "No . . . You're not that much older than I am."

"I was sixteen," Rosemary said. "I wasn't even sure how it happened. Or who your father was . . ."

Genevieve glanced at the wall of glass. "Is it Whit? He said he knew you when you were kids."

"I wish it was him," Rosemary said. "I don't know if I should tell you this right now . . . with everything you've been through." What if she was too fragile?

"Tell me now," Genevieve insisted. "Tell me while I'm all messed up—because I don't think it can get much worse for me right now." Tears slipped out of her eyes and trailed down her bruised face. "He was so mad when you showed up, so determined to kill you. It's my fault you got hurt. I screwed up so badly, Rosemary."

"I screwed up seventeen years ago," Rosemary said. And she told her daughter about the night she was conceived.

Genevieve shuddered with revulsion, and her throat moved as if she was gagging. "Oh, my God . . ."

"I'm sorry," Rosemary said. "So sorry . . . if I'd known, I never would have given you to them. If I'd had any idea what kind of monsters they were . . ."

Genevieve shook her head. "No, I can't . . . I can't believe they raped you. God, you must hate me." She shuddered again and tried to tug her hand free of Rosemary's.

But Rosemary held tight. "No!" she exclaimed. "It killed me to give you up, but I was so young . . ." Tears coursed down her face now. "If I was older, I would have kept you. I would have raised you."

"But how could you even look at me?" Genevieve asked, the tears continuing to flow. "Is that why you didn't visit very often? Was it too hard to see me?"

"That was how Abigail wanted it, probably so I wouldn't tell you about the trust."

"I don't give a damn about the money," Genevieve said. "It's all the lies and what they did to you . . ." Her voice was hoarse, maybe from her screaming earlier, maybe from the tears rolling down her face.

"I'm so sorry," Rosemary said, wishing now that she hadn't told her, that she'd waited until she was stronger. "I—"

Genevieve tugged free and ran from the room.

Rosemary had been so afraid that she'd lost her daughter when she'd spent the past two weeks worrying about where she was and what had happened to her. She hadn't realized that after she'd found her she might lose her all over again.

Whit lost his breath as Genevieve slammed into him in the hallway just outside ICU. He grabbed her shoulders to steady her, and she flinched and cringed as if fearing he was going to hurt her. He wanted to hug her close, but he forced himself to step back from her. But he didn't let her go either, not when seeing how upset she was.

"She told you," he surmised.

Her tear-reddened eyes widened in horror. "You know?"

He nodded. "I was there when she found out. She let Dr. Cooke hypnotize her, so she could finally learn the truth. And it devastated her. Worrying about you, thinking that body we found could be yours, devastated her, too. She loves you—so much that she risked her life for yours over and over again."

She flinched. "I didn't want her to get hurt."

"I know," he said. "You saved her life today." Or was it yesterday? The day had lasted so damn long.

"I love her," Genevieve said through sobs.

"Then give her a chance to explain why she gave you up," he urged her. "She was so young, and Abigail manipulated her."

"I know that," Genevieve said. "I know that better than anyone."

"Then why are you running from her?" he asked. "Nobody loves you like she does. Nobody."

"But how can she love me?" she asked, her pretty, bruised face twisting with a grimace of self-disgust.

"The same way my mother loved me," he said. "I, too, was conceived in rape. My mother didn't tell me until I was older than you are. And even then she only told me because she was dying and I begged her to tell me the truth about my father. . . ."

Genevieve gasped. "I'm . . . I'm so sorry . . ."

He'd hated now that he'd put his mother through that, but he'd wanted to know what the truth was in the rumors he'd heard so many years. "When she told me how I was conceived, I realized how much she loved me. So much that she kept working for the man who'd raped her so that he would support us." Once he'd learned the truth, though, he'd vowed to never accept another dime from that man.

"I wish it was you," Genevieve said. "I wish you were my dad. . . ." Then she broke away from him and rushed down the hallway.

He started after her—until he noticed that the sheriff had caught her. He would stop her from doing anything reckless. Whit needed to check on Rosemary now. As upset as Genevieve was, he could only imagine how bad Rosemary was feeling.

When he stepped into the room, he found her crumpled over in the bed, her face in her hands. Sobs racked her slender frame, making her shoulders shake. He put down the railing on the side of the bed, sat beside her, and pulled her into his arms. "It's going to be okay," he said. "She's going to be okay. She's damn strong. So damn strong . . . she gets that from her mother."

Rosemary's breath hitched then steadied, and she pulled her hands away from her face. "She's going to need to be strong."

"She has been," he said. "She's smart, too. She survived captivity with that kid."

"What happened to him?" she asked.

He shook his head. "He didn't make it."

She gasped. "What happened to him? Did you kill him?"

"Not me."

"Genevieve?"

"No," he said. "Furniture isn't the only antique the Pierce sisters have in that house. They had an old revolver, too."

"Evelyn shot him?"

He shook his head. "No, Bonita was the one who snuck the gun out while Genevieve was arguing with him. And when I threw a chair through the window, she fired at him."

"Oh no . . ." Tears pooled in her eyes again. "That poor woman. She's already been through so much. And if he really was her grandson . . ."

"She actually seemed fine," he assured her. "I'm not even sure she realized what she did."

Rosemary sighed. "She and I have that in common. I've made such a mess of things," she said. "With Genevieve . . . with you . . ."

"I'm here," Whit reminded her. "And I'm not leaving you again—no matter what you say to me."

"But—"

He pressed his finger across her lips. "I love you," he said. "I've loved you for all these years. I just didn't think

I deserved you, that I deserved any happiness . . . since I lost Deborah and Isabella, too."

"Why would you think that?" she asked, her blue eyes brimming with tears.

"I thought that I didn't deserve happiness because I brought my mother so much pain," he said. "Like Genevieve, I am also a product of rape. That's why I could have never hurt you like that. It's why . . ."

She pressed her hand over her mouth to either hold back another gasp or a cry. Fresh tears glistened in her beautiful eyes. "I'm so sorry I ever thought that about you. And when I told you that you were forcing yourself on me, I just wanted you to leave so you wouldn't get sucked into a scandal."

"I know that now," he said. That she'd been protecting him . . .

"I still don't want that for you," she admitted. "My life is such a mess now. I don't know if Genevieve will ever forgive me."

"I already talked to Genevieve," he said. "She's worried about you forgiving her—"

"For what?"

"For being a constant reminder of your rape," he explained. "I told her about my past and about how much my mother loved me even after what happened to her. I assured her that you love her like that, more than anything."

She shook her head. "Not more than you . . . but, Whit—"

He leaned over and pressed his mouth to hers, kissing her deeply. Loving her totally. But she pressed her hand against his chest and pushed him back.

"But your campaign, your career—"

"Means nothing compared to you," he said. "I won't let

you push me away again. I won't give you up. And if you care for me at all, you won't ask me to do that."

"I love you," she said. "That's why I don't want to hurt you."

"You'll only hurt me if you keep pushing me away," he said. "I love you too much to lose you again."

"You won't," she assured him. "But do you mind if I stay on the island for a while? I feel like I should keep working at the hall, like I can do some good there, maybe with Genevieve if she'll stay, too."

"Let's ask her," he said as he caught a glimpse through the glass of the young girl. He motioned for her to join them as she'd motioned for him earlier. As slowly as the wall of glass slid open after Genevieve pressed the button that activated it, she moved, but she joined them.

If she had any lingering doubts about how her real mother felt about her, Rosemary dispelled them when she reached up from the bed and hugged her daughter closely.

Genevieve clung to her, too, until Rosemary pulled back and cupped her bruised face gently in her hands.

"I love you," she told her daughter. "So I'm leaving this up to you. I'd like you to stay here and live with me."

"You want me to stay with you?" Genevieve asked, stunned.

Rosemary nodded. "Of course."

"With us," Whit said. He had no intention of letting Rosemary go again.

"If that's okay with you," Rosemary told her daughter.

Genevieve nodded and wrapped her arms around Rosemary again, hugging her close.

Whit would have hugged them both . . . if he wasn't worried that Genevieve would recoil. She was fragile yet. But Rosemary wasn't. She was strong and certain.

Over her daughter's head, she told him, "I love you."

"And I love you." So much that he cared only that they were together from now on—no matter where the hell they were.

The sheriff stared at the screen of his laptop until it went black. Despite or maybe because of all the notes he'd taken, he had no idea what to include in his report. Evelyn claimed she'd fired the fatal shot, but that wasn't what Whit and Genevieve had said.

Or Bonita . . .

"I hit the target," she'd told him with a cheery smile.

The target had been Teddy Bowers's heart.

"Bullseye," she'd murmured. "He's not my baby. Not my baby . . ."

Evelyn had shaken her head. "She doesn't know what she's saying. . . ."

Maybe that was true. But Whit and Genevieve knew. Bonita had probably fired the fatal shot, but she'd done so in self-defense and in defense of the others. Deacon had no intention of pressing charges against her or Evelyn, so it didn't really matter which one he listed as the shooter.

He sighed as he held his fingers over the laptop keyboard. Genevieve hadn't been too choked up about her kidnapper dying. But she didn't believe he'd been involved in the death of the other girl.

Deacon glanced down at the report lying under the notes on his desk. The coroner's report . . .

While he didn't know who that girl was, he knew she'd been murdered. Despite the condition of the corpse, the coroner had found evidence of a wound through her skull that the coyotes couldn't have caused unless they'd had a special tool.

What the hell kind of tool had it been? Ice pick? Letter opener? He needed to find it for a match. He needed to find a killer, too, if he shared Genevieve's belief that Teddy Bowers wasn't responsible for this murder.

She'd claimed that he'd been really sweet with her at first—until she'd wanted to leave him. Then he'd gone crazy, especially when Rosemary had showed up trying to find her. He'd focused all his attention on trying to kill Rosemary because he'd already felt like he'd been denied other things that were his birthright.

Like the hall . . .

Who the hell would want to stake a claim to that or to being a Bainesworth? The kid must have been crazy. Eventually Deacon would find out once Whittaker Lawrence helped him get those warrants for DNA.

Deacon sighed and tapped his keyboard until the laptop screen flickered back to life. And if the guy was so crazy that he'd tried to kill Rosemary, he might have killed that other woman.

Whoever she was . . .

But if Teddy Bowers wasn't her killer, then there was another murderer on the island. And maybe the corpse Deacon had found hadn't been his only victim.

What about his wife . . . ?

Had she really killed herself?

At least Deacon could wrap up the case regarding Genevieve . . . thanks to the Pierce sisters. But as for the other deaths . . .

Deacon had a lot of work left to do, a lot of investigating . . . but he wasn't the only one investigating. That damn reporter was sticking around, too.

Look for the next thrilling romantic suspense novel
by Lisa Childs,
coming from Zebra Books in Fall 2021!

Connect with

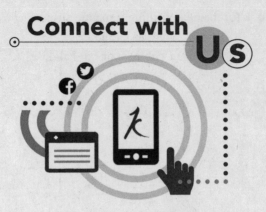

Visit us online at
KensingtonBooks.com
to read more from your favorite authors, see books
by series, view reading group guides, and more.

for sneak peeks, chances to win books and prize packs,
and to share your thoughts with other readers.

facebook.com/kensingtonpublishing
twitter.com/kensingtonbooks

Tell us what you think!

To share your thoughts, submit a review,
or sign up for our eNewsletters, please visit:
KensingtonBooks.com/TellUs.